Transitions

Ruth Reynolds

A Wings ePress, Inc.
Modern Historical Novel

Wings ePress, Inc.

**Edited by: Heather O'Connor
Copy Edited by: Jeanne Smith
Executive Editor: Jeanne Smith
Cover Artist: BJ Haynes**

All rights reserved

**Wings ePress Books
www.wingsepress.com**

**Copyright © 2017 by Ruth Reynolds
ISBN 978-1-61309-704-5**

Published In the United States Of America

**Wings ePress Inc.
3000 N. Rock Road
Newton, KS 67114**

Dedication

To all the strong women who have faced and dealt with the transitions in their lifetimes.

A special thank you to Laura (another strong woman), who helped and supported me all along the way.

Foreword

On the night of Sunday, May 31, 1942, three Japanese mini submarines entered Sydney Harbour with the intention of sabotaging the ships that lay there, including USS Chicago, which was moored at the Garden Island shipyard.

It had been known for some time there was Japanese submarine activity up and down the eastern coast of Australia and although there had been some sightings, combined US and Australian forces had failed to locate them.

The three mini subs had arrived clamped to the afterdecks of mother subs that waited for them off the coast, although there was little hope of the minis returning unscathed after their planned attack on Sydney.

One of the subs never reached the harbour, having been caught in the antisubmarine net that stretched across the entrance. Knowing their eventual fate, the two officers on board blew themselves up. The other two subs made it into the harbour. One, damaged on entry, was later detected by USS Chicago and disabled by depth charges, following which its two crew members shot themselves. The third sub was detected by Chicago and several other ships in the harbour, all of which put down depth charges. The mini sub retreated for a while and when things had quietened down, fired off two torpedoes aimed at USS Chicago.

Both of these missed their target, one running ashore on the side of the harbour, the other hitting and sinking the ferry Kuttabul, which was being used as sailors' sleeping quarters. Nineteen Australian and two British sailors were killed and several others injured in the explosion and eventual sinking of the ferry.

The mini sub managed to avoid further detection and slipped out of the harbour, its eventual whereabouts posing an ongoing mystery that was not to be solved for more than sixty years, when recreational divers discovered it sunk off the coast.

Anyone who was old enough to be aware of what happened would always be able to relate where they were and what they were doing on the night the Japanese came into Sydney Harbour, for prior to that the inhabitants of the southern city had experienced nothing of the war that was raging in the Pacific and Europe.

In comparison to what was happening overseas, Sydney's experience was pretty insignificant. However, it was something that had been expected, although there were many who scoffed at the thought that the conflict would progress so far south. Since the invasion of Singapore in February 1942 and the bombing of Darwin in March of that year, the entire eastern coast of Australia had been put on alert, having been told to expect an attack or an invasion at any time.

One

Sydney, May 31, 1942

At their home in suburban Leichhardt, the Sherwood family became aware of what was going on in the harbour that Sunday night in May when the air raid siren sounded not long before midnight. This was something they had become accustomed to in the regular daytime practices; however, this was the first time the siren had sounded in the night.

The roar of distant explosions made it clear to them this was not a false alarm, as did the sight of searchlights sweeping the sky, anticipating an aerial attack.

Like everyone else in Sydney, they turned on the radio, hoping to find out what was happening, but received little specific detail, other than advice that citizens go to air raid shelters. Hearing this, Minnie Sherwood hastily boiled the kettle, made tea and filled the thermos bottles that had been kept handy in anticipation of an emergency such as this. Meanwhile, Tom, her husband, went to the shelter in the back yard, removed the corrugated iron cover and dropped a ladder down into the depths. He hurried back inside, gathered up armfuls of blankets and said to his wife, "You'd best get the kids up, love, I'll be down there sorting things out."

Angie, aged six, and her sister Shirley, two years younger, were long asleep, so the first they knew of the situation was when they were roused by their mother, armed with a torch, calmly telling them they must get up and come with her. Blinking at the unaccustomed light, Angie came awake almost immediately, all too aware even at that young age of what her mother meant. Little Shirley, who always slept like the dead, refused to budge and turned over in her bed. Minnie shook her head and said to the older child, "She'll have to be carried. Will you be all right, love? Your dad's in the back yard. Can you go out there and call him? I'll need some help with Shirley."

Proud to be trusted with such an important task, Angie found her slippers and, wearing the dressing gown her mother gave her, padded through the house armed with the torch her mother had passed on to her with the words, "You'll need this; it's really dark out there."

The lights were on in the rest of the house, for the windows were covered by blackout curtains; outside, the yard was black as pitch. As Angie came out the back door, her father emerged from the hole in the ground, looking to her like some sort of giant bear. He nodded when she passed the message on and took the torch from her, saying, "You stay in the kitchen like a good girl. Mum and I will be back pronto. Then we'll get Gramma up and all go down the shelter. It'll be a bit of an adventure, won't it?" Nodding sleepily, the child looked at the kitchen clock, its luminous hands telling her it was nearly midnight, at which she was torn between pride at her ability to use her recently acquired time telling skills and the thrill of being up and about at such an hour.

Her parents returned almost immediately, Tom carrying the bundled up child who had not stirred throughout the disturbance. "You go down there, love; I'll hand her down to you," he said to his wife. He handed the torch to Angie, "Shine it on the ladder for your mum; you're being a great help to us tonight."

When her mother was settled at the bottom of the pit, it was Angie's turn to descend the ladder, refusing her father's offer to carry her down. She had no intention of being treated like a baby as her sister was. Her father squatted at the top of the pit, looking down on those below. "I'm going to wake Mum now," he said. "I'm amazed she isn't up already, with all this racket going on."

Gramma, as Tom's mother was universally known, slept in an improvised bedroom on the back veranda of the house. She had only been with them for a few months, having been dragged kicking and scratching from her home in Manly, an oceanfront suburb. With fears of imminent invasion, many of the beachside residents had fled to relatives in the outer suburbs and the Blue Mountains to the west. Anti-landing craft defences and barbed wire had been laid along all the beaches to the north and south of Sydney Harbour as fears grew of a Japanese invasion, similar to what had happened several months before in Singapore. Gramma dug in her heels and at first refused to move from her home; however, Tom, mainly under pressure from his sister who lived in South Australia, had finally persuaded his mother to come to live with him in their inner suburban home. At first they had needed to keep an eye on her, as she grabbed every opportunity to try to escape back to her former home, but eventually she discovered that she enjoyed being involved in the day-to-day activities in the house and had settled down quite happily along with her old cat, Blackie.

Tom knocked on the improvised door of his mother's sleeping quarters and entered to find Gramma lying awake in bed, her cat snuggled up against her, sound asleep. Gramma refused point blank to move. "I'm not going down in that place and nothing on this earth will make me do it," she announced. "I'd rather die in me bed along with Blackie than go down into that hellhole. I've lived this long without being killed by the Japs and if they want to get me now, they're welcome. Whatever happens, I'm staying right here, so you might as well go off and leave me to it."

Frustrated, Tom tried to reason with his mother, but finally shrugged his shoulders, deciding that he wasn't going to go through another to-do like he'd survived in getting her here from Manly. If she was dead set on staying put, then so be it. His main responsibilities lay with his wife and two small daughters and if Gramma wanted to take her chances, then that was her decision. He went out into the night, climbed down the ladder and set to helping his wife in making their improvised accommodation more comfortable.

He and his son, Johnny, who was out at band practice that night, had dug the shelter, following an instruction sheet supplied by the government. It was really nothing much more than a trench in the ground, its walls lined with corrugated iron. There were shelves built into one side, which they had stocked up with candles and a hurricane lamp, as well as some tinned food, Nally Ware plates, cups and a few utensils. Minnie moved all of these aside, making an improvised bed on the shelf for little Shirley, who still slept on, totally unaware of the change in her surroundings. The floor was lined with old linoleum, which was quite damp to the touch, so Tom returned to the house and brought out some cotton floor rugs, which made it a bit more comfortable for those seated on the kitchen chairs he had brought down while his wife was in the house rousing the children. He had also brought a kerosene heater, which at first they were reluctant to light, worried that the fumes it gave off would be dangerous in the confined space. Finally, when he saw that his wife and daughter were shivering with the cold, he lit the heater, then climbed the ladder and partially pushed back the corrugated iron cover they had pulled over when they settled in the shelter. He settled Angie on his knee, trying as much as possible to keep the child warm with the heat from his body.

"It will be a battle between the cold from outside and the heat from the heater, but I think as we are close to it, we will get some advantage in the long run."

It did seem to help a little, so they sat there quietly, bundled up in blankets, talking about what had happened. Minnie was worried about Johnny at band practice and their older daughter, Sandra, who was staying the night with friends from work. Tom, although he too was worried, assured her that Johnny would have headed for the nearest public shelter and that Sandra would be safe and sound in her friend's shelter, for virtually all homes in Sydney now had them— some much more glamorous than theirs. The older children were safe, he assured her.

"We're lucky this thing isn't full of water," Tom remarked, looking around him. This was fortunate, for a regular task on many weekends had been bailing out the water that seeped into the shelter from the surrounding ground. An unusually long dry spell had allowed it to dry out, so the family was at least spared the prospect of spending hours in water up to their knees. The only remaining sign of the damp was the linoleum, which although it smelled a bit, was sufficiently protected by the mats Tom had brought from the house. He handed Angie over to his wife and spent a fruitless fifteen minutes fiddling with a battery-operated crystal radio set he had installed in the shelter.

"Batteries must be flat again," he said. "It would have been nice to know what is going on out there." He finally gave up on the task and settled back in his chair, trying to get as comfortable as possible—it looked like there was a long night ahead. Angie returned to her father's lap, warm and snug, at first following the conversation or gazing up with interest at the stars in the cloudless sky, which she could see through the gap in the roofing. She had never seen the stars at night, only read about them in her storybooks. Finally, the lateness of the hour, coupled with the excitement of the evening, took its toll and she fell fast asleep in her father's arms, not to wake until the all clear siren sounded hours later.

Back inside the house, as soon as the sounds from the back yard quietened down, Gramma dislodged the sleeping cat, left her room and crept barefoot into the kitchen. She poked around in the cupboards, checked out the ice chest and removed the remains of an apple pie that Minnie had made for supper. Looking around guiltily, she hacked off a piece, crammed it into her mouth like a naughty child, and weighed the odds of whether she could take the remainder back to her den. She toyed with telling them that the Japs had broken in during the night and stolen it—but decided that it was not a story they would swallow. Next, she headed for the cabinet where she knew Tom had a cherished bottle of Scotch whisky, given to him by a visiting American serviceman. No luck there, for Tom had suspected for a while that someone (and he felt pretty sure it was his mother) was sneaking the odd nip from the bottle. The cupboard was securely locked, so Gramma had to make do with a swig from the milk jug. Not as satisfying as the forbidden spirit, but it would have to do. She poured some milk into a saucer for Blackie and scuttled back to her room. The cat had moved into her spot on the bed and complained when she moved him, but calmed down when he saw the treat she had brought him. Quiet descended on the house, as old lady and cat nodded off to sleep together.

When the all clear sounded, the family returned to the house. While Tom settled the two girls down again in their beds, Minnie put the kettle on for tea. They had by mutual agreement decided to wait up until young Johnny got home. This was one of the first times they had allowed him out on his own and his mother was worried, even though her husband urged her to be sensible.

"What possible harm could he have come to?" he asked. They had already turned on the radio and heard the news reports. It was obvious that nothing that had happened could have in any way affected their son—for the band practice was at the local Trocadero Hall, a mile away from where they lived. They had only a short wait, as Johnny quietly opened the front door just minutes after they sat down with their tea. He seemed surprised to find them waiting up for him and a bit offended that they should have thought he was anything other than fine.

"I'm not a kid," he said. "I would have gone straight home when the siren sounded just as we were breaking up, but the air raid warden made me go into the shelter. It was obvious the Japs were nowhere near here; it was all a lot of fuss over nothing, if you ask me."

"Tell that to the mothers of the boys who were killed," said Minnie, angry now that she knew her son was okay. "I just hope our Sandra didn't have any crazy ideas like you."

"You know Sandra is with Vera's family," said her husband. "They would have all done exactly what we did—so don't you start worrying about her, too. Sandra is in good hands."

~ * ~

Sandra was in fact not in anyone's hands—at least not at that moment. She was snuggled down in a double bed at the Ambassador

Hotel in the city, miles away from her friend Vera's home, where her parents thought she was spending the night. When the siren first sounded, she was about to succumb to the advances of Lieutenant Casper Freeman of the US Navy, after dancing and drinking with him at the famous Prince's nightclub. Vera had never featured in her evening at all, other than as a useful alibi for her whereabouts. The two girls had worked out similar arrangements before, each using the other as an excuse when they wanted to hit the town in circumstances they knew would meet with parental disapproval.

Sandra had met Casper just over a month before, when she and Vera had gone into town to the movies. They were heading for home when Casper and his friend stopped them, asking directions to one of the many nightspots that had proliferated in Sydney since the start of the war. Naturally the boys invited them to join them, which they did, but only for a short while, as both of the girls knew they would have trouble explaining any late arrival home. Casper had then and there asked Sandra for a date on his next night off. They had met several times since and Sandra was swept away by his boyish good looks and excellent manners.

"He treats me like a lady," she confided to Vera. "Not like those local jerks, who are too mean to even buy you an ice cream at interval."

Tonight he had bought Sandra a slap-up meal, before taking her to Prince's nightclub, a place she had always wanted to go, but so far had never been. Light in the head from his attentions and the champagne cocktails he had plied her with, she willingly agreed to go with him to the room he rented on a semi-permanent basis at the Ambassador. She had no illusions about his intentions, but decided that being eighteen, it was high time she discovered what "it" was all about. Vera, who was much more experienced in these matters, had thrilled her with breathless stories of the wonders of sex. Tonight, she had decided, would be the night—after all, he had already told her she was the only girl for him and that, she thought, was almost a proposal of marriage. When the war was over, as it surely must soon be, she had dreams of him taking her home with him to Chesapeake, Virginia, which sounded so much more glamorous than boring old Sydney.

Sandra had worn her very best brassiere and scanties in anticipation of the occasion and was actually stripped down to these by Casper, who was every bit as keen as she to take their relationship to the next stage. And then to her disgust the air raid siren sounded. Undeterred, Casper was in the process of removing her scanties, assuring her that he loved her saying, "Ohmigod, you are beautiful. You know I love you my darling, Ohmigod!" However, when the sounds of explosions reverberated around the room, it stopped him in his tracks. He left the bed and went to the window, looked out at the searchlights that spanned the sky and said, "Shit, something is really happening out there. I'm going to have to return to base."

Hastily he grabbed his trousers and the shirt he had discarded on the floor near the bed. He sat on the bed to put his boots on, repeating, "Shit! Why did this have to happen tonight of all nights? I'm sorry, sweetheart; I have to leave you. You go downstairs...they'll tell you where the air raid shelter is and when it's over, get yourself a cab home." He reached into his wallet and drew out two five-pound notes, "This should be enough for the fare."

"I'd rather wait for you," she said, determined that she wouldn't be robbed of her night of bliss.

He shook his head, "I won't be back tonight, I'm certain of that. Right now I gotta go." Then, as the sound of a louder explosion rang out, he grabbed his coat, "Sorry, baby...you don't know how sorry I am."

"But, when will I see you again?" Sandra asked, almost in tears.

"I'm off on Tuesday. Wait for me on Bebarfald's Corner," he said, hastily stuffing his wallet into his back pocket. "Seven thirty, I'll be there if I possibly can. I love you," he said, hastily kissing her on the cheek and leaving the room almost immediately.

Sandra sat there on the bed, her scanties still halfway down her legs, clutching the two notes Casper had thrust into her hands. Bewildered, for it had all happened so quickly, she threw the money on the end of the bed, heaved a great sigh and set to pulling her panties up to where they should be. Sobered by what had happened, she looked at her surroundings for the first time, taking in the furnishings and the bathroom which opened off the room. She had never been in a real hotel before and certainly never anything as posh as this, with its own bath and toilet. On the bureau stood a half-full bottle of whisky, something she had never tasted. Well, she decided, if she couldn't have her night of love, she might as well experience life. She found a glass in the bathroom, poured herself a slug of the spirit and topped it up with water from the tap as she had seen her dad do. It tasted like medicine, but sent a warm glow through her body as she sat on the bed and considered her next move. She couldn't go home, they wouldn't expect her and there would be difficult questions to answer if she did. Sandra had no intention of going looking for the shelter, so unless something drastic happened, she was staying right where she was.

Walking into the bathroom, she looked at the bath, sitting there inviting her to take advantage of a leisurely soak. At home she was limited to four inches of water and was screamed at if she stayed in it longer than ten minutes. Here was hot water on tap, as much as she liked and nobody to tell her she had been in the bathroom too long.

She turned on the taps and watched as the bath filled to unimagined heights—what a pity she didn't have any bubble bath like they had in the movies. Then, remembering the small bottle of perfume Casper had given her when they met that evening, "Passionate Impulse," it seemed the very thing to add to the occasion. She opened the bottle and sprinkled a few drops in the water, shed her underwear and climbed into the bath. Finally, when her skin had wrinkled up like an orange and the water was growing cold, she reluctantly climbed out and wrapped herself in one of the towels that stood on the shelf— oh the luxury of a fluffy white towel...nothing at all like her mum's threadbare striped ones.

Sandra dropped the towel on the floor and climbed into bed, pulling the covers up to her neck. She had never been in bed naked. It felt so strange that she hopped out and retrieved her slip from the floor, where Casper had dropped it when he started to undress her. Back in bed, she snuggled down, luxuriating in having a double bed all to herself. This evening had not turned out as expected, but it was heaps better than being at home, where someone was always telling her what to do. Here she was her own master. She drank down the last of the scotch in one gulp, turned out the light and almost instantly fell asleep.

~ * ~

Next morning, Sandra woke as she always did at seven, looked around in surprise at the strange surroundings, then the memory of where she was and of what had happened last night came back to her. What a pity, she thought, that I have to work today. It would have been lovely to wait there until Casper came back. She knew that was impossible, as she had already been in trouble at work lately, for, as her Auntie Kath worked there too, it was inevitable that news of any absenteeism would make its way back home.

She delved down into the bottom of her bag, a large one, as she had come straight from work on the previous evening. In there was her uniform, rather screwed up—but who cared—she didn't work as a fashion model (unfortunately). Last night's dress and shoes went into the bag, her sensible work shoes came out, her overcoat went over the uniform and she was ready to go. At the bottom of the bed the two five-pound notes still lay. She scooped them up and stuffed them into her bag. What a windfall! Fancy Casper thinking it would cost that much for a taxi; it was true what she'd heard, those Yanks had no idea how much anything cost. That was more than she earned in several weeks at that awful job and it certainly wasn't going to be wasted on taxis, when there was a perfectly good tram to catch to where she was going. This would buy the red dress she had been admiring in the Chic Salon and a pair of shoes to match into the bargain. If she hurried, she could get them before the new clothing rationing came into force. It was due in a few weeks, so this was perfect timing. Her evening may not have worked out as planned, but this unexpected windfall helped to ease the pain.

Sandra thought of leaving a note for Casper, but could see neither paper nor pencil anywhere, so she took one last look around the room and let herself out into the corridor, closing the door behind her. When the lift came, it was already occupied by a couple of snooty looking women, who looked down their noses at the girl. She stood there clutching her coat around her, trying to look as if she belonged. The women left the lift on the first floor, one remarking to the other, "Dreadful the types one sees here these days. It really brings the tone of the place down."

Humiliated, Sandra stood in the corner, for the lift driver had obviously heard the remark, too. Before he started the lift again, he smiled at her reassuringly. "Don't you pay any attention to those old bags, love. They're no better than you and me and don't have the manners to know it. You take care now; it's pretty chilly out there this morning."

Cheered by his words, Sandra smiled at him in thanks, walked through the hotel lobby with her head held high, and set out for another day of boredom at work. Her romantic adventure was over, at least for now.

Two

The morning after

Tom and Minnie were up early on Monday morning, anxious to hear a bit more of what had happened the night before. The radio gave only scanty details, but that was not surprising, as details given out over the air were strictly censored so as not to give too much information to the enemy.

Minnie started cooking breakfast as Johnny came into the room yawning and running his hands through his already untidy hair.

"Wish I didn't have to go to work today," he said. "It turned out to be a much later night than I expected; I'd have loved to sleep in just this once."

"There's a war on, son. We can't just take days off because we feel tired," his father said. "I'm sure that everyone in Sydney feels as tired, but I'll bet there won't be too much absenteeism today."

"Just the same, I think I'll keep Angela home from school today. It was a pretty disturbing night for a six-year old," said Minnie, as she set the plates down in front of the two men. "It won't do her any harm to have a day at home."

Once the men left for work, Gramma emerged from her den, closely followed by the cat. It was on the tip of Minnie's tongue to make a comment about the apple pie, for the absence of the sizable hunk the old lady had eaten was very obvious. She knew it was pointless taking on her mother-in-law; it was easier to let it go, as any argument always ended up in a deadlock. Most of the time an uneasy truce existed between the two women, for Minnie had not forgotten what a rough time she'd endured when she and Tom were first married and had lived for a while with Tom's parents. As Gramma was long since widowed and on her own, Minnie felt sorry for her most of the time, but found her eccentric ways increasingly difficult to live with. Tom, who had wanted his mother living with them no more than she, was often impatient with the way Gramma refused to toe the line, but Minnie usually stood up for her except when the old woman had been at her most vexing.

"She's been uprooted from her home; it's not an easy thing for someone her age to cope with," she had said on many occasions, when Tom was all steamed up over one or another of his mother's escapades. Most of them were funny in retrospect, but when she did things such as walking out to the letterbox in her underwear, Tom, whose ideas of what was or was not proper, was pushed almost to breaking point.

"Another episode like that and I'll pack her up and send her to Dorrie over in Hindmarsh. She was the one so set on rescuing our mother from the war; let her see what it's like living with her for a while," he fumed. Of course, he knew that would be almost impossible, for they couldn't trust Gramma to travel nearly nine hundred miles alone. He couldn't take the time off work for the four days it would take to travel there and back, nor could Minnie go and leave the two small children. They were stuck with her for the duration, it seemed.

Gramma helped herself to cornflakes and sat down at the table slurping them up from the spoon and noisily chomping on them, as she had left her teeth behind in the jar beside her bed. Minnie decided she couldn't stay there and listen to the awful noise, so she went to the girls' bedroom to rouse them for their breakfast. It always seemed to her that when the family was at home, the morning meal dragged on for hours before she could finally clear the table and wash the dishes.

She found both her small daughters awake, lying in their beds, while Angie regaled Shirley with a rather embroidered version of what she had missed the previous night.

"And then the Japs dropped a bomb in town, probably blowed up the Harbour Bridge," she was saying as Minnie entered the room.

"Now don't you go filling your sister's head with all your silly stories. They did no such thing and you know it. The next thing will be me having to spend half the night in here because the child has nightmares about it all." She pulled back the bedclothes simultaneously on both beds and pointed to the doorway.

"Up you both get, and into the kitchen with you. You," she pointed at the older of the two, "can stay home from school today. After all the carry-on last night, I want you to have a quiet day. You can practise your sums and Gramma will keep an eye on you while I take Shirley with me to the grocer's."

"I can't stay home today. It's air raid practice on Mondays."

"You had enough air raid practice last night. Anyway, it's too late now for you to get there in time. You are staying home and having a nice quiet day and that's that!"

Recognising the finality in her mother's voice, Angie scampered after her sister, knowing there was no point in arguing further. Secretly, she was happy to miss air raid practice, for it was something she hated. She had been in the toilet block one day when the siren sounded, which meant that the students should assemble in the school yard in class formation, after which they filed into the air raid shelter, which was situated on the other side of the toilets. By the time Angie made it back into the playground. everyone had disappeared, so she was forced to make her way inside by herself. The shelter had only auxiliary lighting, which made it hard to find her way around, and search as she may, she couldn't find her class or her teacher. Finally she succumbed to tears, much to the amusement of some big boys who made fun of her, only making her cry the more. Eventually a teacher investigated to see what all the fuss was about, realised immediately that this child didn't belong to her, used her own handkerchief to wipe Angie's eyes and took her by the hand to return her to her rightful place. Although she usually enjoyed being the centre of attention, she didn't like to earn it by being lost and a cry baby, so Angie was ever after nervous about being late for practice again. A day at home meant she was saved that worry for once.

Angie settled down at the kitchen table, her school work in front of her while her mother and sister left for the shops. She started out reciting her multiplication tables, but when it became obvious that Gramma wasn't paying any attention, she put the book aside and took out her crayons and colouring book. This was much more fun than being at boring old school, she thought to herself. She loved going to school normally, as long as they weren't working on sums...or having air raid practice. Angie had been at school for nearly eighteen months, for her mother had put her in at four and a half—the child was bored at home and needed the stimulation of work and the other children. Not so with her younger sister, who was as unlike Angie as it was possible to be. Shirley was round-faced, plump and blonde, slow of movement and not a fast learner. Angie on the other hand, was whip thin, with dark eyes and hair, constantly on the move and incessantly curious about the world, both at home and elsewhere. Minnie had decided to keep Shirley at home until the next New Year, when she would be three months past her fifth birthday. By then she would hopefully be sufficiently mature to cope with the full day at school and the hustle and bustle of the playground.

The two younger girls were almost a generation apart from their older siblings. There had been two other children between Johnny and Angela—a boy who was stillborn, the other a little girl who lived for four months and was found dead in her cot one morning. Traumatised by these experiences, Minnie had planned to have no more children and when Angela came along, her mother was constantly in fear that something would happen to her. This fear went out the door very quickly, as the baby was obviously thriving, ate well, slept well and progressed in leaps and bounds. Shirley, two years later, was as different from her sister in behaviour as she was in looks, a fussy eater, a grizzly colicky baby, who only slept for short periods of time. At four she still was a picky eater, although what she ate obviously was well absorbed, for unlike her skinny sister who ate everything she could get her hands on, Shirley was a picture of well-nourished health. Her poor sleeping habits as a baby were a thing of the past; the child had long afternoon naps and went out like a light in the evenings. As they had discovered the night before, not even the threat of a Japanese invasion could rouse her from her sleep.

Minnie often wondered how two children from the same parents could be so different—but then in retrospect, the same could be said of her two older ones. Sandra, the oldest, had been a pretty, sometimes stubborn little girl, hopeless at school with no ambitions of being anything other than a carbon copy of her girlfriends. Johnny, nineteen months younger, had been the good student, quiet, musical and introspective. He had hoped to be a professional musician, but there was no money for lessons and when he reached school leaving age, his father had found him an apprenticeship in the factory where he worked. It broke Minnie's heart to see her son's musician's fingers scarred and dirty from his work. She saved every spare penny she could and was hopeful that, once Shirley was in school, she would find some work, anything, just to get in the extra money that would allow her son to go back to school for the Leaving Certificate he would need to get into the Conservatorium of Music. Of course, it would have to wait for the war to be over—the only compensation for where Johnny was working was the fact that he was in a protected industry. The rumours were getting stronger that all eighteen-year-olds would be conscripted soon and with Johnny's eighteenth birthday less than a year away, Minnie slept more soundly knowing he would not be sent to war.

That evening when the whole family was together again, they sat around the dinner table talking of their experiences from the previous night. Sandra came up with a convincing story of her visit to Vera's family, thanking her lucky stars that they lived sufficiently far apart that the two sets of parents would never meet to compare stories. The two five-pound notes were still tucked safely away in her handbag, where they would stay until her Saturday half day off, her first opportunity to buy the coveted red dress.

Minnie dished up the remnants of the apple pie with generous helpings of custard to make up for the small servings of pie. "I'm sorry there's not much for anyone. I could have sworn there was more left than this," she said, looking piercingly at Gramma, who sat there with an innocent face, busily tucking into her helping of dessert.

With the meal over and the washing up out of the way, Tom turned on the radio for the evening news. Naturally last night's attack featured strongly, as did the recent British bombing of Cologne in Germany. Tom nodded approvingly, "That'll serve those Huns right for what they've done to the Poms," he said when he turned the volume down.

"All of it seems a bit like an eye for an eye," remarked Minnie. "It seems to me that it's always the ordinary people in their homes that suffer in war. I don't like those Germans more than the next person, but I'll bet they don't have any more say in what goes on than you or I do. I'd like to bet that it's the same with the Japs, too."

"You'd better not go saying things like that in public," said her husband. "You'll have us all put away for the duration, if anyone hears you spouting ideas like that."

Minnie shook her head, "Anyone with half a brain in their head would be thinking the same thing. Where did war get us the last time? It'll be the same this time round, nothing will be settled, just people's homes destroyed and fathers and sons lost forever. They should put women in charge of the world, if you ask me. We wouldn't go declaring war all the time. That's the problem with you men... whenever you don't like something all you want to do is go off and kill one another. That's what they should do—hand it all over to the women. We'd sort it out without all that killing and bombing!"

Having heard all this several times before, Tom made no attempt to argue, opting instead to change the subject.

"Shouldn't those girls be in bed?" he asked. "They had a disturbed enough night last night and it's back to school again for you tomorrow, young lady," he said to Angie. Minnie took the hint and hurried the girls off to bed, returning just in time to sit down with Tom and Johnny to listen to their favourite radio serial, Yes, What, a ridiculous, but extremely funny story of the goings-on in a fictitious schoolroom run by the long-suffering teacher, Mr Pym. Sandra had already gone to her room to read an old copy of Photoplay magazine she had borrowed from Vera. She considered herself much too adult for all that nonsense going on in the kitchen.

In the bedroom across the hall Angie lay awake, listening to the sounds from the adults and thinking over the events of the past twenty-four hours. Shirley as usual was already fast asleep, but Angie still was far from ready to succumb. She had enjoyed her day at home, for although she loved school, she missed the day-to-day activity in the house. Being at home was never boring, for there were so many visitors who came there on a regular basis. "The Mans," as Shirley called them.

There was the milkman, the bread man, the iceman...he was Angie's favourite since one day in summer he'd chipped a piece off the block of ice he was delivering for Angie to suck on. Mumma had hit the roof when she saw it, saying it was unhygienic. "And anyway, she'd paid for that ice." Still, Angie liked the iceman, for beside that he always winked at her when he came into the house, the great block of ice perched on a hessian bag on his shoulder. Then there were the others... the rent man—they'd had to hide with the door closed once when Mumma didn't have enough to pay him, having had a rather unwise wager with the local SP bookie—the clothes prop man, with his long poles for holding up the washing line, the Rawlings man who only came around occasionally, his suitcase full of all sorts of interesting ointments and pills and potions, as well as the life insurance man—two and sixpence a week—there used to be the postman, who came twice a day, but only once on Saturdays, but he had gone into the forces and now there was a post lady, who rode a big red bike and never said hello to little girls like her predecessor had.

And there were the "boys"—the grocer's boy who delivered the food order, the butcher's boy, who always smelled of meat, and the boy who came around on Saturdays to collect her parents' bets—two bob each way—on the horses. One boy who nobody was pleased to see these days was the telegram boy...for too often he brought bad news of someone fighting overseas.

Life at home for a little girl was never boring.

Three

As you sow...

The weeks went by and Sydney shivered in a cold winter. Sandra spent as much time as possible with Lieutenant Casper Freeman and finally discovered for herself that the wonders of sex were initially not exactly what she had imagined. The first time hurt a lot and she was disgusted to discover what a messy business it all was, but once she became accustomed to "it"...found it quite enjoyable. Casper continued to shower her with presents and she finally screwed up enough courage to bring him home to meet her family. At first she was nervous about it, as she thought he would find them awfully ordinary. On the contrary, like so many of the visiting Americans, he was happy to be in a home setting again, and after the first visit, Casper became a fairly regular caller at the house. Tom became his friend for life when he was presented with a bottle of Scotch...for Minnie, there was always a box of chocolates and a smaller one for Gramma. The two little girls climbed all over him, something Sandra hated, but Casper seemed to enjoy the experience. He hid chocolate bars in his pockets and encouraged them to "go search for them." On the whole, Lieutenant Freeman was a great hit with the Sherwood family.

Casper was based in Sydney on a semi-permanent basis, instructing the locals on some new radar equipment. Towards the end of July he remarked to Sandra that he had heard whispers his stint in Australia would soon end and he might be heading back to Honolulu where he had been for most of the war. Convinced that a proposal of marriage would be coming any day, Sandra thought fondly of how she would knit warm gloves and balaclavas for him—being totally ignorant of the climate in Hawaii—and how she would wait for him faithfully until the end of the war when he returned to whisk her off to the fabled United States.

As the winds of August swept through the city, Sandra was hit with two discoveries that brought her down to earth in a crash. The first was made one evening when, having come straight from work, Casper had retired to the bathroom to take a shower. His wallet lay on the bedside table and knowing he would be gone a while, Sandra picked it up and opened it out of curiosity to see what was inside. Lots of money it seemed, his ID cards, and at the back a pocket, which contained what were obviously photos and letters. Knowing she shouldn't look, Sandra could not help herself, for Casper had on the whole not been very forthcoming about his home and family. The first thing she found was a letter, which she put aside for later, more interested in the two photos that accompanied it. One was of Casper with an older couple, obviously his mother and father. The second was also of Casper and it took a second or so for the significance of the others in the photo to sink in. Beside him, his arm wrapped around her, was a young woman holding a baby. Shocked, Sandra turned to the letter, written the previous month, and read no more than the opening line, My darling husband. She dropped it as if burned and fought for breath as her dreams disappeared in one fell swoop. Casper was married!

Sounds came from the bathroom of Casper readying to emerge, so she quickly reassembled the letter and photos and replaced them in the wallet, which she returned to the bedside table. She knew she couldn't say anything, for her mother had from an early age impressed on her the fact that it was tantamount to sin to snoop in other people's property. She quickly gathered her belongings, made the excuse to Casper that she felt unwell, which was pretty true, dressed as quickly as possible and left the room.

On the tram going home, her thoughts ran round and round her head, for the other discovery she had made was one she had been trying to ignore for days. She was pregnant.

When she missed her first period. she thought nothing of it, putting it down to the fact that she had so recently started having sex. She was now a week past the next one and already changes to her body had worried her enough that she had visited one of the doctor's surgeries near the hospital where she worked. An examination had confirmed her fears, and in the days since she had been trying to summon up the courage to tell Casper. Until today's discovery, she had been sure he would marry her immediately.

Her mother, she was equally sure, would be completely furious with her, as Sandra had heard her mother only recently carrying on about Nancy Grogan down the street who "had to get married." Minnie had expressed her thoughts about what a disgrace it was and she wondered how Mrs Grogan could hold her head up in public with a daughter who had brought such shame on the family. Sandra leaned her throbbing head on the window—what on earth could she do now?

A week passed and she was unable to bring herself to the point of telling her mother. Her parents asked about Casper, at which she mumbled something about his being on duty. Minnie suspected there was something wrong in the relationship, but knew better than to ask questions; it was obvious that Sandra was upset about something and she felt sure it would come out eventually. At first she had no further suspicions, for Sandra was always having "moods" about something or other, but then she started to notice a difference in the girl's behaviour. Sandra had always been a hearty eater, but these days just picked at her food. She spent long hours in her room and showed no interest in going out or doing any of the things with Vera that had taken up her time before she met Casper.

Minnie still had no idea of what was afoot, until one morning when she was alone in the kitchen and Sandra was in the outside toilet that was just on the other side of the door. When she heard the sounds of her daughter being violently sick, all the pieces came together; Minnie hadn't gone through six pregnancies without being able to recognise the signs. She stood at the sink looking out the window, waited until her daughter came back inside, took a deep breath and followed Sandra to her bedroom. She knocked on the closed door and entered to find the girl sitting on her bed, her head in her hands. Minnie sat down beside her and put her arm around the girl's shoulders.

"How far gone are you?" she asked.

Sandra made no pretence of denial, for by this time she was too distraught to do other than answer her mother's question.

"About eight weeks, I think. Oh Mumma, what am I going to do?"

"You're going to marry the mongrel that did this to you. Was it Casper?"

Sandra's head snapped up. "Of course it was Casper; there hasn't been anyone else. He was my first. But Mumma, I can't marry him. He's married already."

Furious, Minnie took the girl by the shoulders. "Why in the name of all that's holy did you take up with a married man? It's bad enough you were sleeping around; I thought you knew better than to get involved with someone else's husband."

"I didn't know—he didn't tell me," Sandra cried, then went on to tell her mother of how she had found out.

"And what excuses did he give when you told him? What did he say about the baby?"

Shaking her head, Sandra replied, "He doesn't know about the baby. I didn't say anything to him; I was too shocked and upset."

Minnie leapt to her feet, "Well, he's going to find out quick smart; and a lot of other things too. But right now we have to think about you—do you want to have the baby? It's your choice and we will stand by you, whatever you decide."

Sandra burst into tears. "I'd love to have babies one day, but not now. I don't even feel grown-up myself. How could I look after a baby?"

"There's plenty your age and younger looking after babies and lots of them don't even have families to support them. But that doesn't prove or solve anything. You can't get married, we know that—now you have to make the decision whether you want this baby or not. If something else has to be done, we can't afford to waste any time."

"You mean get rid of it? Isn't that dangerous?

"It's either that, or you have the baby and give it up for adoption. There are no other options; your whole life would be ruined if you had an illegitimate child. And yes, I know abortions can be dangerous, but I also know there are decent places where things like that can be done. I'm not talking of some old lady with a crochet hook in a back alley. Your Auntie Kath has been around hospitals all her life; she would know of good places, I'm sure of that."

"Auntie Kath! I don't want her to know—I don't want anyone to know. Can't we keep it a secret?"

"Well, if you decide to have the baby, everyone in the family is going to know. But if you decide to get rid of it, then we have to get help. We can't tell your father; he'd half kill you and then kill Casper, which I think would be less than that one deserves, but I don't fancy spending the rest of my married life with a husband in jail. My sister Kath is not the dragon you always seem to think she is... she knows how to keep her mouth shut and she's our only hope in this mess. First you have to decide and decide in a hurry. Do you want to have this baby or not?"

Sandra shook her head. "No Mumma, I don't. It sounds a dreadful thing to kill a little baby and I know I'll feel bad about it all my life, but I think the only way to go is to have the abortion."

Minnie nodded her head, and briefly hugged the girl who was sobbing into her shoulder. "Well that's that. Now we have to decide what to do first."

She stood up. "You get yourself dressed; we're going to visit Lootenant Casper Whatshisname. He's got a hell of a lot of explaining to do. No…on second thoughts, I'll see him. I think it best you have no more to do with him."

It was a Saturday and after sitting down with a cup of tea, Minnie decided to see her sister first. If she were to confront the lieutenant, she must have some sort of idea how much all this was going to cost. She had little spare money and she knew that abortions, particularly in a proper clinic, did not come cheap. She was pinning all her hopes on Kath having more knowledge than she. Her sister was a smart woman who had never married and had made a good career working as a dietitian in hospitals all over Sydney. She knew many doctors and nursing staff and was a far savvier person than Minnie, who had married young and had little experience of the world outside her own little family. She knew for a fact that Kath had had several abortions herself in the past, something that had shocked Minnie at the time, but would serve her well in the current situation. She told Sandra of the change of plans and asked her to mind the two little ones while she visited Kath at home. Sandra, who would normally find some excuse to get out of child minding, gladly agreed, thankful that her predicament had been taken out of her hands, at least for the time being.

Fortunately, it was Kath's day off and she was at home doing her housework when Minnie arrived. Visits such as this were so unusual that Kath left off what she was doing and sat her sister down at the kitchen table. "Now tell me what's wrong; it must be something pretty bad for you to turn up like this on a Saturday morning."

Minnie told her the whole story, finishing with, "I have absolutely no idea of where to take her…I certainly can't ask Doctor Norris a question like that. Then I thought of you; I know you've been to places like that before."

Kath smiled ironically. "The black sheep of the family does come in handy now and then, I see. The silly little idiot, I wondered why she seemed half asleep the last few days. Just you give me a few minutes to change and put my hat on; we'll go down the street and I'll make a few phone calls. Those places don't take weekends off these days, there's so much business for them since the Yanks arrived."

True to her word, Kath quickly found the information she needed and made an appointment for Sandra there and then. The operation was to be the next Tuesday and would cost fifty pounds, a huge amount that sent Minnie's head reeling. If Casper didn't come up with the money, what on earth would she do?

"He'll pay," said Kath. "Don't you worry about that. Otherwise, you threaten to take it to his superior officer. The US Navy doesn't look too kindly on their officers going around impregnating the locals. In the meantime, you keep Sandra home from work; I'll fix it with personnel. And don't you worry about the place she's going...they'll take better care of her there than they do in the public hospitals; they know what sort of trouble they'll be in otherwise. She'll need to get a taxi home, so make sure you get extra from him for that."

Minnie thanked her sister, gave her a hug and headed home, the details of Sandra's appointment safely tucked away in her handbag. Next step would be to confront the lieutenant.

This task was made easier when Sandra admitted that she had a key to Casper's room at the hotel. He had given it to her early in the relationship and she hadn't yet thought to return it. Neither Tom nor Johnny were around that day, for they both worked overtime in the morning and were heading to a football match in the afternoon. Afterwards, Tom would be at the pub with his mates and Johnny would have gone off somewhere with his friends, so Minnie had the whole day free to go into town without any questions asked. Sandra was by then fed to the teeth with the demands of her young sisters, but could not complain in the circumstances, so had no alternative other than to agree to stay on as babysitter.

Four

Retribution

On the tram heading for the city, Minnie's stomach churned at the thought of the task ahead. She didn't know her way around town very well and, even armed with a rough map that Sandra had drawn for her, she had a few false starts before she finally found the Ambassador Hotel. She had never been in a hotel—other than the Ladies Parlour at the local and that didn't count, so it was with trepidation that she climbed the steps and walked into the lobby. Sandra's instructions told her exactly where to go, so she made her way across to the lifts, trying to look as if she belonged there and certain that every eye in the place was upon her. Waiting for the lift to arrive, she expected at any moment to be challenged by someone asking her what she was doing there. She entered the lift, gave her floor to the driver and stood there, sure that he could hear her heart pounding. Down the corridor she went, searching for the number on the key she held in her sweating hand, knocked on the door and waited. No answer—good, Casper was not at home.

Minnie looked stealthily up and down the corridor, turned the key in the lock and entered the room. Somewhat surprised that it was nothing out of the ordinary—she hadn't quite known what to expect, for like her daughter, she had never been in a hotel room before—she did a quick check of the room and the adjoining bathroom and finally took a seat on a chair under the window. There she would wait, if necessary until hell froze over, for Casper to return.

It was quite a long wait, but he eventually came. Minnie had started to nod off through boredom when she was roused by the sound of a key turning in the lock. She prayed to herself that Casper would be alone and her prayers were answered. He almost fell over when he came into the room and saw Minnie sitting in the chair under the window. Struck dumb by this totally unexpected visitor, the American just stood there looking at her. She spoke first. "I suppose I'm the last person you expected to see here."

Still unable to speak, he nodded, then regained his composure and said in an almost normal voice, "Mrs Sherwood, what are you doing here? Has something happened to Sandra?"

Minnie rose to her feet. "I suppose you could say that. Something I'm sure your wife would be very interested to hear, Lieutenant."

The American drew a deep breath, his face paling noticeably. "My wife? What makes you think I have a wife?"

"You should have been more careful where you leave your letters if you wanted that to be a secret," Minnie said, seating herself back in the chair. "I suggest that you sit yourself down, young man. You and I have a lot to talk about."

At first he started as if to speak, then shrugged his shoulders and sat on the bed facing her. He made no further attempt to talk and sat through Minnie's discourse without comment, his only reaction being a gasp when he heard about the pregnancy. Although she had originally intended to lay into him with a vengeance, Minnie found herself recounting everything in calm tones, finishing with the words, "Now what have you to say to all that? We welcomed you into our home and you took advantage of an eighteen-year-old girl." He seemed about to argue, so she raised a hand to silence him. "Now, before you say anything, it is obvious that she was no unwilling party to what went on here. That is between her and me and I've already spoken to her on that count. She is just as guilty as you and I realise that. What I can't understand or forgive is why you allowed this to happen, knowing you had a wife and a child back home."

All aggression faded from his face. He hit his hands on his knees and raised them helplessly in the air.

"I knew it was wrong. I haven't been home for over a year; it gets so lonely in a strange place. I know it's no excuse, but it gets so lonely."

"Then why couldn't you find other ways to fix that loneliness? There's plenty out there willing to do that, why pick on a young girl from a decent home?"

"I didn't go looking for Sandra; it just happened. I've tried the other type and it felt so dirty. I took every precaution I could, but obviously it didn't work. I am very fond of your daughter and this was the last thing I wanted to happen. I'm so sorry."

That he was genuine Minnie felt no doubt, finding that all her anger had dissipated when faced with this young man, who in spite of everything she couldn't help liking. This, she realised, was probably a scene being played out on countless other occasions; an otherwise decent young man who was as much a victim of war as anyone else. Casper ran his hands through his hair and then looked up at her. "What is going to happen? What can I do to fix things?"

"I've talked it over with Sandra. There were several things she could do and I left it completely up to her. She has decided to have an abortion. I don't like the thought, but that's her decision and it's probably the best one in the long run." She stood, walked over to the young man and laid a hand on his shoulder. "I'm here today as much as anything to ask you for the money. We don't have any and you must be responsible for that. The other thing is to say to you that you must never see Sandra again." He opened his mouth to speak at that and she shook her head, repeating, "Never."

He sat for a moment without speaking; then nodded in agreement. "I know you are right. I will hate not seeing her or knowing what has happened to her. I want you to know that I love my wife, but if I weren't married, I would marry Sandra and be a good father to her baby. I never wanted this to happen; I never thought it would and

I know it was stupid and irresponsible of me. I should have guessed when Sandra disappeared the way she did that something was wrong, but I never even thought it was because of something like this. My mom would kill me if she knew what I've done—I don't think she would have been as kind to me as you have. You tell me how much money you need and I will get it for you. It so happens I have a fair bit of cash on me right now; how much is it going to cost?"

He thought it unwise to tell her where the money had come from. He'd spent last night in an all-night poker game and had come away with over a hundred pounds in winnings. Funnily enough, his intentions for the afternoon had been to shop for something for Sandra. He had intended to take the gift to her home, anxious as he had been at her unusual absence. The furthest thing from his mind was that the money would go to Sandra in this way.

Taking a deep breath, Minnie told him how much, expecting at least some argument. She was surprised when he took out his wallet and counted out twelve five-pound notes, saying, "Are you sure that's enough?"

Minnie took the money, thinking that she had never in her life held so much money at one time. She had to harden her heart when she saw how devastated the boy was; at the same time she was filled with relief that the confrontation had gone so well. She could go home and set about straightening out her daughter's life.

She made one concession to the American before leaving, something she would never tell Sandra. He begged her to let him know that everything had gone well and she promised to write to him and tell him the outcome, as long as he gave her his solemn promise that he would make no attempt to contact Sandra again. He agreed, gave her his Service number and told her that he had just found out he was to return to Hawaii in the next few weeks. Minnie kissed him on the forehead where he still sat on the bed and left the room without a backward glance.

When she reached the street, she found she was shaking so much she would have given anything for a brandy, but compromised by finding a cafe and having a strong cup of tea with lots of sugar in it.

She couldn't afford to go to pieces at this stage; there was a lot to face in the next few days, not the least being the fact that she must keep everything a secret from her husband. It was going to be very hard to keep on an even keel without giving anything away; Tom must never know and it was up to her to make sure he didn't.

Sandra spent most of the time between then and Tuesday in her room. They had agreed that as far as the family was concerned she was ill, which would allow them to keep up the pretence in the days after the operation. When pressed by Tom for details, Minnie told him "female problems"—which was true in a way and effectively silenced any further questions, the workings of the female body being something virtually unknown to Tom and most men of his generation.

Minnie had no intention of allowing her daughter to go alone on Tuesday and decided she would give the excuse that she was taking Sandra to a specialist in town. She and Sandra left the house for a while on Monday, ostensibly to visit their local doctor and she was then able to tell Tom and the others that he had referred Sandra to the specialist. Nobody questioned this, but there was the problem of the two little girls on Tuesday morning, for Minnie and Sandra would have to leave long before Angela went to school. There was no alternative other than to leave Gramma in charge and all that Minnie could do was hope and pray that the old lady wouldn't do anything stupid. That was a risk she would have to take.

Five

The solution

Early on Tuesday morning they left the house as if they were about to catch a tram to the city, but as soon as they were out of sight, Minnie steered her daughter towards the shops and the taxi rank. They had ten pounds of Casper's money for that purpose, so why not take advantage of it? Sandra had not been allowed to eat or drink that morning and was so nervous and feeling so ill, it seemed wise to get to their destination as soon as possible.

The address Kath had written on the piece of paper turned out to be an anonymous-looking, large Victorian house in a comfortable middle-class suburb. Nothing on the exterior suggested that it was anything other than a private residence. Hoping that Kath had not made a mistake, Minnie rang the doorbell, her daughter's sweaty hand gripping her arm.

The door was opened promptly by a woman who could have been any suburban matron. She smiled at the two standing nervously on the doorstep and said, "Won't you please come inside." Obviously, they were in the right place. She asked their names; Minnie gave the fictitious name Kath had made the booking under, at which the woman nodded and showed them into a room, where two other women were sitting quite far apart, obviously not together. The younger one, who was about Sandra's age, looked up only briefly and lowered her head. The older of the two, who looked to be in her forties, had brightly dyed hair and wore way too much makeup for daytime. She smiled at them quite cheerily and said, "Good morning, dears. Lovely day, 'int it?"

Minnie weakly returned the smile but could do no more than nod; Sandra sat next to her, nervously twisting her handkerchief round and round. She glanced once at the other girl, who looked up briefly and again lowered her head. Silence reigned in the room until the woman returned and asked both of the young girls to come with her. Sandra rose and turned, expecting her mother to follow. Minnie shook her head. "No love, I can't come; I don't think they will allow it," she said while looking towards the woman for confirmation.

"I'm sorry, dear; your mother will have to wait for you here. She can come in later, once you're ready for her." The woman gently steered the two girls from the room.

Minnie looked nervously at her watch, then checked again—it was only nine o'clock; it seemed as if the day had gone on for ages. The other woman smiled at her. "Your daughter, is it? Is this her first time?"

Shocked, Minnie replied, "Of course it is; she's only eighteen and I sincerely hope it will be her last." Then, thinking she had sounded a bit abrupt, she asked, "Has your daughter been in there long?"

"Me daughter?" said the woman in a puzzled tone, then laughed and shook her head. "No, love, it's me having the op, not any daughter; I don't have one."

Embarrassed, Minnie was about to try another subject, when the woman came into the room saying, "Mrs Johnson, could you come with me, please?" Both women looked at one another, then Minnie realised this was the name they had booked under. She jumped to her feet. "Is she all right? Has something happened to Sandra?"

"Nothing has happened," said the woman reassuringly, taking her arm and leading her from the room. "It's just that we need to have the money up front and your daughter says you have it."

Minnie was ushered into an office. She hastily opened her handbag and took out the roll of notes. The woman counted them, then said, "Thank you, Mrs Johnson. You can return to the waiting room. We'll call you when Sandra has had her operation." Minnie left the room and returned to the other to continue her wait.

Sandra and the other young girl sat side by side on chairs like condemned prisoners awaiting their fate. The other girl was taken away first, leaving Sandra waiting alone, until the woman returned and showed her to a room at the far end of the corridor where there were two hospital beds, each surrounded by curtains. The woman pulled back the curtains on one, handed her a hospital gown and told her to take off her clothes and put on the gown.

"Nurse will be with you in a minute," she said, pulling the curtains back around the bed.

Sandra did as she was told, then sat on the edge of the bed almost numb with terror at what was about to happen. A nurse came into the room, spoke briefly to the person in the other bed—the other girl, Sandra assumed—then pulled the curtains back from Sandra's bed, saying, "Into bed you hop; I'm going to shave you now."

Horrified, Sandra's hand went to her head. The nurse laughed, "Not there, silly, I have to shave you down there for the operation." This she went about doing, chatting to Sandra all the time, who just lay there enduring the humiliation and wishing the whole thing were over and she was back home in her own bed.

The preparation over, the nurse left the room. Sandra lay in the bed, wondering if she could somehow escape, when a tremulous voice came from the other bed. "I'm so scared. What are they going to do to us?"

"I'm scared too," said Sandra. "I never thought anything like this would ever happen to me. I wish it was all over."

"Is that your mum out there with you?" asked the girl. "I wish mine was here; I haven't told her. We're Catholics, we...she doesn't believe in all this. I'm so frightened, this is a terrible sin. I'm only eighteen... how old are you?"

Sandra, used to her mother's practical outlook on life, suddenly found herself a lot more at ease. She was still worried about what was to come, but her resolve had returned and she felt for some reason a lot older than the other girl.

"I'm eighteen, too. I suppose it is a sin, because it's against the law, but I really have no alternative. I don't think it's fair to bring a baby into the world that isn't wanted. I would have kept it if the father could have married me, but he couldn't."

"My boyfriend says we are too young to have children; he's nearly eighteen, too. I wanted to get married, but he doesn't want to just yet—he's borrowed the money for this and I'd much rather spend it on things for the baby." The girl was openly crying.

"I'm sure we've both done the right thing," said Sandra, as the nurse came back into the room and pulled back the curtains. She said, "Come along, dear; doctor is ready for you now."

Sandra started to follow through the doorway, then turned back on an impulse and poked her head through the curtains. "I know we're doing the right thing," she told the sobbing girl. "I just know it—we'll be all right."

She was shown into a spotlessly clean room, bare of furniture other than a high bed and a cupboard, on top of which was a tray holding instruments and bottles. The nurse helped her onto the bed and said, "I heard what you said. Good, you've got the right attitude. You will be fine." Then, indicating the man who came into the room, "This is Doctor... he's going to give you a little injection; you'll go to sleep and when you wake up it will be all over."

Sandra, who usually was terrified of needles, endured it all with her newfound confidence. Told to count backwards from ten, she complied and woke to find herself back in her bed in the other room, still counting. The nurse stood by the bed, smiling. "You can stop counting now, it's all over and everything went well. I'm going to get your mother in soon; you just lie there and rest for a moment."

Groggily, Sandra looked to the other bed. It was empty, the covers turned back, waiting for its occupant to return. She was trying to collect her thoughts to ask the nurse about the other girl, when her mother came into the room, worry written all over her face.

"Don't worry, Mum, I'm fine; the nurse told me so. I'm so glad it's all over. When can we go home?"

"Not for a while yet," said the nurse, who had followed Minnie into the room. "You have to wait for the anaesthetic to wear off. In a little while I'm going to bring both of you something to eat and a cup of tea. Then, if you are feeling well enough, you can certainly go home." She smiled at them both and left the room.

Minnie brought a chair to the bedside, pulled the curtains around them and sat holding Sandra's hand. "I can't believe how calm you are. You were so frightened before; they must have given you something to calm you down."

They were disturbed by the doctor entering the room. He shook Minnie's hand and felt Sandra's pulse. "How are you, young lady? Nurse has told you that everything went as expected." To Minnie he said, "The anaesthetic we used is sodium pentothal...it wears off much more quickly than ether and usually causes less nausea. It also has a residual calming effect, so your daughter will sleep well tonight and should have minimal discomfort. I'll look in on her again in a little while and if she continues to progress as well as at present, she can go home quite soon."

Vastly relieved, Minnie thanked the doctor and sat holding her daughter's hand, while Sandra slipped in and out of consciousness. Ten minutes later, the nurse arrived with tea and biscuits. With her mother's help, Sandra sat up and sipped the hot tea—never had a cup of tea tasted so good. She realised that she was hungry and asked for one of the biscuits, which she ate, saying, "I wish I had something more; I feel as if I haven't eaten in ages."

"First things first," her mother said. "I'll feed you anything you want once we get you home. We've a taxi ride ahead of us, so I think biscuits will be enough for the time being."

An hour later, they were sitting in the cab on the way home. The hospital had asked if they had transport, then called the taxi for them. As they walked down the steps to the car, Sandra noticed a young man pacing up and down outside. I'll bet that's the girl's boyfriend, she thought. I wish I could tell him she'll be all right.

Minnie would have preferred not to have the taxi pull up outside the house but knew that Sandra was still too shaky to walk far. She had decided to tell the family that the specialist had done some sort of procedure on the girl and that would explain her being in bed and the fact that they had taken a taxi home.

Everything in the house was as normal. Shirley sat on the kitchen floor stroking Gramma's cat; the old lady was sitting near her, knitting something in khaki wool. She made no comment when the two entered the house and went straight to Sandra's room. Minnie told Sandra to undress and get into bed and left her to go to the kitchen. She thanked Gramma for minding Shirley.

"Angie got off to school okay?" she asked.

Gramma grunted in assent, but made no comment, concentrating on her knitting—she was turning the heel of the sock and that was always a tricky operation.

Even though she felt as if the day had gone on forever, it was only just past lunchtime. Minnie made lunch for everyone and took a sandwich to Sandra's room. The girl was asleep, so deciding not to disturb her, Minnie left the plate on the bedside table and tiptoed out of the room.

She was at the sink washing up, when Gramma piped up, "She got rid of it, did she?"

Minnie froze and took a deep breath, then said in as normal a voice as she could muster, "What are you talking about?"

"The baby. That's what I'm talking about. You think I don't have eyes in me head? Tommie may have fallen for your specialist story, but not me. I know where the two of you've been today. It's that Yank that's the father, I suppose."

Minnie put down the dish mop and sat herself at the table facing the old woman. It was pointless denying the truth. She took the knitting from her and clasped her mother-in-law's hands in hers.

"Gramma, Tom must never know. It would break his heart and cause untold trouble. If Sandra has any chance of getting over this and having a hope for the future, nobody must ever know. Can I trust you to keep this to yourself?"

"Of course, I know that. Us women have to keep together sometimes. Men aren't as strong as us, none of 'em are. I might be a silly old woman, but I know what's what and I love our Sandie as much as anyone. Her secret is safe with me. The girl's all right, is she?"

Minnie rose and hugged the old woman. "Yes, she's fine, just a bit shaken up. And she's going to be okay in the future. This has been a tough lesson that I'd hoped she never would have had to learn, but deep down I think she's really a good girl, just a bit silly at times." She smiled and added, "I suppose we all are."

Nodding in agreement, the old lady picked up her knitting. "You're right there, Minnie me girl."

~ * ~

Sandra had no problems in recovering and was back at work two days later. She was nervous about facing her Auntie Kath and said so to her mother. Minnie assured her that Kath would say and do nothing and that Sandra was to act as if nothing had happened.

Kath, when she saw the girl simply said, "You're back then. Are you feeling better?" Sandra answered "yes" and, relieved, went about her work, feeling glad that bridge had been crossed. Strangely enough, she felt happy to be back at work and found herself taking an interest in the job, something she never done before. More than anything else, she felt relieved and thankful that her life had been put back on track. She put thoughts of Casper out of her mind, but no longer felt anger towards him, realising that she was as much to blame as he for what had happened. She wanted to thank her mother (and even Kath) for what they had done for her but didn't have the words to do so. At home she tried in other ways to show her feelings, helping out with chores when previously she had evaded them and even taking an interest in the two younger girls, something she had never done in the past.

Even Tom noticed this change in attitude. He remarked to Minnie one Sunday when Sandra had taken the girls to the park, "Our Sandra is really growing up, isn't she? It's funny how these things happen overnight."

Minnie smiled to herself, thinking at what cost to all involved! She answered, "I suppose it happens to all of us eventually. With Sandra it just took a bit more than most."

True to her promise, Minnie wrote to Casper Freeman, telling him that Sandra had survived the operation okay, telling him that she bore him no grudge, and wishing him well.

Several weeks later, a letter with an American stamp came addressed to Mrs T. Sherwood. Inside was a postcard from Hawaii. There was no message and no signature—just two words. "Thank you."

Six

On holiday, December 1944

Minnie sometimes thought she had lost her identity completely. It seemed that nobody called her by her given name anymore. To the neighbours and all the tradespeople she was Mrs Sherwood, to her husband she was "love" or "darl" and sometimes "mother." Her children called her Mumma, her sister called her Sis, her mother-in-law usually called her nothing at all. She was often hard pressed to remember the last time someone had actually called her Minnie. In a way, she thought, you lose your identity when you get married. You used to be a person in your own right; suddenly you are just an anonymous wife and mother. It seemed like only yesterday that she was someone sought after; at school she had been a star pupil, top of the class—someone to look up to. When she left school there were her girlfriends and the boys she met at dances... all of these called her by her name and she was still someone. Tom did too, when they first started courting, but it seemed that the moment he put the ring on her finger, she stopped being her own person and became his wife. Still, in spite of that, she felt happy with her lot in life; she loved her husband and children and wouldn't dream of it being any other way. When she compared her life with her sister's she knew she wouldn't swap places for anything. Although she had hoped to take a job once Shirley was at school, she had abandoned that idea, as Gramma's health had deteriorated and Minnie did not feel she could leave the two girls in her care. This would have to wait until they were a few years older.

These thoughts ran through her head as she sat on the beach at Manly Pool, trying to distinguish her two small daughters from the hordes of other children who frolicked on the water's edge. It was school holidays and she had taken the girls to stay at one of the guest houses that lined the harbour's shore. Tom and the two older children had stayed at home and usually joined her on the weekend. For now, time hung heavily on her, used as she was to being busy from morning to night. No cooking to do, precious little washing, for the girls spent most of the day in their swimsuits, and the sheets and towels were supplied in the boarding house where they were staying.

Yesterday, just for a change, they had taken the ferry over to the city, wandered around the ferry wharves, bought ice creams and caught the next ferry back to Manly. The girls loved the ferry. They held their breath as the engines were turned off for the craft to float quietly through the submarine boom that stretched across the harbour—no running around allowed, for quiet had to be maintained in case a waiting sub was out there listening for sounds of shipping above. Then came the excitement of crossing the Heads, the ferry rocking side to side as it ploughed through the waves that rolled in from the open sea. Angie loved this, but little Shirley wasn't too sure about it. She clung to her mother as she watched the horizon disappear, holding her breath and only letting it go when the ferry righted itself; ready to attack the next wave that hit. These adventures over, there came the part that both girls loved best. The musicians started to play. To the adults on board they were just a group of old blokes, with a squeeze box, a clarinet and a violin. To the girls they were something wonderful, real men who made real music...and they played all the songs that everyone knew, "Daisy - a bicycle built for two," "Cecilia - Does your mother know you're out?" and because it was wartime, the old WW1 favourites "Rose of No Man's Land" and "Lili Marlene"—which the

Allies had stolen from the Germans—as well as the current hit, the nonsense song "Mairzy Doats and Dozey Doats and Little Lambsy Divey." The girls knew most of these songs and completely without embarrassment sang along with the music—much to the amusement of those around.

When the musicians moved on, the girls followed them. Minnie let them go, for they would come to no harm on the boat and she knew they would come skittering back in no time—hands held out for pennies, as the musicians were circling the boat, taking up a collection from the passengers. On one trip, the man with the money box allowed Angie to carry it for him, rightly thinking that the passengers would be more than usually generous, just to see the excitement on the eight-year-old's face as the coins fell into the box.

Another part of the fun of a trip on the ferry was to go to the lower deck and inspect the huge engines that drove the ship. These were exposed in all their glory, their shiny brass pistons working up and down; the noise was ear-shattering, the smell of oil almost overwhelming. Minnie thought that all things considered, for the price of one shilling for herself and a penny for each of the girls, a trip on the Manly Ferry was the best entertainment that money could buy.

At the weekend, with Sandra and her new boyfriend minding the girls, Minnie and Tom went to the other end of Manly to inspect Gramma's house. It had been abandoned, its windows boarded up since Tom had taken the old lady to live with them early in 1942. This was the house where Tom and his sister had grown up and it saddened him to find it in such a derelict state. He had tried at first to rent it out, but there were no takers, renters being every bit as wary about living on the ocean front as were the homeowners when the threat of invasion had been so strong two years ago. It would probably be lettable now, for there had been only one other scare since the night the submarines came into the harbour. A month following that, a submarine had fired on the eastern suburbs of Sydney and again in Newcastle, but these days the Japanese were too occupied in other parts of the Pacific to worry about Sydney and its surrounds.

The house was a semi-detached, single-storey brick cottage, built around the turn of the century. It had a small front garden and a larger one at the rear. Both of these were overgrown with grass and weeds to almost waist height and the front veranda was littered with old newspapers and other rubbish. Tom pushed the litter aside and opened the front door with the key he had brought along, together with a torch, as he knew that visibility inside would be almost nil with all the windows covered up with sheets of timber taken from old tea chests. With no ventilation for nearly three years, the house stank of damp and cats' urine. The reason for the latter became immediately apparent, as two alley cats that had been asleep on the old sofa in the front room fled in fear of the sudden intruders.

"I wonder how they got in," said Tom, as he made his way down the hallway. "Phew, this place smells disgusting."

At the back of the house, his question was answered by the sight of a broken window in the kitchen. The boarding on this window had been pulled away, obviously by human hands, and the room was littered with the remains of old meals that had been eaten on dishes from the cupboards. Whoever had broken in had long since left, having made no attempt to clean up their mess.

"You'd think the dirty mongrels would have washed the dishes before they left," he said to Minnie, who had followed him into the house, a handkerchief held to her nose in an attempt to keep out the smells.

"Maybe we should try to clean it all up." Minnie looked around her in disgust. "But how can we? There's no gas, so we can't heat any water. This mess needs more than cold water to get it clean."

Tom shook his head. "No, it would be impossible. Let's heap all the stuff in the sink and cover it with water. It won't make it any pleasanter a job when we eventually do wash them, but at least it might make it easier." He started picking up plates and cups, then paused, saying, "Maybe we should just toss it all out?"

"That's Gramma's best china they've used," said Minnie inspecting one of the plates. "It's too good to throw away. We'll clean off as much as possible for now and leave it all for another time.

Without the gas on, there really is nothing more we can do." She looked around the house, memories flooding through her mind of the early days of her marriage, when she and Tom had moved in with his mother and father. What a rough time Gramma had given her in those days, envying the girl who had taken her only son away and relishing the chance to make her life a misery.

When Tom told her that he was bringing his mother to stay with them, it had taken every bit of Minnie's forbearance to accept the fact that her tormenter from the past was being brought into her home. At first she'd intended to get some of her own back, but when she saw how frail Gramma had become in recent years, it hadn't been in her heart to be anything other than generous to the old woman. In the two years since Sandra's abortion, the relationship between the two women had become a lot better, to the degree that Minnie had almost forgotten her past troubles.

I should be glad that her house has become such a mess, she thought, but I'm not—only sad.

To Tom she said, "Let's not tell Gramma about all this; it would break her heart." Tom nodded in agreement, for his mother had become even frailer—both mentally and physically—in recent times, since the death of her beloved cat, Blackie. He had offered to get her another cat, but she refused, saying that nothing could take her Blackie's place, and anyway she'd wait until she went back home after the war. That she would never go home again was very apparent to both Tom and Minnie—these days she could hardly get out of bed to eat her meals. Tom and Sandra had only been able to join the family this weekend because Johnny had generously agreed to stay home and keep an eye on his grandmother.

"I'm going to try to board up this window again," Tom said. "But first we'd best check and see there's no more intruders in the place. Cats, I mean," he said as Minnie looked fearfully around. They went systematically though the house, checking every nook and cranny, and in the process noticing that the two-legged visitors had helped themselves to anything removable, "Or hockable," Tom muttered.

He went to the shed and came out with a hammer and nails and a rusty scythe.

"I'll clear up some of the yard while I'm here too," he said. "Darl, while I'm doing the window, how about you clean up some of the mess in the front yard? Once we've done all that, we can burn off some of the rubbish in the old oil drum in the back yard." Minnie set to gathering up all the loose paper. In the long grass, she picked up more than a dozen empty soft drink bottles. These she took into the kitchen and rinsed out. She searched around and found an old basket in one of the cupboards and piled the bottles into it. These she would take back to the shops and get the tuppence back on each bottle. Why throw them out when there was a refund given on old bottles? Fancy throwing them away, she thought. Some people have more money than sense.

The window once again secure, Tom attacked the long grass. Minnie walked along behind him, gathering up armfuls and piling it all into the back yard incinerator. It was impossible to do much of a job with the old scythe, but at least the worst of the growth was cut down and the rest of the mess around the house tidied up. When they finished, Tom found some matches in the kitchen and lit the incinerator. They stood by watching it burn, both feeling hot and filthy and longing for a bath, which would have to wait until they returned to the guesthouse. Neither of them relished a cold bath, dirty they may be, Spartan definitely not, even in this warm weather. They hunted around and found that, luckily, there were some clean towels in the linen cupboard. There was no soap in the bathroom, but Tom found a dried-up cake of Sunlight Soap in the washhouse. It lathered well enough to allow them both to have a good wash—at least they would look respectable when they walked back through the streets, even if they still felt hot and sticky. Minnie, much to Tom's amusement, gathered up her basket full of bottles. They locked up the house again, took a last look at its vastly improved appearance, and made their way back to the guesthouse, where Sandra was impatiently awaiting their arrival.

"You've been four whole hours," she complained. "What on earth have you been up to?"

"We've been working like slaves," said her mother. "Think yourself lucky we didn't come and make you pitch in and help. Gramma's house was a shambles and we couldn't just go off and leave it like that. And don't you go saying anything to her about it, my girl. I don't want her getting all upset. Where are your sisters?"

The girls, it appeared, were in their room, happily playing with cut out dolls that had been in their Christmas stockings. These were their favourites—Plain and Pearl, the Woolly Sisters. Each girl had her own paper doll; Angie had Plain, Shirley, Pearl. Sandra had helped them by cutting out the dolls; they were now doing the same with all the different outfits that came with them. Angie had taken on the task of cutting out Shirley's doll's clothes as well as hers...for when they previously had cut-outs, Shirley had always managed to accidentally remove the tabs at the top that attached the clothes to the dolls. As this was inevitably followed by misery of unimaginable proportions, Angie thought it best to help out rather than have to endure her sister's floods of tears.

Minnie dutifully admired their handiwork; then as she still felt hot and uncomfortable, said to them, "How about you put those away for later and we all go down the pool for a swim?"

Ten minutes later, the whole group was heading towards the Manly Pool, past the Fun Pier, where the dodgems cars and the giant Ferris wheel lay idle. The only activity in there at this time of day was in the penny arcade. Next to this was the Manly Aquarium, above its entrance a giant jawbone of a shark, so threatening that the two little girls gave it a wide berth. Then at the entrance to the ferry wharf was the Fish and Chip shop, "Please can we have some chips?" begged the little girls.

"Not before you go in the water," said their mother, a statement she was forced to repeat as they passed Burt's Milk Bar at the other side of the wharf entrance, this time to a plea for ice cream.

"Time for all those things later," she said. She shook her head in refusal to the street photographer who always haunted the wharf area, as she herded her children down the steps towards the sand. Tom, who had grown up on this beach, dived straight into the water, leaving Minnie to remove sandals, dab noses with zinc cream and stow their belongings together. She headed for the water, a child on each hand, grumbling to herself that she always seemed to be the one who was stuck with the children. Sandra, with Cliff, her boyfriend, had left them at the steps and headed along the boardwalk that ran along one side and for the full length of the pool. This boardwalk had two sides, divided by a fence. On the harbour side of the fence was the promenade, which ran all the way from the ferry wharf to the shoreline at the far end of the pool. At intervals along the way were steps running down to small mooring wharves where speedboats offered the intrepid a ride for five shillings. These always did a roaring trade when the Americans were around.

On the pool side, the boardwalk sported two diving boards; one quite low, the other much higher up. Only the experienced or the foolhardy ever dived from the higher board, for particularly at low tide, even the lower one was a fair distance from the water. In the pool were two pontoons, popular with the young of both sexes, as they offered an opportunity for each to eye the other and for the boys to show off. The first and smaller pontoon was ideal for sunbathing away from the shore and the children who ran around kicking sand in all directions. The second one, towards the end of the pool, was a much more splendid affair. It had a water wheel and a slippery slide—something that Angie had been agitating to be allowed to try. Even if she could have taken the child out there—for her swimming was at best rudimentary—Minnie would not feel safe taking her little girl on the slide. She was hoping that Tom would oblige, but had not made any promises to her daughter, for she wasn't sure her husband would be willing.

Once Tom had cooled off by swimming out to the boardwalk, he called out to Sandra and Cliff, who sat with their feet dangling over the edge.

"Come on in, you scaredy-cats. You'll never get wet sitting up there."

"She's the scaredy-cat, not me," called back Cliff. "She thinks that if she jumps in she'll ruin her hair."

"Then you come in, I'll race you to the far pontoon," Tom called back.

Cliff looked at Sandra, who shrugged. "You go...I'll go back to Mum." She stood and watched the boy jump into the pool, then turned and headed back towards the sand, studiously ignoring a wolf whistle from an American sailor, who leant over the fence, watching the passing parade.

On the water's edge, Minnie stood watching the two swimmers, head to head making their way across the pool. Although Tom had more than twenty years on the younger man, she knew that it was a rare person who could beat her husband in a race. He had been surf club champion when they met and had won every medal in the swimming races when he was at school. Although he was now in his late forties, he was still a very fit man, who cycled the five miles back and forth from his work every day. In the end it was a dead heat, although Minnie suspected Tom had slowed down a bit so as not to make the younger man feel uncomfortable. Tom really liked Cliff, as did Minnie—they both had high hopes that something would come of the romance, as the lad fitted into the family as if he'd always been there.

Sandra had met Cliff at work. About a year ago she had left the hospital, when she heard through the grapevine of a job at a factory in walking distance from home. She had never quite felt comfortable working with her aunt since the Casper business, although Kath had never mentioned it and went out of her way to make the girl feel at ease. Regardless, the new job was a step up from the rather menial work Sandra had done in the hospital kitchen, for she was now working in an office as assistant to the accountant. Her parents were amazed when she was given the job and even more so when she seemed to be making a success of it.

"I don't understand," said Minnie. "When she was at school, she was hard pressed to add two and two together; now she keeps the ledgers, and if she's to be believed, actually balances them. There must be more to our Sandra than we thought."

Apparently, there was, for six months after she started, she was given a rise in salary, something almost unheard of in the economic climate of the day.

Cliff Jacobsen was a year younger than Sandra and had gone to school with her brother John. He was in his final year of apprenticeship as an electrical mechanic in the same company as Sandra, working on the wiring and maintenance of the lifts they manufactured. Sandra had seen him in the local area and even remembered him coming to their home years ago with Johnny, when both of them were working together on a school project. She knew who he was, but had shown no interest in him, as she looked on him as just a kid. Unknown to Sandra, he had always harboured a crush on her and when he discovered they were working at the same place, found every possible excuse to run into her. It was only after the factory Christmas party several weeks earlier that Sandra had thought of him as anything other than part of the furniture.

She had rather overindulged in the festivities and, tipsy almost to the point of collapse, sat by herself in a corner, wondering if she would be able to walk across the room to get outside for some air. One of the older men saw her sitting there and grabbed the opportunity to try to kiss her, very much against her wishes. Cliff, who had been watching her all day, trying to get up the courage to approach, immediately came to her rescue. He grabbed her assailant by the shoulders and pulled him away, saying, "You leave her alone. Can't you see she doesn't want anything to do with you?"

The man started to protest and shook Cliff's hands off, turning back to Sandra, who, overcome by everything, promptly passed out. Cliff to the rescue—he picked up the unconscious girl and carried her from the room and outside into the fresh air, making as little fuss as possible, for he thought it best that management knew nothing of the state she was in. Sandra regained consciousness the moment the cool air hit her and then proceeded to lose the contents of her stomach. Cliff held her head and comforted her, went quickly to a nearby tap and wet his handkerchief, then wiped the distressed girl's face and forehead, telling her all the while that she would be okay. One of the other girls had noticed them leaving and had followed them outside, so he asked her to find Sandra's handbag and bring it out to them.

He left her friend sitting with Sandra, went out to the main road and hailed a passing taxi. With the other girl's help, he loaded the crying Sandra into the cab and gave the address of the boarding house where he lived. Knowing she would not want to go home in such condition, he took her to his room, removed her shoes and laid her on his bed. She fell asleep almost immediately, only waking as the sun was going down. All this while, Cliff had sat by the bed, watching the girl lying there and thinking how beautiful she looked, even with her tear-stained face and smeared makeup.

Sandra woke with a start. In shock, she looked around at the strange surroundings and then at Cliff sitting by the side of the bed. Memory came back of what had happened at the party and, embarrassed, she jumped to her feet. "Oh, I'm so sorry," she said. "I spoilt the whole party for you." Looking around, she asked, "Where are we?"

"At my place," he said. "I knew you wouldn't want your mother seeing you like that, so I brought you here, so you could have a rest and freshen up before you went home." Nervously, he took her hand. "Do you feel all right now? I was just about to wake you; I thought they might be worried about you not being home yet."

Sandra looked at her watch and, surprised to see that it was almost seven o'clock, she said, "I must have slept for hours and you waited all that time. How kind of you. It must have been awfully boring for you."

It was then Cliff's turn to be embarrassed, as he thought to himself that not for one moment had he felt bored, being so close at last to the girl he had dreamed about for years. He knew he could never say that, even if he'd had the words to express his feelings, so he returned to practicality, picked up Sandra's shoes and handed them to her.

"I'll bring you a basin of water and leave you alone for a while. You might like to freshen up and then I'll see you get home all in one piece."

He took her home in another taxi—hang the expense—and saw her to the door. Before she left him, Sandra reached up and kissed him on the forehead. "How can I thank you for being so kind to me? I'm sure no other boy I know would have been as good as you have."

Realising that this was his only chance and being determined not to lose it, Cliff rallied his courage and said, "How about you come to the pictures with me on Saturday? That would be thank you enough."

Sandra, to his immense surprise, said yes. He felt like shouting out loud but restrained himself and said in as calm a voice as he could muster, "Okay, I'll pick you up at seven then." After the girl went inside, he stood at the closed door with a silly grin on his face, then turned to walk away, feeling as if he were floating on air.

After the Saturday date, at which he felt a lot less nervous than he had expected, Cliff asked her if she would like to come with him to Carols by Candlelight the following night in the Domain. Sandra again agreed to go out with him, for she had found herself liking his company and really enjoyed being the subject of his obvious devotion. From there it had just progressed naturally, each feeling as comfortable in the other's company as if they had known one another all their lives. Her brother Johnny had at first given her a rough time about it, but as he really liked Cliff, he soon shut up and, like the rest of them, welcomed him into the family.

To be accepted into a family atmosphere was something new for Cliff—he had been brought up by an elderly aunt, who had been a loving but stern substitute mother to the young boy whose parents had died in a train crash. He had known nothing of the banter and competition that exists between siblings and, at first, found the often rowdy climate in the Sherwood household a bit overwhelming. Minnie and Tom liked him right from the start and although he had only been around for a short while, his presence at Sunday lunches and family outings was now taken more or less for granted.

All those thoughts ran through Sandra's head as she sat with her mother on the sand watching the two men race against each other. When they returned, panting from their race, Minnie took her husband aside and asked him if he was willing to take Angie out to the pontoon. Tom was more than happy to oblige, as he was anxious to see the young ones being at ease in the water. The older two were like their mother, not able to do much more than stay afloat, and he realised that he had fallen down on the job where they were concerned. So, he was determined to make up for that with his two youngest daughters.

With Angie clinging to his back like a limpet, Tom breast-stroked his way out to the pontoon. Up close, the slide looked a lot bigger and scarier to the little girl and she clung to her father's legs, no longer sure that she really wanted to try it.

"I'll be coming down with you," Tom reassured her. "I'll be with you all the way and will catch you when you hit the water." He picked her up and held her to eye level. "Are you game?"

Never one to miss a dare and determined to show off in front of her younger sister, Angie nodded and took a deep breath. Tom gave her a hug, then placed her on one of the steps up to the slide.

"I'll be right behind you," he said. "When you get to the top, sit down and I'll grab you before we go down the slide." The child climbed the steps, not daring to look down until she was at the top. The water looked a terrifying distance away and, had her father not been right behind her, she would most likely have climbed back down again. Tom sat himself behind the standing child, then pulled her down in front of him. Angie clung to the side rails, scared to let go, even with the reassuring presence of her father holding her around the waist. Tom gently pried her hands away from the railing, saying "Are you ready?" When she nodded, too numb with fear to speak, he said, "Here we go," and pushed off down the slide. After the lengthy preparation, the actual ride down the slide was all too brief and, before she knew it, Angie was under the water. She surfaced spluttering and frightened, until her father's strong hands grabbed her from behind. At once she felt safe and immediately wanted to do it again. "Please Daddy, can we go up again?"

Tom lifted her onto the pontoon and pulled himself up next to her, shaking the hair out of his eyes. He laughed and gave her a hug. "No doubt about you, you're a game one." He lifted her to her feet and nodded in the direction of the steps, "Okay, away we go."

Angie needed no prompting this time and raced up the steps, turning to look triumphantly back at her smiling father. "I want to learn to swim so I can do this by myself," she said. "It's the best fun I've had—ever."

"I think you might have to wait a year or so before we allow you up here by yourself, but once I get you down again, I'll do something about the swimming part.

"Are you ready?" he asked again, this time receiving an enthusiastic "Yes."

Angie would have kept on riding the slide for as long as her father would take her, but after a third trip he shook his head. "I think that's enough excitement for today. What about we go into the shore and I'll give you your first swimming lesson?"

They returned to the shore where the others stood clapping, all except for Shirley, who, feeling left out of things had retreated behind her mother's legs. Tom announced that he was going to teach his daughter to swim, totally forgetting in the moment his other child, who was on the verge of tears. Not so Cliff, who realised the situation, picked the little girl up and swung her in the air.

"Would you like me to teach you to swim, too?" he asked.

Thumb in mouth, Shirley nodded, still a bit in awe of this newcomer to the family. He took her hand and led her down to the water and stood there talking to her to get her confidence up, while Minnie and Sandra looked on.

"He's a good boy, that one," said Minnie to her daughter as they sat on the sand together. Sandra nodded in agreement and uncharacteristically took her mother's hand.

"He is...I think so. I'm very lucky to have met him." Then, squeezing her mother's hand tightly, she sighed and said, "Thank you, Mumma."

"Whatever for?" said Minnie in a gruff voice, well aware of what her daughter was thinking about. Then, feeling it best to leave well alone, she pulled up the straps of her swimsuit and said, "How about we try some of that water, too? I can't remember the last time I could just have a dip without at least one child hanging on to me. Are you coming?"

Sandra planted a kiss on her mother's cheek and jumped to her feet, stuffing her long hair into a bathing cap. Cliff hadn't been too far wrong there—she had only washed her hair that morning and didn't want to have to go through the process again of setting it all in pin curls. They had big things planned for the coming night.

When the men returned with the two small children, they joined them in digging an immense hole in the sand, which constantly filled with water, caused by waves made by the nearby departing ferries.

"We're digging right through to China," Tom said. "Any minute now, a Chinaman is going to pop his head out of the hole and ask us what we're up to." Angie, who knew this was just said in fun, giggled and continued digging, but little Shirley was rather worried at the prospect and refused to dig any further until her father picked her up and cuddled her, telling her it had only been a joke. She reluctantly returned to the task, but obviously was still not quite sure about it. Tom guiltily hoped that it wouldn't be the source of nightmares for the child; he had forgotten just how gullible she always was.

~ * ~

The following weekend, Tom and Minnie returned to Gramma's house. Tom had noticed a kerosene heater in the lounge room. If he could get it going again, they could use it to heat some water to wash the dishes and give the place more of a clean-up. He bought a can of kerosene at the hardware store, took the heater out into the yard and after trimming the wick, put it all back together and filled the tank. In the kitchen, he lit the heater and set a large pot of water on top. As they waited for it to heat, they busied themselves scraping the mess off the plates and when the water was hot enough, Tom poured it into the sink, while Minnie retrieved the Sunlight soap they had used the previous week. She broke off some pieces and put them into the soap saver on the window ledge; after that it was only a matter of making lots of suds in the water and washing all the dishes. Tom found a clean tea towel in the drawer and set to drying up as Minnie washed. They had set another pot of water on the heater and used this to mop up the floor, after Minnie swept the other detritus left by the intruders out the open kitchen door.

Everything in the kitchen was clean and tidy and smelling vastly better. They walked around the rest of the house and decided at that point there was little more they could do, for thanks to the efforts of the squatters and the cats that had followed them, most of the furniture and bedding was suitable only to be thrown out.

"That'll have to wait for another time," said Tom. "Let's get back to the kids. We're supposed to be on holidays—let's enjoy what little time we have left."

This was the last weekend of the holidays, as the children were soon to return to school. That night they made the best of the time left with the girls and Johnny, who had come with Tom this weekend, for Sandra had volunteered to stay at home to keep an eye on Gramma.

The five of them made their way through the crowds that thronged the Manly Corso, down to the ocean front, where the children begged to take one last look at the Wishing Well, which stood in a wired-in enclosure on the beachfront and included a model of the Manly Hospital. It had been built as a moneymaking venture for the hospital up the hill, with the intention that the generous and the superstitious would throw money through the mesh, in the hope that it would buy the granting of their wishes. The two little girls threw their pennies into the well, their eyes tightly closed as they wished for what Angie, the avid reader, called their heart's desire.

Back they went to the Amusement Pier on the harbour frontage, to give the girls a last ride on the merry-go-round and the giant Ferris wheel, from the top of which they could see all the way to the Harbour Bridge. Angie wanted to go on the Ghost Train, a ride that scarily burst through a door to seemingly dangle over the harbour, only to go through another door and back into the dark. By this time, Shirley was asleep in her father's arms, so Tom and Minnie decided it was time to call it a night. Leaving Johnny playing the pinball machines in the penny arcade, they took the girls home to bed.

Monday was Australia Day—or Anniversary Day, as most people continued to call it—and a public holiday. The family had planned to leave for home early in the morning, but the two little girls begged to be allowed to have one more day on the beach. Tom and Johnny were leaving early, as they wanted to attend the Australia Day march, so they agreed to take the bags home with them, leaving Minnie and the girls to follow later in the day.

Before the men left, the whole family rose early and crossed the road to the harbour frontage to watch a spectacle that happened there every day of the week. Each morning, the fishermen who had been out all night in their boats brought their catch in to shore and cleaned them on the sand, before taking them off to the shops and markets. What a sight it was, the silver fish flapping in the sunlight, surrounded by screaming gulls and a few stray cats, all fighting for the heads and entrails thrown down by the fishermen. Tom bought a couple of flatheads from one of the men, which he took back to the house. He wrapped them in several sheets of newspaper and then in some greaseproof paper he begged from the landlady. No longer likely to leak, or smell of fish, he packed them into one of the suitcases to take home for dinner that night.

After breakfast, they said their goodbyes to the landlady and the friends they had made among the other boarders and made their way towards the ferry wharf. After they had waved Tom and Johnny off on the ferry, Minnie and the girls walked around the side of the wharf where, at great risk to life and limb, young boys were diving for pennies thrown by onlookers.

"I'm going to do that when I grow up," said Angie, thinking of how exciting it would be.

"You most certainly will not," her mother said emphatically. "It's much too dangerous and anyway, you don't see any girls doing it, do you?"

"I don't see why girls can't do it, too. I think it would be fun."

"You'd proberly get squashed by a ferry," piped up Shirley, ever the cautious one. "I think those big boys are very silly."

"Your sister is right; it is very silly as well as dangerous and I'm surprised the authorities don't put a stop to it," said Minnie, as she marshalled the girls away from the wharf and led them towards the adjoining poolside.

For once, Minnie didn't shake her head at the street photographer, who was in his usual spot at the top of the steps. The resulting shot, which featured in the family album for many years to come, showed the three of them, the wharf in the background, with Angie grinning widely and Minnie looking down at Shirley, who at first had stubbornly refused to be in the photo and was hanging her head, wearing what her mother always referred to as her "not best pleased" look. This reminder of what was to be the last time the family holidayed together—albeit in patches—would always bring back memories to Minnie of their wartime stay and of that final day of their holiday.

Minnie had dressed the girls in their swimming costumes, with their going home dresses over them. She packed their underwear into a small knapsack, which would hold the wet cossies and a beach towel on the way home. She had decided not to go into the water herself, as it would have meant a trip along to the dressing sheds at the other end of the pool. The girls could be undressed on the beach, but she couldn't. So, she removed her sandals and sat rather uncomfortably on the sand while the children frolicked in the water, trying to perfect the dogpaddle that they been had taught by the menfolk.

Why did I let myself be talked into this? Minnie thought to herself. I'm going to be in a lather of perspiration all the way home. Finally, as the sun rose higher in the sky and she felt more and more uncomfortable, she decided to call it quits. The girls had had their last swim and she felt it was time for them to make their way home before all the crowds, who would pile onto the ferries later in the day.

Called reluctantly from the water, the two small girls stood impatiently as their mother removed their swimsuits—modestly behind the towel—and dressed them in their underwear and frocks. Socks and sandals could wait until they reached the taps up above on the concourse, so Minnie wrung out the wet swimsuits as much as possible and packed them away in the knapsack. With nearly an hour until the next ferry, she gave in to their pleas for one last paddle.

This proved to be an unwise decision, for although Shirley obeyed her mother's warning to stay on the water's edge, she clumsily lurched right into the path of a youth running past, who accidentally knocked her full length into the water. He pulled the wet and bawling child to her feet and delivered her with many apologies to her mother. Having witnessed the whole episode, Minnie assured the boy that it wasn't his fault and set to dealing with her wet and sobbing daughter.

"Why didn't someone warn me at an early age never to have children?" she muttered to herself as she removed the dripping dress, singlet and panties and tried ineffectually to wring them dry in the only towel she had with her, while Shirley sat by her side, her modesty rather inadequately covered by her mother's jacket, her crying diminished to an occasional deep sob. Minnie gave up on the heavy cotton singlet and redressed the child in just her wet panties and frock, which, being cotton, looked as if it had been slept in.

Completely fed up with everything, a hot, annoyed and thirsty Minnie herded the girls up the steps, washed the sand off their feet and left them to put on their socks and sandals, while she took a drink from the nearby water bubbler. Then, drinks for the girls and they headed towards the wharf, Shirley complaining all the way about how uncomfortable she felt and how everyone was looking at her.

"They're looking at you because you are making such a carry-on," snapped her mother, completely at the end of her patience. Then, realising she was taking out her own discomfort on the child, she looked at her watch. With twenty minutes left until the ferry's departure, there was enough time to buy some lunch before they left. They made the ferry in plenty of time, armed with newspaper packages of their favourite potato scallops—slices of potato dipped in batter and deep fried—not really the most desirable lunch, but by then Minnie was more interested in peace than in nourishment. All she wanted was to get her children home, have a good wash and a peaceful cup of tea. This had hardly been the end to the holiday that she had imagined.

Shirley complained all the way home that she felt itchy and that her panties were rubbing and then put the cap on the day by announcing on the tram she was going to be sick. Off they got at the next stop while the child threw up in the gutter, followed by a long wait in the sun for the next tram.

Angie had done nothing to help her mother's state of mind by making unnecessary comments all along the way. As her sister brought up her lunch, she muttered, "She shouldn't have gobbled her food so quickly. I knew she would get sick."

In retrospect, Minnie realised that she should not have fed the child such a greasy meal when she was about to travel. Her head was starting to ache from the hot sun, so she simply snapped at the older child.

"I don't need you sticking your nose in things, Miss Perfect. How about you do something helpful and get that towel out of the knapsack so I can clean your sister up a bit."

Shirley getting sick on trams and trains was not something new, and Minnie could have kicked herself for not bringing with her some sort of receptacle just in case. At least then they could have stayed on the tram and would be almost home by now.

When they finally arrived home, Minnie, with a raging headache, searched through the house. Nobody was home except for Gramma, who was snoring away in her bed. On the hall table was a note from Tom.

I missed the Australia Day march but thought I'd catch up with some of the boys at the Pub. I'll be home early, Tom.

Minnie snorted as she crumpled the note and threw it in the bin. She had no illusions about Tom's "home early," for from past experience she knew that catching up with the boys always led to a long session and a late arrival home by a husband who was more than three sheets to the wind. "The boys" were World War One veterans like Tom, who had missed the call up this time round because they worked in protected industries. Early in the war Tom had decided to enlist, but Minnie, who usually placidly accepted her husband's ideas, firmly put her foot down. "You did your bit last time round," she said. Although her husband cracked hardy about it, she was all too familiar with instances of him waking in a sweat after nightmares about the horrors of the trenches more than twenty years ago. Tom had said he would think about it and said no more on the subject, much to Minnie's relief.

Although she would have liked some help with the girls, at least it meant that she had only them and Gramma to worry about, as there was no sign of either Sandra or Johnny, which usually meant they would stay out all evening.

Enough of all that; her immediate thought was to have that longed-for cup of tea, which was postponed when she entered the kitchen, by the sight of the ice chest drip tray overflowing all over the floor. She paddled through the water and emptied the tray, noticing as she mopped up the water that obviously this was not the first time it had happened recently, for the linoleum was completely saturated, right through to the floorboards beneath. That job done, Minnie made the tea and opened the ice chest to get some milk, which was not to be, for the milk jug had a nasty scum on top—there was no need to smell it; it was clear that the milk was sour. Obviously, Sandra hadn't thought to put the bottles out for the milkman. Black tea was better than none and, as the only alternative was powdered milk, she took two aspirin for her headache and swallowed the tea as if it were medicine.

From the girls' bedroom came the sound of squabbling. Her patience completely at an end, Minnie stormed into the room. "You girls are to stop that right now. No, I don't want to hear who did what to whom," she said as Angie started to complain. "I want you both to quieten down. I am going to lie down and have a rest and if I hear one sound coming from this room, I will paddle the behinds of both of you. You find something to do that doesn't make any noise and stay here until I tell you to come out. I've just about had my fill of both of you today."

That said, she left them alone and went to her room, pulled the blinds down and lay on the bed with a sigh. Not one to nap in the daytime, she actually fell asleep—the heat having finally taken its toll. She woke to find it almost dark; no noise came from the girls and by the looks of it, nobody else had come home yet. She felt a bit better, but her head still ached and she decided it was mainly because she had hardly eaten anything all day. Nobody else was going to do anything about that—so she knew it was up to her to get moving and make a meal for herself, the girls and Gramma. She would worry about the others if they finally turned up.

She found the two girls sitting on the floor playing Snakes and Ladders, all thoughts of argument long since gone.

"Good girls. I knew you could behave if you really tried," Minnie said to them. "I'm going to run a bath for you and then we'll have some nice fish for dinner."

With the girls splashing in the bath, she went to the kitchen and turned on the radio to get the six o'clock news. She opened the ice chest to take out the fish. No fish.

"What the...?" said Minnie, then realised something she had missed previously. There had been no signs of the two suitcases that Tom and Johnny had brought home with them.

"Oh no," she said as she walked all over the house and then out to the back veranda. There were both suitcases, right where Tom had dumped them when he came home. They had sat there all day long, cooking in the blazing sun. She opened the case that held the fish to discover a sodden, stinking mess that had soaked right through the layers of paper and into all the clothing. The mess went into the garbage tin and the smelly clothes into the laundry tub to soak, following which she returned to the kitchen, wishing her husband were there right that moment so she could murder him.

From the radio came the plummy tones of the ABC announcer. "As we lead up to the news, the next record will be Paul Robeson singing, "As you come to the end of a perfect day.""

"Bloody hell," muttered Minnie to herself. "That would be all I need," she said as she switched the radio off.

Seven

Manly, 1946

Angie sat on the front veranda steps, her book turned face downwards on her lap, one hand holding a dandelion she had plucked from the garden, the other resting lightly on the back of Bob, her dog. Her thoughts, however, were with neither of these, for in her mind she was miles away in another country and another time. What, she wondered, would it have been like to be a child in Dickens' England? She was halfway through reading Oliver Twist and, try as she may, it was hard to imagine the life that Oliver and others had to endure. How lucky she was to live in the twentieth century and always to have been in the care of a loving family. And to live in the best place in the world—for this is what she felt sure Manly was.

Much had changed in the Sherwoods' lives in the past two years. Sandra had married Cliff and several months ago a new baby arrived in the family. Gramma had died not long after her cat Blackie, and the newlyweds lived with the family for a while. It was a bit crowded at first, for Sandra's old room really was only large enough for one. Minnie finally decided to turn the lounge room into a bedroom for the young couple, for as she rightly said, the family hardly ever used it. Activity in the Sherwood family had always centred round the kitchen and the large dining table, where they ate their meals, read their newspapers, listened to the radio and played cards. Nobody really noticed the loss of the formal sitting room, for formality was not a part of their life.

Then, last year, the war had ended. First the victory in Europe, which was celebrated only half-heartedly, for the Japanese forces had yet to be defeated. It was just a month or so later that the Americans dropped atomic bombs on Hiroshima and Nagasaki—which effectively ended the war. Minnie took Angie and Shirley to a Newsreel theatre in the city to see a documentary showing an atomic bomb explosion, which probably had not been a wise move. For months after, Shirley refused to sleep in her bed and insisted on sleeping under the card table that stood in Sandra's old room (presumably for protection from rogue bombs). Angie didn't mind that at all, for it meant that she had the bedroom to herself and was free for a while of her sister's constant chatter.

Several months later, it was Angie's tenth birthday and it was then she received the only gift she had wanted—and had begged for—for years, in the form of Bob, her beautiful Red Setter/Labrador puppy. He had the temperament of the Lab, the slimmer body and colouring of the Setter and adored Angie with every bit of the passion that she returned to him. Shirley, who wanted a pussy-cat—and usually gave Bob a wide berth because she wasn't too sure about dogs—had been assured that she would get a cat when she too turned ten. It was Minnie's hope that in the interim the child would forget about it, for she always seemed to be the one who cleaned up the messes and remembered to fill the water bowl. Angie, on the other hand, never had to be reminded to take Bob for walks; the very first thing she always did when she arrived home from school was to fix a length of rope to his collar and proudly parade him through the streets to the football oval.

Now that they had moved from Leichhardt to Manly it was to the beachfront that she headed, to walk along the sand and throw sticks for Bob, which he tended to chew up rather than fetch, but fetching was something she was sure he would learn in time.

The move to Manly was not one lightly taken. Tom, who had grown up on the northern beaches, had been keen to make the move when his mother died and he inherited the house in half share with his sister Daphne. To everyone's surprise, there was a substantial amount of money in Gramma's Commonwealth Bank savings account—there was much conjecture about this, but they never did find out just where and how Gramma had accumulated it. Suddenly Tom was a property owner, albeit only half a house, and had money in the bank for the first time in his life.

Tom proposed that they pay his sister rental for her half of the property and move there, but Minnie rightly pointed out that the two bedroom semi was much too small for all of them, so it was rented out to a couple happy to have a roof over their heads in those times of short accommodation. Then, in quick succession, there were changes to the household.

First, Johnny announced that he was moving to Melbourne to take up an offer of a spot in a jazz band and Minnie's plans for her son going to the Conservatorium went out the window. However, she was happy that he had found a job doing what he loved, even if it was so far away. Next, Sandra found that she was pregnant and told her mother that she and Cliff had decided to look for their own house, now that the baby was on the way. On hearing this, Tom immediately pointed out that now the place in Manly would be plenty big enough for them and the two girls, but Minnie needed a lot of persuading. The move meant taking the girls away from their school and friends and on top of that she would be far away from Sandra, who would need a mother's help when she had the baby.

Tom agreed to compromise, and they stayed on in Leichhardt for another year, until Sandra had given birth to little Andrew and had been steered through the first shaky months of motherhood. In the interim, the lease on the house in Manly expired and Tom used his inherited money, aided by Minnie's savings which were no longer needed for Johnny's education, to buy his sister's share and own the Manly house outright. For several months they spent weekends camping in the rundown house, gradually bringing it back to its former glory.

Although they had cleaned it up for letting, there was still much to do. The moulded metal ceilings were intact, but the walls were covered by multiple layers of wallpaper and paint and the bathroom and kitchen were badly in need of upgrading. They found that there was enough room in the bathroom to install an inside toilet—something neither of them had ever had—so they luxuriated in the thought that there would be no more trips outside in the winter cold, or at night. Those modern additions paved the way to making the wrench of the move a lot easier to bear in Minnie's mind. Tom even found that he had enough money left over to splurge on a vacuum cleaner, an electric refrigerator—so goodbye to overflowing water trays—and wonder of wonders, an automatic Westinghouse washing machine, with its own electric wringer. "No more boiling up the copper for the weekly wash," said Tom, but Minnie wasn't at all sure about that; she couldn't see how sheets and towels could get really clean without a good boil up. She'd keep the copper for the time being and see how this washer went.

Finally, Tom managed to do something he had always wanted, work near the water. He found himself a job working on the ferries, right there on his doorstep. To Tom and to his small daughters this was the greatest job in the world. No more noisy machinery shop, no more grease and grime—he got to travel back and forth across the best harbour in the world, breathing in fresh air and salt spray. For the girls it was the greatest thrill imaginable, for when they travelled over to town to visit Sandra, Cliff and little Andrew, they could make the journey on "Daddy's ferry," Angie's only regret being that she was not allowed to take Bob, who was forced to stay behind in the back yard and had to be regaled with the day's adventures when she arrived home and took him for his walk.

Skeptical at first, Minnie reluctantly had to agree that the move to Manly had been a wise one. The girls slotted seamlessly into their new school and made new friends effortlessly, while Minnie found she could buy anything she wanted in the department stores in Manly, without the need to travel to the city. Because the surrounding areas were still semi-rural, she could catch the bus out to Brookvale, past the Warringah golf course, to buy fresh produce from the Chinese market gardens at the junction of Condamine Street and Pittwater Road. It was proving to be completely different and better in many ways from life in the inner city suburbs.

Now a day at the beach was as simple as a walk down the street, or a half hour's journey to any one of the other golden beaches along the Warringah peninsula. If they became bored with all that Manly had to offer, it was a simple matter to hop a bus to Collaroy Beach or all the way up to the old tram terminal at Narrabeen. Summers were no longer a stew in the inner suburbs, for even on the hottest days there always seemed to be a sea breeze blowing.

The end of the war brought many changes to Australia, with servicemen returning from overseas, often finding their womenfolk vastly changed from those they had left behind. For the first time in their lives, women had been given independence, taking on and succeeding in jobs that in the past would never have been considered "women's work." With the men returning and wanting their old jobs back, many women found their newly won independence had flown out the door. Those who had happily lived the life of a housewife before the war had found that there was a life outside the kitchen sink and laundry tubs and now, with their husbands back home, they were expected to slip back into their old role with no complaints or regrets. After years of being the ones making the decisions, paying the bills and living an independent life, they had to defer again to the will and whims of men and many found this new situation rather hard to accept.

The men were vastly altered too, for as well as wearing the trauma of years of fighting, they too had become accustomed to a very different life. At first ecstatic at being home and away from the constant fear of being shot or blown up, many of them found it hard to go back to the old routine of going to work every day. None of them missed the war, but many of them missed the travel to new places and the mateship they had found among their fellows. Life in the suburbs with children they hardly knew, a wife who for the first time questioned their decisions and expected to sometimes have a life of her own, was not the utopia they had dreamed about in the years in the jungle or in Europe.

Many marriages foundered. Many men found themselves without work, for it was too early for new businesses to have formed and much of the flush of work during the war had been created by the war itself. Coming as it did right at the end of the Great Depression, the war had caused many businesses large and small to flourish—but there was no pre-war prosperity to return to—none had existed.

There was also a measure of resentment among the returned servicemen towards those who had not gone to war and had led what was thought of as a "cushy" existence. Food rationing, which had been imposed during the war, continued to be in force while non-rationed items such as ham and bacon were slowly becoming more available as the need to ship all supplies overseas diminished. Other rare items such as cream biscuits and chocolate bars sold out almost as quickly as they hit the shelves to a population starved for such luxuries. Things were improving, but they were taking their time.

There was much publicity about the comparatively luxurious life of the Australian populace compared to those in Britain, where there had been no recovery and scarcity of even the simplest things was rife. Australians were urged to send parcels of non-perishable foodstuffs to relatives and friends in Britain—and many families complied, making up their "Bundles for Britain," then sewing them up into calico packages and posting them off...in many instances to people they had never met.

People who had been used to frequent blackouts and brownouts during the war found that little had changed now that the country was at peace. Homes with electric stoves kept a constant supply of candles and canned heat on hand, for it always seemed to be around mealtime that the power went.

Although those scarcities and inconveniences hit the Sherwoods as much as anyone, they suffered few of the problems that affected many other families. Minnie was a dab hand with the sewing machine and turned out new and revamped clothes for herself and the two girls, while Tom, whose job required nothing more than an old pair of trousers and a navy singlet, had few needs on the clothing front. Most of his shirts were pre-war and had lasted the distance very well, as Minnie simply turned the collars when they started to wear. For rare formal occasions Tom had one good shirt and his pre-war suit, which he proudly said fitted him perfectly still.

The high point in the week for the two small girls was the Saturday matinee at "the pictures." Now that they were older they were trusted to go alone, their money tied into handkerchiefs in their pockets, or in the case of Shirley, secured with a safety pin—things always seemed to get lost out of her pockets. Each had enough for the cost of entry and a chocolate-coated ice cream from the lolly boy who came around at interval. With Australia still a year or so behind overseas, most of the films were either pre-war or wartime, but it was for the cartoons and the serials that the girls waited with excitement. Shirley loved the Mickey Mouse and Donald Duck cartoons best, but Angie preferred the heart stopping serials. Her favourite was Jungle Queen, a glamorous lady who lorded over her native followers dressed rather unsuitably in what looked like a long white nightgown. For nearly three hours they were lost in another world, to emerge blinking into the daylight, making their way home excitedly talking over what they had seen. These movies were as real to them as anything that happened in their own back yard.

The films and serials they watched provided material for many of their games, with each vying to play the heroine. Because it was her favourite, Angie always insisted on being the Jungle Queen—dressed in an old slip of Sandra's—and because Shirley complained at being left out, Angie created a special part for her as the Jungle Princess, and although she knew it wasn't authentic, just the fact that she was a princess more than satisfied little Shirley.

Princesses were very much in the news and these featured very strongly in the lives of the two girls. Among their prized possessions was a book about the two English princesses, Elizabeth and Margaret Rose. Those two had assumed almost star status since their father was crowned king in 1937 after the abdication of his brother. The book had belonged originally to Sandra, who had much to their excitement, given it to her sisters when she no longer wanted it. Although the two princesses were now young adults, Angie and Shirley pored for hours over the photos of them as children, marveling at the thought of life in a palace and realising they seemed to have been just two little girls like them. The newspapers and magazines were full of conjecture as to when and whom the young Princess Elizabeth would marry, for, as heiress direct to the British throne, a suitable marriage was imperative for the production of future heirs. Nobody even considered the possibility that the next-in-line, the flighty Princess Margaret, would ever be a suitable candidate for Queen of England. In spite of that, the pretty Margaret was everyone's favourite, but it didn't stop the public interest in marrying off Elizabeth before she eventually became queen.

One thing noticed by the whole family about their new home in Manly was the difference in the local population. Because beachside Manly was a combination of retail centre, holiday resort and residential area, the makeup of the population was a lot more eclectic than the inner western, working-class suburb they had left behind. Tom, who had grown up in this area, found it very different from his remembered childhood home, for the war had considerably changed Manly as much as it had the rest of Sydney.

The Sherwoods' home was at the end of a block of semi-detached houses. Their house was attached to a similar one, its only inhabitant being Mr Gibson, a retired bachelor in his sixties, who spent most of his time at home, dressed in a flannel vest and trousers held up by fraying suspenders—this outfit in winter being supplemented by a scarf and decrepit plaid dressing gown. He showed no interest in his new neighbours to the point of unfriendliness and incited the ire of Angie by throwing stones at Bob when the dog ventured into his yard. For this action Angie dubbed him Mr Nasty, and although she chastised the girl for saying this, Minnie could not help but think it was a title he richly deserved.

The neighbours on the other side were notably more pleasant; however, in many ways they were no more suitable than Mr Gibson. This house, situated on a corner, differed from those in the rest of the street, being large, freestanding and two-storeyed, whereas the others were traditional turn of the century single-storeyed, semi-detached cottages. The corner house was owned by Mrs Anthea Spiteri, operated ostensibly as a boarding house, although it quickly became obvious it was more than that. Mrs Spiteri was a large, rather blousy, overly made up woman, who appeared to have neither husband nor children. She did, however, have six or so lady "boarders," none of whom went out to work, but spent their days at home, often lying in the sun in the back yard, reading magazines, their hair in curlers, chatting and giggling together like a group of school girls. At night the house was a hive of activity, with gentlemen callers coming and going and music playing well into the early hours. All of this was done with great circumspection; the music was never loud and except for a couple of occasions when one or other of the callers rang the Sherwoods' doorbell, asking for Maisie or Florrie, none of next door's activities impacted on Minnie and Tom much at all.

In the early days when Minnie first twigged to what went on next door, she worried about the effect on her two young daughters, but quickly realised that the people in the house offered no threat to her children. The "ladies" were always polite and friendly whenever they met in the street, showed great interest in the two children, and at Christmas time even went so far as to take up a collection and present the two girls with beautifully dressed dolls, which Minnie knew must have cost a fortune. Although she disapproved of their way of life, she was sufficient of a realist to accept that this was something that had gone on from the beginning of time. Having lived through the Great Depression and two world wars, Minnie was all too aware that in order to survive some people had to seek a living in ways that may not appeal to others. Another thing that altered her outlook was the niggling thought that her newly won affluence could well have been due to activities not unlike what went on next door. There had never been an explanation found for how Gramma, Tom's mother, had managed to have a house fully paid for and a quite substantial amount of money in her bank account. Tom's father had not earned much money, working as a labourer all his life. He had died quite young and

Gramma had never to their knowledge gone out to work. To Minnie it seemed that the possible source of her money could only be due to Gramma either being a kept woman—by whom, she wondered—or to some form of prostitution. She had never voiced these thoughts to Tom, although she often wondered if he had put two and two together and reached the same conclusion.

Regardless of whether he had, Tom was a lot less accepting of what went on next door, questioning on several occasions why such things could be allowed to happen in among respectable, hard-working people.

"I don't understand why the police don't shut them down," he complained to Minnie.

"Someone has to put in a complaint first," was the reply. "They're quiet, clean and tidy. I'm sure Mrs S pays all her bills, why would anyone complain? I certainly hope you have no intentions of doing so. The last thing I want is to have another unfriendly neighbour. You just leave well enough alone—mind your own business, the way they mind theirs!"

Minnie had her own ideas about why there was never any official action against the ladies next door. She hadn't mentioned it to Tom, who would have been horrified, but she had noticed that one of the few daytime callers to the house was the local police car. Whether this visit was to take advantage of the favours of the ladies, or for something more of a monetary nature she had no idea. What she saw was enough to convince her that what went on next door was well and truly under the protection of the local law.

Eight

On the job

With her two girls settled into their new school and only a small house to look after, Minnie found time lay rather heavily on her hands. The long hours spent hand washing all the clothes were a thing of the past, as the new washing machine coped very efficiently with this task in a fraction of the time. When she saw how cleanly it washed the clothes, Minnie overcame her doubts about its ability to handle the linen and towels and eventually used the old copper only occasionally to boil up extra-dirty items. She had read somewhere that the simple process of hanging the wash in the sunlight would remove any germs that remained after the wash, so she decided there was no real reason to submit herself to the arduous task of lifting the dangerously hot and heavy washing from the copper into the laundry tubs to manually rinse and wring them out. Her refrigerator allowed her to buy perishables in more than the two day's supply that the old ice chest had necessitated, so she could, if she wished, shop only once a week for the household's supplies. The Hoover cleaner whizzed over the carpets doing a much better and quicker job than she had ever been able to do with her hard broom. So Minnie happily embraced this new age of labour-saving devices and realised that the women of the future need not necessarily be tied to house and home. But this didn't solve the problem of too much time on her hands.

She thought of doing charity work but decided that could be something for the future. With two growing girls there always seemed to be the need for money for something or other and often she was really scraping for funds by the end of each pay week. Minnie decided to find a job. She knew that Tom would object to this if she asked him, so the obvious thing would be to find the job first and tell him later. He was less likely to make a huge fuss if confronted with a fait accompli.

She had learned typing and shorthand at school but had never used them. Her experience in the three years before her marriage had been as a shop assistant—so that was the obvious way to go. Never one to mess around once she had made up her mind, Minnie did the rounds of the local department stores. She drew a blank at the first two, where she was simply told there were no vacancies. Her third attempt, at the largest store in Manly, brought her an interview with the personnel manager, who asked her a few questions and gave her an application form to complete.

"We are always finding vacancies, with such a shifting population. We will be in touch if anything suitable should come up," he said, rising and shaking her hand.

Several weeks later, when Minnie had almost forgotten about it, she received a letter in the post, asking her to come in for a further interview. Her heart racing, Minnie hastily dressed and made her way to the store's employment office. She was interviewed by a different person, a rather formidable woman, who asked much the same questions Minnie had answered on the previous occasion, making notes as she went along. Questions answered, the woman read back through what she had written, tapping her pen on the desk as she read, while Minnie sat opposite her in nervous silence, clutching her handbag in her lap.

Finally, the woman put the form aside and looked up again at Minnie, who by this time was beginning to wonder whether she was doing the right thing.

"You have two children," said the woman. "Would this not pose a problem for you, working until five pm?"

"I don't think so," Minnie replied. "I've thought it through—they are not little children, one is nearly eleven, the other is nine. They are good sensible girls, they start school just around the corner from here at much the same time I would start work. My husband is a shift worker and often is home in the afternoons, but even if he wasn't, there would only be a break of an hour or so before I came home. I know I can trust them to stay at home and do their homework until I arrive."

"And is your husband happy with this arrangement?"

"Oh yes, he is fine," Minnie replied, mentally crossing her fingers at the lie.

The woman picked up the paper again, holding it in one hand, the other resumed tapping the pen on the desk, while Minnie resisted the urge to reach across and snatch it from her hands.

Finally the woman laid down the pen, unclipped the form from its clipboard and looked up at Minnie, "We will give you a try out," she said. "I have to admit that I still have some doubts about the age of your children. Young children do tend to be always catching things and we frown on too much absenteeism." She held up a silencing hand, as Minnie started to explain that her children never got sick. "On the other hand, we are finding that married ladies are much more reliable staff than the young ones, who tend to be always taking off and leaving. I particularly like the fact that you are an experienced seamstress—the vacancy we are hoping to fill is in our Dress Materials department. We need someone sufficiently knowledgeable about sewing to be able to advise our customers on fabrics and making up from paper patterns. Do you think you could handle this type of work?"

Right up my alley, thought Minnie, pleased at the thought of being paid to do something she had done unpaid for two decades. She smiled in relief as the woman smiled back at her in return and suddenly seemed less formidable.

"Oh yes, I'm sure I could handle that. I love sewing and really enjoy helping people," Minnie replied.

"Then that's settled. If you don't mind, I will take you down to the department and introduce you to Miss Robson, who is the department head. She will explain some of your duties and give you full details of starting times and what we expect you to wear. Please report here at 8.45 next Monday and we will take the rest of your personal details for our records. Welcome to Master's Department store. You will find us to be a friendly, family-owned company, where we like to look on our employees as part of that family."

Minnie sailed home, elated at the prospect of being a working woman, her elation fading somewhat when she faced the prospect of breaking this news to her husband.

To her surprise, Tom raised very few protests that evening when she nervously told him about her job. He had sensed Minnie's restlessness for some time and suspected that something along these lines was afoot. He was a bit doubtful about the girls coming home to an empty house in the afternoons, but Minnie pointed out to him that it would only be on alternate weeks. His shift work meant that he would be home in plenty of time on one week and it would only be on the other that the girls would return to nobody at home. There might be nobody there she remarked—but there was always Bob— who although he loved the family to distraction, was most unfriendly to anyone unfamiliar.

More surprising was the reaction of her two daughters. They acted as if their world were coming to an end, for they both had a mental picture of their mother waiting at home at any time of the day—whether they were there or not. Minnie sat them down and explained the difference her job would make to their lives in the long run. The extra money would mean more clothes, toys and treats such as trips to the Royal Easter Show and the Blue Mountains, and mean that money could be put away for future holidays. Feeling somewhat guilty, she bribed them with the offer of extra pocket money and when they realised the benefits, they suddenly changed from being against their mother's new venture to enthusiasm and interest. She allocated each of them small tasks to do around the house and promised that if they did them properly she would reward them for their efforts.

Minnie's first working week was hard going. She hadn't realised how tiring the job would be, having to learn about the store's procedures, the stock, and dealing with her superior. Miss Robson proved to be a difficult taskmistress, lacking in humour and compassion for errors and after the first day, Minnie was ready to throw the job in, feeling that she would never be happy and never make her boss happy, either.

The next day, when she reluctantly turned up for work, two of the other girls in the department called her aside.

"Come to lunch with us today," said Mary, a woman about her own age.

"We think it's time you had the talk—we give it to every new girl." This came from Rebecca, a tall, smartly turned out woman, who was in charge of the paper patterns department.

"But, I have to go to lunch when Miss Robson tells me, how can I be sure I go at the same time as you?"

"Don't you worry about that—you find out what time your lunch break is and we'll swap around with the others so we all go at the same time."

At 1:30 pm, the three of them sat together in the store's lunchroom, Minnie bursting with curiosity over what they had to say.

"Eat first, then talk," said Mary as she opened her packet of sandwiches. They ate; then with cups of tea in front of them, the other two sat back in their chairs and relaxed.

"Minnie," said Mary, lighting a cigarette, taking a deep draw and exhaling the smoke before continuing, "we thought it best to tell you here and now that you're not alone. We saw how miserable you looked as you left yesterday—and because we felt exactly the same way at first, we decided to have this little talk before you give up, as so many others have in the past."

Rebecca took over from her friend. "We've all run the Miss Robson gauntlet, so we know what you're going through. Tell me if I'm wrong—right now you think you are useless, incompetent and will never please her. Am I right?"

Minnie shrugged her shoulders and, smiling wryly, nodded her head.

"We all felt that way at first. Sometimes we still do, because Robbo is so sure she is right and nobody else is. We've found it impossible arguing with her, and if we want peace we just go along with it. Unfortunately, she has worked here since the beginning of time and has no outside interests other than her old mother. She lives and breathes Master's Department Store, and because of that, they think she's the bee's knees. All us others have lives outside; we like our jobs and try to do our best and we've learned the way to survive is to turn a blind eye to everything the old girl says.

"What we wanted to tell you is that we understand, we're behind you, and—trust us—it will get better."

Mary tapped the ash from her cigarette and waved it to take in their surroundings. "This is a pretty good place to work. Not too many shops have a good lunchroom like this, the big bosses are friendly and you'll find most of the staff in the other departments are nice people." She smiled conspiratorially. "As for our department, if we think we won't like any newcomers, we just leave it alone and let Robbo do her work. For those we like, we know that unless we all work together they never stay very long."

"We like you," said Rebecca unnecessarily.

Minnie burst out laughing. "Well, I'm certainly glad to hear that." She sat back in her chair and relaxed for the first time that day. "You're right, of course. I had begun to wonder what I'd walked into. And yes, I was thinking how hopeless I am—it's such a comfort to find I am not the first."

"Only one of many," said Mary, crushing out her cigarette. "We've all been down that road and we've worked out how to look out for one another and enjoy ourselves in the process. Welcome to the club!"

From that moment on, Minnie felt so much better; she relaxed and found the new environment less intimidating. By the end of the second week, she no longer had a sinking feeling as she headed for work and she found she could cope with customers without shaking. When she earned the wrong side of her boss's sharp tongue, she would spy one or other of her friends grinning in the background and would nod and look sufficiently contrite, while smiling inwardly, knowing they were on her side.

Her home routine required some reorganisation; in the process of which she tried to cause as little disruption to Tom's life as possible. She found she no longer had time for home baking, but her extra money allowed her to bring home treats from the local cake shops, something none of the family had ever had in the past. The girls, after their initial worries, found they enjoyed the responsibility of the jobs allotted them, their extra pocket money giving them the chance to save for special occasions. Tom made surprisingly few complaints, for he had always spent time with his girls and was more than happy to officiate on the days when Minnie wasn't there. He saw the change for the better in his wife and was happy to balance that against the occasional late meal and the lack of home baking. If Minnie was happy, then so was he.

More than anything, Minnie enjoyed the comradeship of the women she worked with. She had not had the company of other women since before her marriage; her life had been so closely tied to the family and she had never looked beyond that. With her fellow workers she found the release of sharing stories of their lives, and making friendships that extended beyond working hours. Mary's husband had a car and the two families developed the habit of enjoying Sunday picnics, where the men fished or swapped stories about football and cricket, while the women sat and relaxed, and their children played together or joined in fishing with the men. Her job had opened up a whole new lifestyle for Minnie and she often wondered how she had managed all those years without it.

Her only worry was about her girls on the days when Tom was not at home to greet them from school. The mornings were fine; the girls left for school at the same time as Minnie and they walked together most of the way, for the school was just around the corner from the shops. Although there was always the trusty Bob to stand guard when the girls returned to an empty house, it was still something of a worry to her.

This worry was alleviated in an unexpected way. One day not long after Minnie started work, Mrs Spiteri from next door, accompanied by one of her "young ladies," came into the Dress Materials department. Although they were always friendly in greeting one another, each had kept their distance, knowing instinctively that there was little in common in their respective ways of life. At first, when she saw them, Minnie was inclined to avoid them; then thinking how rude it would look, she walked up, greeted them and asked if she could help. Mrs Spiteri looked surprised at first. "I didn't know you worked here. I hadn't seen you around the house as often as I used to, but didn't realise it was because you had gone out to work."

"I've been here for several months," Minnie replied. "Now that the girls are bigger, I thought it would be good to get out and earn a bit extra to help with the household bills. I found it hard at first and I do worry about them after school, but Tom's there every second week to see them when they come home, and on the other weeks I'm sure they are fine, for Angie's dog would send any strangers packing in no time."

Mrs Spiteri started to speak, stopped and thought about it for a second…then after some deliberation continued, "Would you like me to look out for them? I'll understand fully if you say no, but we are right next door—they are such lovely kids and I'd love to help you out. You've been such a good neighbour and never complained, like some in the street have done." She fidgeted with her handbag, smiled grimly and went on, "I know we aren't your sort of people, but we've most of us had kiddies in the past and we really enjoy having your two next door to us. I wouldn't presume, just keep an eye out for them if you told me the weeks they are home alone. The girls and I would love to do it—but you mustn't feel obligated, I do understand how you must feel about us."

"I feel that you are good neighbours and I thank you for your offer. Tom and I would be honoured if we felt that you are keeping an eye on our girls." Minnie grasped the woman's hands in gratitude and then and there they made the arrangement that she would let them know the weeks that Tom would not be home for the girls. It took a load off her mind, for in spite of saying otherwise, she felt so much better that there would be adults looking out for the girls in the couple of hours before she came home.

Tom was horrified when she told him of the arrangement. This led to one of their rare arguments, as Minnie angrily asked him just what he thought would happen to his daughters when someone who obviously cared about their safety was keeping an eye on them.

"What are you worried about?" she asked. "Do you think they will try to recruit our daughters into a life of sin?"

"No, of course I don't. I just don't think it would be suitable for someone like that to have anything to do with our children."

"Someone who has been a mother herself? Someone who cares enough to offer to help us out? Tom, you are being completely unreasonable." Minnie marched from the room in anger, went to the kitchen and started washing the dishes with much crashing and banging.

Finally, Tom, who in the long run was a reasonable man, followed her into the kitchen.

"I suppose you are right," he said. "It's because I don't much like what they do. I just have a natural suspicion of anyone who would choose to live that way."

"Sometimes circumstances force people to do things they would rather not," said Minnie, sorely tempted to add, like your mother, for instance. But that was a road she knew she would never go down.

Nothing more was said by Tom on the subject and Minnie thought it best to say as little about it as possible. On the quiet, she took the girls aside and told them that Mrs Spiteri next door would be keeping an eye on them when their father wasn't home.

"You already know never to answer the door when we aren't at home and never to talk to strangers. If anything should ever go wrong, if either of you are hurt or feeling sick, I want you to know that you can always knock on Mrs Spiteri's door. She and the nice ladies who live there will always look after you until I come home."

The need for help from next door never arose and neither Mrs Spiteri nor any of her ladies imposed in any way on the agreement, but Minnie's sole remaining worry about going to work disappeared and everyone, even Tom, settled into a comfortable routine that worked really well for the whole family.

Nine

Three years later

It was a Saturday afternoon in early November, 1949. Minnie had been to work that morning and was in the back yard hanging out the washing. Tom had left for his afternoon shift, Angie was visiting one of her friends from high school and Shirley was at swimming practice. To everyone's surprise, Shirley, who had never excelled at anything, had proven to be an excellent swimmer, much better than her usually more athletic sister. She had joined the swimming club some months ago and was every bit as successful as her father before her—taking out all the prizes and winning races against girls much older than herself. Happy to see her youngest child take the forefront for once, Minnie encouraged her and tried to be there for her races whenever she could. Tom, of course, was over the moon—anything to do with the water had always been paramount in his life and Shirley's success brought back to him his glory days when he had been the Manly Surf Club champion. Although they were totally different children, throughout their childhood the two girls had always been good companions to one another. Since Angie had moved to high school earlier in the year, Shirley had felt rather left out of things; however, her success in the water had done a lot for her self-esteem and she had made some new friends into the bargain.

Minnie hummed to herself as she shook out the wet garments. Bob, Angie's dog, lay in the sun occasionally snapping at flies, which had hatched out early this year due to the unseasonal warm weather. Although his owner still loved him, Bob no longer received the undivided attention he had when Angie was younger. At thirteen, her interests centred on other pursuits, top of the list being her newly acquired friends at school. Because of her academic ability she had been sent to a special high school on the north shore, rather than the local one, which was adjacent to the primary school that Shirley still attended. Most of Angie's friends came from a different background than hers; their fathers were mostly businessmen and, although she still loved her father, she was reluctant to reveal the fact that he was a deckhand on the Manly Ferries. She had, of course, not mentioned this to either of her parents and when her mother asked why she never brought any of her friends home, she always managed to evade the question. No fool, Minnie suspected she knew the reason, but because there was no solution to the problem, she decided to leave well enough alone and let the child find her own answers. Of course she never mentioned any of this to Tom, for being the straightforward man he was, she knew he would never understand and would be deeply hurt to hear that his daughter was ashamed of his way of making a living.

With almost all the wash on the line, Minnie was contemplating what she would do for the rest of the afternoon. As always, there were innumerable things to do around the house, but they could wait. On the way home from work she had bought the few groceries she needed from the corner store, so the rest of the day was her own and her main inclination was to have a rest and read the magazine she'd purchased at the local newsagency.

Bob suddenly leapt to his feet and ran to the side passage barking loudly—at the same time, Minnie faintly heard the front doorbell ring. Who could it possibly be at this hour? she wondered as she made her way into the house and down the hallway. It was too early for either of the girls and Tom would be at work until about eight that evening.

Through the frosted glass of the front door she saw two dark shapes. I do hope it's not someone trying to sell something, she thought. Minnie hated saying no to anyone, and door-to-door salesmen were becoming something of a nuisance lately.

She opened the door to find two large policemen standing there.

"You've come to the wrong house; Mrs Spiteri is next door," she said, gesturing in that direction and starting to close the door.

"I'm sorry madam, we're not looking for Mrs Spiteri," said the older of the two. "We need to speak to a Mrs Sherwood, who we believe lives at this address."

"I'm Mrs Sherwood." Minnie's heart started thudding. Had something happened to one of the girls?

"May we come in?" said the sergeant.

"Yes, of course." Minnie showed them into the sitting room. They gestured towards the settee and Minnie collapsed into the seat, unable to speak. It was already obvious to her that something had happened; the serious faces of the two police told her that before they spoke further.

"Is your husband Thomas Sherwood?" asked the sergeant. Minnie nodded—still speechless. Tom—what had happened to Tom?

"I'm afraid there has been an accident. It involved a person who carried the identification of Thomas Sherwood at this address. It involved his bicycle and another vehicle."

Minnie finally spoke. "Is he all right? Where is he? Oh God, tell me he's not hurt too badly."

"I'm very sorry to tell you that your husband is deceased. He died immediately at the scene—we think it may have been his heart, for he veered into the path of the van and although it happened right outside the ambulance station, they were unable to revive him. I'm very sorry to bring this news. Is there anyone else in the house with you, Mrs Sherwood? This has been a terrible shock to you, I know."

Numb, her ears ringing, Minnie shook her head. "No, I'm alone. My daughters are both out for the afternoon. Tom—are you sure? It couldn't be him; there's never been anything wrong with his heart." Then, in a flash, a recent conversation with her husband came back to her. It had been Tom's fifty-first birthday and he'd grinned and remarked that at least he had outlived his father.

"He dropped dead at fifty—never had a day's illness in his life. He just went out without any warning. His heart just stopped." Unless the police were wrong, exactly the same must have happened to her husband. Minnie knew instinctively that there had been no mistake; her Tommy was gone. What would she do now?

The police were very kind; they asked if there was anyone she wanted notified and she explained that Sandra lived on the other side of the harbour. As neither she nor her daughter had telephones, the police offered to contact the Leichhardt station and have them tell Sandra what had happened. Not prepared to leave her alone, they suggested they bring her neighbour in to stay with her until someone in the family could come.

Mrs Spiteri came in immediately, took the weeping Minnie into her arms and told the police that she would stay there for as long as she was needed. The sergeant gave her details of where Tom had been taken and said that someone would have to conduct a formal identification in due course. He wrote his name and phone number on a piece of paper and he and his colleague left, again expressing their condolences to Minnie, who stopped crying long enough to thank them for their kindness.

Sandra arrived by taxi about two hours later, fortunately before either of her younger sisters arrived home. She had left little Andrew at home with Cliff and assured her mother that she would stay with her for at least that night. Cliff intended to borrow a car from a friend and would be there tomorrow to help them out and to join in a conference on what they should all do in the immediate future. Mother and daughter clung to each other, each mourning in her own way the loss of a good man, who had been a wonderful father and a loving and faithful husband.

When it came close to the time for the two young girls to arrive home, they made a conscious effort to pull themselves together, for they both knew how hard it would be to break the news to Angie and Shirley. They must keep up a strong front, to assure the youngsters that their world had not ended with the loss of their father and that the rest of the family would look after them and do as much as possible to keep their lives on an even keel.

There was, of course, no easy way to tell the girls that the apparently hale and hearty father they had seen that morning was dead. All four of them wept together and when Minnie suggested the two girls sleep with her that night, they climbed into bed, one on either side of her and cried themselves to sleep, while their mother lay awake for hours looking at her sleeping children and wondering what the future held for them all. She wished she could go to the other room to comfort Sandra, who was every bit as upset as her sisters, but she couldn't move for fear of disturbing her two young daughters.

Cliff arrived the next morning and, as usual, proved to be a huge asset. He calmly assessed the situation and handed the care of Andrew over to Angie and Shirley, rightly assuming that the little boy's antics would partly serve to take their minds off their loss. He contacted the police and volunteered he would conduct the formal identification as Minnie was in no state to do so. Because of the circumstances of death there was to be an autopsy, so no funeral could be arranged in the immediate future, and after a family conference it was decided that Minnie and the two girls would return with Sandra and Cliff to Leichhardt for at least the next few days. They had no phone contact for Johnny in Melbourne and as the post office was closed until Monday, they had to wait until then to send off a telegram telling him of his father's death. One came back almost immediately, asking for funeral details and telling them he would be there as soon as possible. They despatched a further telegram explaining the holdup due to the autopsy and it was agreed that John would come to Sydney when the funeral had been arranged.

Before she left for Leichhardt, Minnie had called on Mrs Spiteri to thank her for her kindness; she also told her of their immediate plans and asked a further favour. Could she look after Bob until they returned? It would be crowded enough in the car with three adults and three children and even if they could fit the dog in, there was the problem of how to get him back, as they would doubtless be travelling by public transport on their return. Assured that the dog would be fed and walked while they were away, Minnie returned home to organise the packing of enough clothes for a stay of several days—she doubted if she would be able to stay away longer than that.

They stayed with Sandra until the end of the week.

"Stay with us a bit longer," Sandra urged Minnie.

"I can't," her mother replied. "The last thing I need at this point is to lose my job. It's no longer just for luxuries; from here on I need the money to put food on the table. They've been very understanding, but they won't be forever. Besides that, the girls need to get back to school. End of the year exams are coming up and they can't afford to miss those."

Sandra nodded in agreement. "I suppose you're right, Mumma. Besides, I suppose the sooner their lives return to something approaching normal, the sooner they will adjust to life without Dad."

They arrived home to be greeted by an ecstatic Bob, who thought he had been deserted, although his rotund stomach proved he certainly hadn't wanted for food while they were away. The house seemed so empty without Tom, with constant reminders everywhere. Although friends and neighbours did everything they could to make it easy for them, nothing could fill the void left in their lives. Minnie realised that she must keep the family going, so she did everything in her power to help her daughters. Her grief had to be confined to the privacy of her bedroom; in the light of day she must keep up a brave face for their sakes.

The autopsy verified the police officers' theory—Tom had died of a heart attack. The funeral was held at St Matthew's Church in Manly, just doors from Minnie's workplace. The turnout was amazing; there were friends from his youth, from the Manly Surf Club, his old army mates, his co-workers from the ferries and dozens of people Minnie had never met. All the ladies from next door attended, decorously dressed for once; several of Minnie's friends from work came, including the usually gruff Miss Robson, who hugged her and told her they were all thinking of her. Johnny arrived from Melbourne the night before the funeral, bringing with him his girlfriend, Anne, someone they hadn't previously known existed. She was a shy, gentle girl, obviously very taken by Johnny, and was universally liked by all the family. Johnny confided to his mother that he intended to propose to Anne when they returned to Melbourne, which made Minnie happy to think her son would be settled down with such a lovely girl.

Minnie's foresight in paying regularly into an insurance policy for her husband over the years brought welcome dividends, covering the funeral costs and leaving her with a reasonably sized nest egg that would be put aside for the future. Having always been a thrifty housewife, she had managed to save quite a tidy amount from her earnings over the past three years—so there was no immediate worry about money. Unlike many husbands, Tom had always included Minnie in the household's financial affairs—so she was not like many widows, who, confronted with the reality of paying bills and managing a bank account, were thrown into unknown territory at a time when they were most vulnerable. As soon as things settled down, Minnie worked out a budget for herself and the girls. She found that they could manage quite well on her wages.

One luxury she allowed herself was to install a telephone in the house. Cliff was working on maintenance at the General Post Office in the city, earning a much better wage than before, and Sandra had been thinking for some time of getting a phone herself. After Tom's death, when loneliness became a constant for Minnie, it was a huge comfort to be able to pick up the phone and call her daughter. Telephone lines were still as scarce as hen's teeth in Sydney, but through his job, Cliff was able to speed things up for both of them, for not a great deal had changed in some ways from wartime—sometimes contacts and a bit of palm greasing was the only way to avoid months and even years of wait for some of the simplest things.

The telephone meant that not only could Minnie keep in touch with Sandra, she could call her sister Kath, whose company she had missed greatly since she moved away. To everyone's surprise, Kath, the confirmed spinster, had at the age of forty-three, through her job at the hospital, met a widower with two young children. Within three months, she had married him, left her job and settled down to a life of being a wife and mother—exactly what she had always told her sister she would never do. Her husband was an orthopaedic surgeon with a good practice, as well as being a visiting consultant at several hospitals, so Kath's lifestyle was very different from the one she had lived in her tiny, semi-detached house in Leichhardt. The two children, a boy and a girl, were both in boarding school, where he had placed them after his wife died. They were happy to stay in their schools and equally happy to enjoy Kath's cooking when they returned home for holidays. Minnie was very pleased to see her younger sister settled down, for she had always worried about her situation, with nobody to care for her in her old age. With her characteristic frankness, Kath had laughingly remarked to Minnie that even if her stepchildren wouldn't, there would be plenty of money to pay someone else who would.

Now that Minnie's wages were needed for living, not just for extras, she valued her job even more. But the monetary side was probably not the main thing she appreciated, for if it hadn't been for the friendship and continuing support of her fellow workers, she knew she would have been beside herself in the lonely hours without her husband. As her girls grew they became more independent, having their own friends and interests, and it made a huge difference to Minnie's life to have someone with whom she could take in the occasional movie, or sit down for a quiet chat over a cup of tea. At weekends, she was still automatically included in any activities that Mary and Fred were planning and, especially if her girls had other plans, she made a point of going along, rather than sitting at home alone with just the radio to keep her company.

The first Christmas without Tom promised to be a hard one for all the family. He had always been the life of the party, dressing up as Santa Claus and keeping up a family tradition of filling the pillowcases they left on their door handles on Christmas Eve. Minnie rather dreaded the whole process this year, but Sandra, having given some thought to a way of making the day as special as possible for her two sisters, came up with a brilliant idea.

"Why don't we rent a house up the mountains?" she said. "It would be a great break for all of us and because it will be something different, it won't bring back too many memories of Dad to Angie and Shirley."

Although she could ill afford the time off for the holiday, Minnie realised what a good solution it was to something that had been worrying her ever since she'd started thinking about the approaching holiday season. Fortunately, she had a week's holiday due and as the Dress Materials department did virtually no business in the holiday period, her employers were more than happy for her to take the time off.

The Blue Mountains west of Sydney, although traditionally more popular in winter, have many attractions in the warmer months. One factor in their favour is that, although the temperature is high in the daytime, it cools down to a much more comfortable degree overnight. Summer nights in Sydney can be exhausting, particularly when the humidity is high—so the prospect of this, coupled with all the sights and interesting bush walks, was something that they all looked forward to. Although the girls had been to the mountains on day trips, they had never stayed overnight and there was much excitement about spending a week in this completely different environment.

The place they were renting was a fair distance from the train station, and with all of their luggage, they found it necessary to take a taxi. It pulled up outside a rambling, rather run-down old house, surrounded by overgrown gardens. The girls and their small cousin ran ahead of the adults up to the front door and waited, hopping from one foot to the other as Minnie fumbled with the unfamiliar lock.

Angie was the first through the door. Full of excitement, she looked around the rather gloomy interior. "Wow, it's like another world!" she exclaimed.

Minnie looked at Sandra and Cliff, both of whom seemed not quite as thrilled as Angie. "Let's hope the other world doesn't come complete with bedbugs," she remarked. "I didn't expect it to be as old as this."

They made a full inspection of the house and found that in spite of its age, the place was quite clean and the beds, although a bit lumpy, seemed fortunately free of any unwelcome visitors.

"Angie's right, it is from another world. I think we will really enjoy living somewhere so different from home," was Minnie's final verdict.

And they did. Circa 1900, the house was packed with interesting nooks and crannies, with lots of overstuffed settees and old-fashioned furniture. The walls were covered with faded prints of the mountains in another age, and framed photos of ladies in ankle length dresses and cloche hats, standing by open automobiles accompanied by blazer clad gents wearing straw hats. Angie thought them quite the tops of high society and made up stories in her mind of being driven around in a vehicle such as that, on the way to a sophisticated party at one of the grand hotels in Katoomba.

The grounds of the house, although overgrown, had obviously been wonderful in their day. The girls spent many hours just wandering among the pathways and making their way through the undergrowth to an old summer house, its paint faded away, but still maintaining the magic of its past glories. There they would sit and for a while forget that they were "too old" for their fantasy games of the past, telling each other what they would have done if they had lived there in days gone by.

Every morning, while it was still cool, they would troupe along the road to the many mountain walks in the area, with pathways winding round the mountaintops to look-outs on the valleys below. Because little Andrew was too small for these adventures, Minnie and Sandra took turns staying home with him. Cliff offered to spell them in these duties, but the two women pointed out that they preferred there be a man with the girls, to keep an eye on them and help them over some of the more tricky and dangerous pathways. There were, of course, moments of sadness, particularly when someone remarked, without thinking, "Dad would have loved this." Minnie was determined not to let this spoil everyone's fun and although she shed an occasional tear alone in her bed at night, she kept up a brave face when she was with the others.

The holiday flew by and eventually they had to pack up their goods and presents and catch a taxi to the station for the train journey back to Sydney. The experience of travelling on a steam train was another adventure for the girls; there was always something new to be seen as the train made its way through all the little mountain villages, past breathtaking views, before finally descending to cross the Hawkesbury River bridge and on to the grassy plains on the other side of the river. The final part of the journey through suburbia was something of a letdown, but the girls were looking forward to being home, to seeing their friends, and to Bob, who had once again been left to the tender care of Mrs Spiteri and her ladies.

~ * ~

With day-to-day survival uppermost in her mind, Minnie found little time to plan for the future, until six months after Tom's death, when she received a proposal which would in the long run affect the whole family.

Early on a late summer Sunday morning, the phone rang—it was Sandra.

"Are you going to be home this afternoon? Cliff and I thought we might pop over and visit you; we have two surprises and an idea we want to discuss with you."

Curious as to what it was all about, Minnie assured her daughter that she would be there. The girls, as usual on a weekend, would be out and about, but she had no plans other than to do a bit of gardening and then put her feet up. In a way she was sorry that her rest would be interrupted, for there was precious little free time in her busy schedule. Still, it was always good to see Sandra and Cliff and, in particular, Andrew, with whom she shared a mutual admiration society.

Minnie waited in the front garden, cutting back some of the bushes that had grown out of control in the hot summer weather, at the same time watching down the street for the family's approach. When they arrived, their means of transport was a surprise—and was in fact the first surprise that Sandra had promised her.

A motorbike and sidecar came down the street, to which Minnie paid scant attention. It was only when Andrew's voice rang out, "Granny, Granny—look at us!" that she realised the motorbike was ridden by Cliff and the sidecar was occupied by Sandra and the little boy.

Laughing and dusting off her hands, she lifted Andrew out of the sidecar and stood back with her wriggling cargo while Cliff dismounted and helped Sandra out of the cab.

"And where did this come from?" she asked. "You promised me a surprise and it certainly is—now I'm dying to know what the other one is."

"Let's get inside first," said Sandra. "I'm dying for a cuppa; the surprise can wait until later."

They sat at the kitchen table with tea and the scones Minnie had made in anticipation of their visit. Andrew, after a drink of milk and a scone, disappeared into the yard to play ball with Bob, who was surprisingly gentle with the little boy.

"Now, you promised to give me a surprise…and you certainly did. I had no idea you were buying a motorbike. But you mentioned two surprises and something else, too, if my memory serves me correctly," Minnie said, as she topped up their cups and leaned back in her chair."

"First things first," Sandra replied. "The other surprise is that Andrew's going to have a little brother or sister—sometime in September—a springtime baby. The other thing I'll leave up to Cliff, for it was his idea in the first place."

Mother and daughter hugged, while Cliff sat there beaming at them. When they sat down again, he assumed a more serious expression and pushed his cup away from him across the table. He looked around the room for a while, seeming to be taking in the surroundings for the first time. Then he spoke. "You love this house, don't you." It was more a statement than a question, but there was some semblance of question in the way he said it. Minnie, puzzled as to why he should say what he had, answered honestly.

"I loved it more when Tom was alive. It's still home to me and the girls, but something went out of the place when Tom died. I suppose it is because it was always his home—he grew up here and it meant a lot to him, so it meant a lot to me because of him. What a strange question, Cliff—why do you ask?"

Cliff was having trouble finding the words and Sandra impatiently took over from him. "Mum, we're worried about you and the girls living here alone and now that we are going to have another baby, we've decided we want to bring up our children away from Leichhardt—somewhere with cleaner air and open spaces for them to play. What we would like is for us all to live together in one house. We love it over here and now that Cliff is working in town, it wouldn't be all that hard for him to travel in to work. Plenty of people from this side of the harbour do it every day."

Taken aback, Minnie, who had expected nothing like this, said, "Darling, how could we possibly all fit in here? There are only two bedrooms and it would be impossible to extend the house, and even if we could, it would cost a fortune. I think it's a great idea—us living together—we all get on so well, but there's just no possible way we could all manage in this little house."

Cliff spoke up again.

"That's the reason I asked you about the house. What we're proposing is that you sell up and we buy something larger together. Your share of the new property would be the money you get from the house sale. I have a bit of money put away from a legacy my aunt left me, and we saved a fair bit while Sandra was still at work. I'm sure the bank would give me a mortgage for the balance. What we're currently paying as rent is dead money; we feel we will never be in a position to save enough to buy a house outright—but we certainly would be able to make payments on our half of a house we all bought together." He shifted uncomfortably in his seat and pushed his chair back from the table. "This is an idea that's been going through my head ever since we came back from the mountains. We all worked together so well as a team and had so much fun together. Sandra and I have talked about it for weeks and it sounds like the perfect situation for all of us. But we don't want to push you into anything; we don't want to force you out of your home. We only want you to agree if you feel the same way we do."

Minnie sat there dumbstruck for a moment. This proposal was the last thing she had considered or expected, but already thoughts were running through her head. There would be so many advantages in Cliff's proposal. Although she was a fairly capable woman, she had really missed the presence of a man about the house, and although she knew the ladies next door kept an eye on the girls until she came home from work, it still was not the ideal situation to leave them alone in the house every day. If the family all lived together, then Sandra would be there in the afternoons and she could work without the guilt that brought her hurrying home to make sure they weren't left alone too long. She looked from face to face of the two who sat opposite her, their expressions reflecting a combination of worry and hope.

"I think it's a wonderful idea," she finally said. Cliff and Sandra, who had been holding their breath in anticipation, expelled it as one.

Sandra leapt up and hugged her mother. "Oh Mum, I'm so happy! I've really missed you and the girls and worried about you so much since Dad died. I know it will work out wonderfully for all of us. All we have to do is find the right property."

They sat there over lunch and throughout the afternoon, drinking numerous cups of tea and discussing the ins and outs of what needed to be done. When the two girls returned home and were told about what the adults had decided, they were overcome with excitement at the prospect of the whole family being together again. When their excitement had died down, Cliff took them for a ride in his sidecar before they all walked down to the beach for an early meal of fish and chips.

After Sandra and Cliff had gone, Minnie sat with the girls and explained the plan to them in a bit more detail. "One thing we've already realised is that we may have to move up the peninsula a bit further in order to find a house big enough for all of us. There are some in Manly, but they would be much too pricey—but wherever we end up, there will still be the beach. You, Angie, will still be able to catch a bus to school and Shirley and I will get to Manly probably as quickly by bus as it takes us now to walk every day. And Sandra will be there for you when you get home from school—you won't have to come home to an empty house."

Now came the hard part—finding the right property would not be easy.

Ten

Moving on

It took three months, during which Minnie spent every spare moment checking every possible house for sale in the area they had chosen. Because of Cliff's commute to the city and Angie's to Neutral Bay, they had decided not to consider anything beyond Narrabeen, which was several miles to the north of Manly. It gave them a fairly large area to choose from, but affordable homes with at least four bedrooms and lots of living space were not readily available in an area that had been until recently mainly holiday homes, most with no more than three bedrooms. Minnie was just about to give up when she received a call from Anthony Butler, one of the estate agents she had been dealing with. "I have what I think will be just what you want," he said.

The house was located at Narrabeen, right on the outer limit of their required area—however it sounded perfect for two families who wanted to live together, but not in each other's pockets. It had been for many years a boarding house, had separate living quarters for the owners and an amazing six extra bedrooms, a living room and sunroom.

"The house is old, but well maintained," said the agent. "It's right on the lake, with huge grounds, and for all that the price is not exorbitant; it has been dropped considerably owing to the lack of interest in something so large." It sounded so perfect to Minnie that she sneaked a morning off work and caught a bus straight out to the agent the next day. "It sounds to me like the sort of place where my late husband and I stayed when we were newlyweds," she remarked to the agent as they climbed into his car.

To Minnie's amazement, the house they eventually reached was the self-same place where she and Tom had spent a week back in 1922. Without even walking through the door, Minnie felt she was fated to buy this house—the coincidence was too large for it not to have been preordained.

The couple who had run the boarding house were long gone—it was in fact a deceased estate, the sale having been held up by the long wait for probate. Minnie was surprised to find that almost all the furniture in the house remained, although blank spaces showed that pictures had been removed from the walls, with the exception of two antique views of the River Nile—and there were no signs of any ornaments. Obviously the owners had removed what they wanted and left the rest of the house untouched, considering the furniture not worth worrying about. Although the interior was musty from being shut up so long, the grounds were in really good condition. The bushes showed signs of being regularly trimmed and the grass had the unmistakable smell of having recently been mowed, which was surprising in view of the fact that the house has been unoccupied for well over a year. When Minnie remarked on this, the agent smiled wryly. "There is one potential problem," he remarked.

"With the house you inherit Jack. He is a World War One veteran who lives in the shack down the end of the garden and has been given a lifetime lease, which is iron tight and can't be broken. The current owners went so far as to take him to the Landlord & Tenants board, but due to the new laws that have been brought in since the war, there isn't a hope in Hades of getting him out unless he wants to move. They even offered to find him alternative accommodation (which I might add may have been well-nigh impossible) but he just wasn't interested. Old Mr & Mrs Carmody promised him a home for life and that's what he intends to have. Unless he defaults on payment of rent—and he has always been as regular as clockwork—he will be here until he drops, or finally decides to move on."

Before Minnie could comment, he continued, "His rent is very low, but that is because the original arrangement was that he would maintain the grounds and do odd jobs around the house. I must say that he has been remarkably conscientious about this—with nobody to oversee him he has, as you'll have noticed, kept the place in tiptop condition. Apparently he keeps himself very much to himself, although he does a bit of work around the district and I've heard nothing but good about him. Jack is one of the reasons the price is so low…a lot of people are put off by the fact that he lives here. Looking at it from a different perspective, having him here is a definite asset. You could do a lot worse, Mrs Sherwood—not too many people have what is, in effect, a live-in maintenance man."

Minnie's heart had sunk at the thought of having a stranger living on the premises. "I don't know," she said doubtfully. "I've two young girls and the little grandson and another baby on the way soon. I don't think I like the idea of some old fellow hanging around the place."

"I know what you are saying and understand your doubts," said the agent. "All I can suggest is that you come down the yard with me—I'm sure Jack is home. Why don't you meet him and decide for yourself. After that, if you're still interested, we can come back here and you can have a more thorough look through the property."

They made their way out the back door, to the steps that led down to the back garden. At the top of the steps, Minnie paused and looked at the view. The neatly mown grass ran all the way down to the lake frontage, where there was a small jetty with a rowboat tied up to one of the piers. "I wonder if it's the same boat Tom and I took out on the lake," she thought to herself as she followed the agent down the wooden steps.

Jack's "shack" proved to be a neat timber construction, freshly painted, with its own little garden planted with various annuals. It wasn't the run down shed that Minnie had imagined, but an obviously well-tended small home. Anthony Butler knocked on the door, which was opened promptly enough to suggest that the occupant had been as interested in his visitors as Minnie was in him. He proved to be a small wiry man of indeterminate age, his face, arms and legs burnt brown by the sun, dressed in a clean check shirt (which Minnie suspected he had donned in anticipation of her visit) and old, but clean twill shorts. He wore no socks, just sandshoes, which had seen better days. He smiled at his visitors cautiously but said nothing.

Anthony Butler spoke first. "Jack, this is Mrs Sherwood, who is interested in buying the house. I thought it would be a good idea for you two to meet."

"How do you do?" said Minnie, feeling uncomfortably like the lady of the manor visiting the peasants.

"I'm very well, thank you," Jack replied. "Won't you come inside? It's hot out there. Would you like a cuppa? I was just about to make one."

Minnie's immediate impression was that he certainly seemed decent enough and seemed as cautious about her as she was with him. They went inside the cottage and, although it was hard to see much detail after the brightness of the outside sun, enough was visible to show that this was a well-kept home—not something spruced up to make an impression. It was unequally divided in two by a partition; one part shut off by a closed door was probably the bedroom, the larger room being a combination living, eating and cooking area. The kitchenette was equipped with a small electric stove, where a kettle was emitting steam, ready to make the proffered cup of tea. Jack took a jug of milk from a small ice chest and two cups and saucers from the cupboard to join his, which was already on the table. As he poured the boiling water into the teapot, Minnie noticed that his hand shook slightly. *He's as nervous and uncomfortable about this as I am,* she thought. Strangely enough, this made her feel a lot better about everything.

Jack was not a man to chatter, but he answered the few questions that Minnie thought to ask, politely and concisely. She noticed on one wall a bookcase filled with old and obviously frequently read books... once again giving her a comfort that she was unable to define. One thing was for certain, this was not some old tramp—but a man who looked after his home and, by the state of the grounds, took his obligations seriously. By the time they had finished their tea and thanked Jack for his hospitality, any doubts that Minnie initially had about him had vanished. Together, she and the agent returned to the house—this time to look at the layout more thoroughly.

The "owner's flat" would be perfect for Sandra and Cliff, having its own kitchen, small bathroom and little sitting room where they could have their privacy if they wanted it. Behind this was a hallway leading to two of the six other bedrooms, and it was obvious even to the untrained eye that it would be an easy job to make a doorway from the flat through to the hallway to give access to these two bedrooms, which would be ideal for Andrew and the new baby. The other four bedrooms were small, but adequate, which would allow one each for Minnie and the two girls, while the final one could be a combination spare bedroom (for when Johnny and Anne came to visit) and serve as a perfect sewing room for Minnie in the meantime. A veranda spanned the front of the house, continuing halfway down each side—on the northern side it was glassed in, a perfect place to catch the winter sun. Next to the southern side of the veranda was a large garage, closed off with double doors. The kitchen and bathrooms were adequate, though far from glamorous, but on the whole the house could not have been more perfect.

"I'd like the children to have a look at it at the weekend," Minnie said to the agent, as he closed the front door and led her back to the car. "I won't say a definite yes—and I have yet to sell in Manly, but as far as I am concerned, this place is perfect." They made arrangements for another viewing on the coming Saturday and Minnie returned home to call Sandra and tell her of the gem of a place she had found. She felt certain that Sandra and Cliff would be as enthusiastic about the house as she was.

Minnie had become very close to her next door neighbour since Tom's death, particularly due to the woman's kindness to her and her family. It had been such a comfort to her to know that there was always someone there to keep an eye on the girls and the house whenever they were away. Mrs S, as Minnie called her, knew everyone and everything in the area; some of the most surprising people managed to turn a blind eye to the source of the woman's income, happy to accept the generous donations she made to any and every good cause. Because of her wide range of acquaintances, it was to her that Minnie turned to ask for the name of the most reliable estate agent in Manly. If they were to buy the property in Narrabeen—and she was already thinking of it as a done deal—she needed to sell quickly and at the best available price.

Mrs S was upset to hear that Minnie was to move. "But I've suspected for some time that you wouldn't stay on for long," she said. "In fact, I've been giving it a lot of thought. I've always liked this little house—so close to my place, but separate from it. And you've done a lot to make it more modern. I think it would be just perfect for me...I would have somewhere to escape from all the chatter that goes on in the big house. When you decide you definitely are selling, come to me—don't worry about any agents. You can get an independent valuation and I'll buy it from you at a fair price. How does that sound to you?"

How did it sound? Minnie was over the moon...no worries about losing the other house, no hordes of people trekking through the current one. Angels didn't come in long robes and wings—they lived right next door, dressed in a floral house frock and wearing altogether too much face paint. She resisted the urge to hug her saviour and said in as calm a voice as she could manage, "I think that sounds like a good idea. I'll get a valuation as soon as possible and come back to you with a suggested price if that's okay. I won't make a definite decision on the new place until the children have looked at it, but I don't see them raising any objections." Then, unable to restrain herself, she overcame her resistance and hugged her kind neighbour.

"Thank you, Mrs S—you are a Godsend. My only regret is that we won't have you for a neighbour anymore. Nobody could ask for a better one."

Anthea Spiteri returned the hug, then rubbed her hand across her eyes. "That's the nicest thing anyone has said to me in more than forty years."

~ * ~

Cliff, Sandra and Andrew met up with Minnie and the two girls the following Saturday outside the old tram terminus at Narrabeen shops. They found that Anthony Butler was out with a client when they arrived, but his wife, who was a partner in the business, was waiting for them, looking rather taken aback at the number of viewers.

"It's going to be a bit of a crush in my car," she said, as she locked the door of the business and ushered them over the road to the parking lot.

"Don't worry, Sandra and I will go in the bike," said Cliff, gesturing towards the motor bike and sidecar that stood nearby.

"Can I go with Cliff?" begged Shirley, who had retained a soft spot for her brother-in-law since the days when he taught her to swim.

"Well, you're certainly too big to sit on my lap in it," laughed Sandra. "You can go in the sidecar instead of me, and Andrew and I will go in the car."

Seating accommodation sorted out, they climbed into the two vehicles and with Mrs Butler leading the way, drove up the peninsula towards the house.

Minnie's heart was in her mouth as they headed towards the front door. She had spent the past few days thinking so much about the house and felt even more than ever it was the right home for the family. If Sandra and Cliff didn't like it, she knew she would feel dreadfully let down. Mrs Butler opened the front door and ushered them inside. "I'll leave you folks to look around. If you have any questions, I'll be out here on the veranda," she said, as she took a cigarette from its pack and lit it, taking a deep draw and sitting herself down on a rickety cane chair that stood near the doorway.

"I'm glad she didn't come in here with her cigarette," muttered Minnie, who hated smoking. "Filthy habit—I'm glad none of you do it." Angie and Shirley, aged thirteen and eleven, giggled together at the thought, while Sandra, who felt the same as her mother, nodded in agreement.

Minnie, having seen the house before, took over the tour of inspection. She led them first through to the flat, remarking as she opened the door, "I thought this would be perfect for you and Cliff, Sandra. You could shut us off and have your own little world—I think that was one of the main things I liked about the house. We would all be so close, but each of us would have our privacy when we wanted it."

Sandra nodded in agreement, which turned to one of approval when she saw the adjoining bathroom. "Oh Mum, it is perfect for us, isn't it! And we'd have our own little kitchen, so I could get bottles for the babies at night, without disturbing anyone else. But where would they sleep?"

Minnie explained her thoughts about knocking an extra doorway from the little sitting room to the hallway. "Come through to the back of the house and I'll show you what I mean."

Meanwhile, Angie and Shirley had taken off on their own voyage of inspection. They ran through the house, squealing in excitement at each new discovery. They were deep in an argument about who would have which bedroom when Minnie and the others came back from inspecting the two back bedrooms.

Having done a general inspection, the family then made a more careful check of each of the rooms. Although the house had an understandably musty smell, there were no obvious signs of damp and a check of all the ceilings found nothing more than the occasional spider web. The girls became bored very quickly with this, and having found some old comic books, were sitting down leafing through them when the adults returned to the living room.

"Well, what do you think?" asked Minnie, sinking into an old stuffed chair, glad to get off her tired feet after being on them all morning at work.

Sandra and Cliff looked at one another and nodded in unison. "We love it," said Sandra for both of them. "It needs some paint and new curtains—but it's perfect, just perfect; we couldn't ask for anything better."

"You haven't seen the back yard yet—wait until you see the rowboat," Minnie remarked, and to Angie she added, "Bob will go off his head with all this room to run around in. Come on everyone; let's look at the rest of our new domain."

She took them down the back steps and introduced them all to Jack, who was sitting on the jetty dangling a fishing line in the water.

"Are there real fishes here?" asked Shirley in excitement. "Could we catch some when we live here?"

"You come to live here and I'll show you how to catch fish. And if your mother will let you, I'll take you out with me when I go prawning one night," replied Jack. "We go out in the dark with a lantern and they come up to the surface to see what's going on—we scoop them up with a net—and there you have a lovely feed of prawns, fresh from the lake. Much better than those ones you get from the fish shop; they're fresh and juicy, like nothing you've tasted in your life."

That did it for Shirley, who long since had grown out of her reluctance to eat and loved her food—prawns being one of her favourites. "When do we move in?" she asked her mother.

Everyone laughed at her enthusiasm. "First things first," said Minnie, "but I think there's a pretty good chance we will be moving in eventually." They said their goodbyes to Jack and headed back to the house...one final look around and they left through the front door to find Mrs Butler sitting where they'd left her, another cigarette in her hand and the squashed remains of two others on the floor beside her.

From then on, it was only a matter of time before the place became theirs. The deal with Anthea Spiteri went without a hitch, that lady insisting on paying the full valuation price. Cliff applied for and easily obtained approval for a mortgage on his part of the property, which they bought as Tenants in Common, rather than the more usual joint tenancy. This had been suggested by the solicitor, as it allowed each party to sell their ownership to the other in the unlikely possibility that the arrangement didn't work out.

Everything went like clockwork and, with the baby's birth only a couple of months away, they finally moved into their new home. Settlement on both the sale in Manly and the purchase had been completed three weeks previously, but when Mrs Spiteri found that they wanted to paint and do some redecorating, she insisted that Minnie and the girls stay put until the new house was completely ready. "I think I can put up with those giggling women for a few more weeks," she remarked. "It gives me more time to enjoy my neighbours before you leave. I'm in no hurry."

A grateful Minnie took a week of her annual holidays and spent the time travelling back and forth to Narrabeen, measuring for new curtains, which she ran up on her faithful Singer sewing machine. At the recommendation of the agent, Anthony Butler, they employed a local painter to paint right through the house. It was an extra expense, but a wise one, for nobody in the family had the time to take on such a large task. It meant that they moved into a house in perfect order, rather than having to spend months making do. It was decided that Sandra and Cliff would use the sitting room in the flat as Andrew's bedroom for the time being—the new baby would sleep in with them when it arrived and they could then take their time in decorating the two back rooms for their children as they grew older. All the furniture in the house had been included in the sale, but with the consolidation of two households, there was little need for much of it. A couple of the old lounges went out into the sunroom and, as most of the rest was in reasonable condition, the local second hand shop was happy to take it off their hands.

Eleven

A new life

One of the happiest members of the two households when they finally moved to Narrabeen proved to be Bob, who as Minnie had predicted, was overjoyed with his new surroundings. He had his own home under the house, but spent little time there, as Jack adopted him as his own and took him on walks and out in the rowboat. In his new back yard, the dog spent his days chasing seagulls and the occasional wild duck that strayed into his domain—it was a dog's idea of heaven.

Angie's nose was slightly out of joint at this turn of events, but as she had more pressing things on her mind, she found little time to think about it—so involved was she in the turmoil of growing up and dealing with life.

The only cloud on Bob's horizon was the presence of the new addition to the family. Not Sandra's baby, which was yet to be born, but the cat, which had come with Sandra and Cliff from their home in Leichhardt. Bob had been used to chasing every feline that dared to enter his yard and when he discovered a furry invader settled comfortably in a chair on the front veranda, he went off his head.

Frankie—named after Frank Sinatra, Sandra's favourite singer—was equally as affronted at the enemy in her province. She had been kept inside for the first few days in fear of her straying away in these strange surroundings. Although Minnie had suggested the old tried and true practise of smearing her paws with butter, Sandra, who agreed with Cliff that there was absolutely no logic in this suggestion, had made sure that Frankie stayed inside the house until she felt completely at home. That the two natural enemies should eventually meet was inevitable and equally inevitable was the outcome of this encounter. Poor Bob, who thought he was doing the right thing by protecting the family from an invader, not only suffered several scratches to his nose, but was yelled at by those he had sought to protect. He retreated to the back yard, tail between his legs, and sought the comfort of Jack, who he was sure felt exactly the same as he on the subject of cats around the place.

Eventually the two animals came to accept one another's presence on the premises. An uneasy truce evolved whereby Frankie claimed the front veranda and garden as hers and Bob stayed most of the time in the back yard with his mate, Jack. On the rare occasions that the two met, their enmity was confined to growling on the part of Bob and much hissing and fur raising from the cat.

Everyone in the family settled down quickly and made the necessary adjustments that must always be effected when moving into a new situation; all, with the exception of Angie. As she grew older and wrestled with the traumas of puberty, Angie became less and less at peace with herself and her family. She felt that of all of them she missed Tom the most. She had been her father's favourite, for she had reminded him of himself in his younger days—fearless, game to try anything and always fiercely interested in the world around her. He had loved Sandra and Johnny, but had little in common with either of them, and Shirley was so quiet and withdrawn that he was always at a loss as to what to say and do with her. He would spend hours with Angie, telling her stories of his experiences in the war, of the places he had been and of the things he had done as a child with his own father. It was he who first explained to her that the stars in the night sky were actually other worlds; it was he who taught her to ride a bike and who took her to the stables behind the bakery to feed the horses with carrots and sugar lumps. Tom had been Angie's hero, her best friend and the one who always knew the answer to her many questions. She missed her father as if something had been torn from her body and although she was old enough to realise that her mother was probably the one who suffered his loss most—she was still sufficiently a child to feel that her loss was most important.

When the suggestion had been made that they move from Manly to the new house, Angie had been as enthusiastic as anyone else in the family. However, when she realised that this entailed selling up the house that had been Tom's childhood home, she was overcome by a feeling of betraying her father. "Can't we keep this house and move to the other one, too?" she had asked her mother. When it was explained to her that they needed the money from the sale, she said no more, but her enthusiasm over the move paled considerably.

Now that she had her own bedroom, free from the constant chatter of her younger sister, Angie spent more and more time alone. Reading, listening to the mantel radio that had been her father's, she became more withdrawn as time passed. This was largely missed by the rest of the family, for there was always so much going on and everyone was so involved in the anticipation of the arrival of the new baby. Cliff was the only one who suspected that all was not well with Angie, for more often than not they left together in the morning, he to board the bus to the city, she to catch the school bus. He found that the girl who had always chattered nonstop was noticeably quieter and far from the cheerful child he had known in the past. With no knowledge whatsoever of the workings of the teenage female mind, he just put it down to her getting older and thought no more of it. With a new baby on the way and plans for the future that promised to change his life drastically, Cliff had little time to wonder what made his young sister-in-law tick.

Angie's schoolwork suffered, too. She had always been top of her class and, although she still completed her assignments on time, sometimes her marks were not much more than a pass—whereas previously she had excelled in most of her subjects. When Minnie saw the school reports she was rather worried, but as did Cliff, she thought that Angie's behaviour was due to her growing up. She recalled how difficult Sandra had been at this age and assumed this was just a phase the girl was passing through.

Finally, the fact that all was not well with Angie was brought home to Minnie when Anthea Spiteri, back in Manly, came into the shop and told her of strange behaviour she had noticed. Angie had taken to hanging around the old house in Manly, stopping off there on the way home from school and standing across the street, looking at the house. Mrs Spiteri had approached her on a couple of occasions, at which Angie immediately headed off down the street. When this had happened several times, Mrs S felt the need to tell Minnie about it. Stunned when she heard what Angie had been doing, Minnie hastened home to question the child about why she was behaving that way.

When confronted, Angie burst into tears and at first could give no coherent reason for her actions. Minnie, knowing there must be something serious behind all this, sat down patiently with her arm around her daughter, waiting for the sobs to subside. Finally, Angie calmed sufficiently to be able to talk and gave a garbled story about wanting to go to where her father had lived, because she was starting to forget what he looked like and thought this would be the way to bring him back into her mind.

Stifling the urge to cry herself, Minnie held her daughter closer and kissed her, saying, "Sweetheart, this is what happens when someone dies. We never forget them—how could we forget your dad? But it's quite normal that we forget exactly how they looked as time passes. We keep a sort of image in our minds, but time has a way of making that a bit dimmer, just as it makes the ache of losing them easier. We don't love them any less... we still have our memories, but we have to go on—and that's what families are all about. We all loved your dad; we all miss him terribly, but we are so much more fortunate than lots of people. At least we have one another. And we have our memories of him—those will stay with us for the rest of our lives. We can't bring him back, but he's always with us, for we'll always think about him. Do you understand what I'm trying to tell you?"

Angie nodded and sniffed, wiping her eyes with the hanky her mother handed her. "I think so," she mumbled, burying her head in her mother's shoulder. She lifted her head and turned to look at Minnie. "It just seemed to me that nobody cared about him anymore, except for me. Oh Mumma, I miss him so much."

Minnie was finding it impossible to hold back her tears. "Darling, so do I. But all the missing in the world can't change things."

Angie, who had stopped, began crying again. "But Mumma, I did an awful thing. I told lies about Dad. I did it and I wish I hadn't and I know I'll always feel bad about it."

"Whatever are you talking about, child? What do you mean lies?"

Angie lowered her head, mumbling, "I told everyone at school he was a ship's captain. I didn't want them to know he worked on the ferries, so I made up stories about him being on a ship and away all the time. It's only since he died I realised it was a bad thing to do. Do you think he would forgive me?"

Minnie strained to keep herself from laughing, for she realised how hard it must have been to confess something that had obviously been weighing on the child's mind ever since Tom's death. She chose her words carefully before replying, "Sometimes we tell what are called white lies—stories for one reason or another that we feel we need to tell, either to make someone else feel better, or for ourselves. Angie, I suspected you were not comfortable telling your friends about your father's job. One of the things we all find ourselves doing, particularly when we're young, is trying to be like the people we mix with. And that was what you did when you told those stories to your friends. I'm not saying it was a sensible thing to do, but if that's the worst lie you tell in your life, I'll be happy. I won't suggest that your father would have been happy about what you did—he was a proud man and never pretended to be anything other than what he was. But he was also a fair man and I'm certain that if he knew you were sorry about what you did, he would forgive you in an instant. And I think he would have had a good laugh about it too—for one thing he always wished he could have been was a seaman—and there you went and promoted him to captain."

Angie blew her nose loudly and looked up at her mother, who had risen from the bed where they had been sitting together. She said in a serious tone of voice, "I'm sure that if he'd been a seaman, he'd have been made captain in no time. He was the cleverest person in the whole world. I feel so much better now after talking to you. Do you really, really think that Dad would have forgiven me?"

"I really, really do," said Minnie.

They talked together for a while about things in general and Angie opened up about what had been going on at school and some of her hopes for the future. Minnie left her feeling reassured that Angie was out of the woods and had learned a valuable lesson from her silly stories. She felt less reassured, however about something that had been on her mind for a while. Today's conversation with her daughter highlighted to her the fact that she had spent so little time with the girls in recent years. By the time she came home from work, they were usually busy doing homework or listening to their favourite shows on the radio, and she was often too tired to do much more than prepare their meal and put her feet up. Certainly now that Sandra was on the scene, they had someone at home with them, but Sandra was always tied up with Andrew and, with the new baby due very soon, she would have even less time to give to her young sisters. Maybe it was time for a change.

~ * ~

They had found that Narrabeen was a little community on its own. Its shopping centre was universally known as the "The Terminus" due to the fact that it was located at what had been the end of the line for the old tram service that ran until the 1930s. There could be found almost everything the locals could possibly want: a post office, newsagency, chemist, library, butchery, fish shop and bakery. As well as a picture theatre, there was a drapery shop, which sold clothing, both men and women's, fabrics and all sorts of haberdashery items.

It was outside this shop that Minnie waited each day for the bus when she went to work and she always passed the time by looking at what was on display in the front windows. Only that morning she had noticed a small handwritten sign. "Part time lady wanted, general shop work, experience preferred. Apply within." Minnie had read it and smiled to herself, thinking, I already have a job; otherwise I could be interested in that, and dismissed it from her mind. Now she thought again. She knew she was not in a position financially to give up work completely—and she really didn't want to; she enjoyed the opportunity to be herself—rather than just a mother. She owned her share of the house and had money in the bank—not enough to keep her for life, but a comfortable nest egg for the future. What she needed was enough for outgoings and day to day living for herself and the girls, with a little left over to save for holidays. A great believer in omens, it seemed to Minnie that the fact she had seen the notice in the window on the very day she had decided to make a change was too much of a co-incidence not to be followed up.

Next morning, she waited on the doorstep for the shop to open. Even though it meant being late for work, she decided not to put it off; to leave it could mean that she might miss out on the opportunity.

She found that the job was for Wednesdays, Fridays and Saturday mornings, with the possibility of extra time when other staff were sick or on leave. The job would bring in slightly more than half what she was earning at present, which was close to what she had calculated she needed to get by on. When the shop owner heard of her experience and interests, he offered her the job on the spot and Minnie, finding him pleasant to talk to and the shop an interesting change from what she had been used to, accepted immediately. Feeling guilty, she headed for Manly, faced with the prospect of having to give notice at the department store where she had worked so happily for several years.

~ * ~

Two weeks later, Minnie started her new job. The department store had been understanding when she explained the need to be closer to her daughters and had given her a good reference. She settled into the new arrangement quickly and discovered it made a vast improvement to her life. Instead of having to leave home an hour before work, she could walk there in ten minutes and was home quickly without the tiring bus journey after a day at work.

Her only doubt had been about Shirley, who usually had travelled with her in the mornings, but her youngest daughter suddenly surprised everyone by announcing that she wanted to change schools. She had struck up a friendship with a girl her own age who lived three doors down and attended the local public school. Minnie was doubtful at first, for Shirley had only a year left of primary school before going on to high school, which would entail her travelling to Manly anyway... but she would be able to catch a special school bus by then. In spite of her quietness she could be very stubborn when set on an idea, and she nagged her mother so much that Minnie, in exasperation, went to the local school and found out that a transfer would be a simple matter, at which she arranged for Shirley to start there after the coming school holidays.

Sandra's new baby was a girl, christened May Dorothea Jacobsen—after Cliff's mother and Minnie's middle name. A healthy eight pounder, she slept through the nights almost immediately, causing virtually no disruption in the household. Angie and Shirley had been too young and lived too far away to take a great deal of interest when Andrew was born, but now at fourteen and twelve they often became willing little substitute mothers for their big sister's baby.

It was school holidays and they had lots of time on their hands, so a frequent undertaking was to take baby May for a walk in her pram, accompanied by Bob, who already had a proprietary interest in this new addition to his extended family. Anyone who stopped to look at the baby was given the once over by the dog and woe betide anyone who threatened his new charge in any way. Although Bob still spent most of his time with Jack, the prospect of a walk with the girls immediately brought him from the back yard, tail wagging and keen for the outing.

Shirley's friend Alicia often accompanied them, so it was a happy procession that made its way down to the shops—to say hello to Minnie if she was at work—then back along the ocean front as far as the riding school, where they stopped to feed the horses with a supply of carrots they'd brought from home. Sometimes they gave in and also took Andrew, who was now nearly three and rather hard to control, but usually they tried to time it with his afternoon sleep, rather than have to slow their pace to accommodate his shorter legs and have to put up with his stopping every few steps to examine things that took his interest. Being substitute mother to a baby in a pram was fun, looking after an active and single-minded little boy was more like hard work.

It seemed that everything in the composite family was complete, so they could sit back and enjoy their new home. However, more changes proved to be on the way.

Twelve

Taking a risk

Minnie was happy in her new job, as was Shirley in her school; Angie had overcome her miseries and Sandra was busy with her two small children. Everyone was content with their lives...the one exception being Cliff. He had been taking a further study course at night school for the past several months, as his long-term ambition was to set himself up in his own electrical contracting business. He passed his final exams just after baby May was born and spent many hours worrying whether this was the right time to take the risk of giving up confirmed paid employment and striking out on his own, now that he had a young family to support.

The technical college he had been attending was in the city and on those days he always rode his motorbike to work, for bus transport in the evening was rather unreliable. Halfway through the course he discovered that Harry Peterson, one of his classmates, lived in Mosman and as it was on his way home, Cliff offered him a lift. They formed the habit of stopping off for a coffee on the way—both would have much preferred a beer, but as hotel closing was the uncivilised time of 6 pm, it was coffee or nothing. It turned out that Harry had much the same ambitions as Cliff, with similar doubts about whether this was the time to make a move, mainly because of his age and lack of experience. Harry was in a better position than Cliff in many ways. He was unmarried, lived with his parents and had a reasonable amount of savings, but at only twenty years of age, his main worry was that he knew nothing about running a business and had even less knowledge about how to set it all up. He needed premises and realised that an electrical business needed both that and someone to answer the phone. Of where and how to go about this he was unsure, but when Cliff suggested they go into it together and told him of his ideas, he readily agreed that pooling their resources was the wise way to go.

Cliff spent many a sleepless night worrying about ways and means and finally called a family conference with his wife and mother-in-law. With their help, he felt he had a viable proposition. The initial premises for the business could be set up in the unused garage adjoining the house—they really only needed a storeroom and workshop—and the garage would be ideal. Sandra was at home most of the time to answer the phone and Minnie would be there four days a week to back her up. Between them, if they were willing, they could handle the phone calls, and Sandra had already proven her bookkeeping skills, so the accounts side of the business would be simple for her. The family would supply the premises and office know-how, and Harry had the money to invest in a van, plus the equipment and stock they would need. But to make all this possible, Cliff needed the approval and help of his wife and mother-in-law.

Sandra, of course, had a fairly good idea of what her husband had in mind, for he had discussed his hopes with her over a period of years. Now that he and Harry had made definite plans, he needed to run them past his wife and mother-in-law in detail—for they were needed to help get the business off the ground and to ensure its ongoing success.

"There's a lot of new people moving into the area," he said. "New homes will be built and all those homes will need electrical work done. Now that people are settled down and have money to spend, I feel there will be a rush to buy all the new appliances that are coming on the market...so we thought we would take on repair work as well as general electrical. After the Depression and the War, people are going to want a few of the luxuries of life and many of those seem to be electrical these days. Besides the installation work, those appliances will be breaking down and someone will be needed to fix them. It won't be easy at first and we won't have a lot of income, but I've managed to save enough to keep us going for six months. If the business hasn't taken off by then, I will go out and get another job...but I really don't think I'll have to."

The women's reactions differed quite strongly. Sandra, with the thought of her two babies, was naturally cautious...but Minnie, who had great faith in the sense and capability of her daughter's husband, was immediately enthusiastic.

"Why don't you sell it all as well as fix it?" she said.

"Sell what? Are you suggesting we open up a shop?"

Minnie nodded. "I'm suggesting exactly that. How far does anyone around here have to travel to buy any of those electrical appliances that are going to be so popular?" She answered her own question. "To Manly, that's where. There's no electrical retailer anywhere between here and Manly—and none north of here as far as Palm Beach. You're right—there are a lot of people moving into the area. They won't just want their homes wired; they will want radios, refrigerators, electric radiators and vacuum cleaners to put in them. Many of them are refugee families—certainly most of those people moving into the Warriewood Valley are. They've been living in migrant hostels where they had no room for things like that and nothing to spend their money on until now. Also, there are people moving away from the western suburbs like we did—so many of them are coming to this area. I don't see how a shop selling all those things could do anything other than succeed."

Cliff sat there open mouthed at Minnie's suggestion. Why hadn't he thought of that?

~ * ~

It was late 1950 and huge changes had occurred in Sydney since the end of the War. In 1945, Prime Minister Chifley had looked at

Australia's position, isolated as it was from the rest of the developed world. The fact that the country had come close to invasion by Japan had illustrated to the government just how vulnerable it was to any outsider. It was obvious that they could no longer rely on the British for support—England, drastically depleted by the war, was struggling to support itself and was begging other countries untouched by the conflict to take in some of its people, many still homeless after the intensive bombing which so many cities had suffered. Europe was even worse off. The war had left tens of thousands of displaced persons, with little other than the clothes on their backs for their homes... and in many cases whole villages no longer existed. Governments struggling to re-establish themselves were totally dependent on the Allies to provide food and accommodation for these refugees. But this was only a short-term solution; homes and jobs had to be found and as quickly as possible. America, Canada, South Africa and Australia, untouched by the conflict, were begged to take in as many displaced persons as they could accommodate.

In Australia, the Prime Minister was saying "Populate or Perish" and this was obviously not something that could be done overnight by natural means. On the other side of the world there were tens of thousands of people wanting homes—and thus began Australia's largest intake of immigrants in its short history. From countries all over Europe they came in shiploads, to be housed in tin army huts and—in the case of those from Europe, used to better fare—fed the awful "English style" food that most Australians ate. After three years of "working for their keep," these people were free to move wherever they wished. From their meagre wages they had salted away money to set themselves up when they left the migrant hostels. Many, coming from urban backgrounds, settled permanently in the cities, starting up cafes and restaurants and, in the process, gradually changing not only what Australians ate, but how they lived. Others, with rural backgrounds, looked for land where they could carry on making a living the only way they had known. They spread out through the country, but areas such as Liverpool, in the west of Sydney, and the

Warriewood Valley, near Narrabeen, had a received a large intake of immigrants—mainly from Italy and Yugoslavia.

~ * ~

As Minnie rightly said, these newcomers were setting up homes. They wanted some of the necessities that American movies had led the people to expect. Someone had to fill those needs—and why not us, she argued?

The thought of a combination electrical sales and contracting business was beyond Cliff's wildest dreams—and, more to the point, totally beyond his means.

"I think it's a wonderful idea, but we will be struggling to find funds to set up the electrical contracting business. There's no way on this earth we could afford to start a shop as well."

"I've got money," said Minnie. "There's Tom's insurance money virtually untouched, plus I've saved a bit in the meantime. I'm prepared to advance you the money, because I believe in you and think you will succeed."

"But what if it doesn't work? You'd lose everything then. I can't let you do it, Mum!"

"It will work. I'm as sure as I possibly could be on that. And if the impossible happens—which it won't—I've got years of work left in me and, by the time the girls are grown, I can stop work and live on the pension if need be."

Minnie pushed her chair back and rose from the table. She walked around to the back of Cliff's chair and grasped him by the shoulders.

"We've all started a new life here and I, for one, feel like a new person. All my life I've done the sensible thing, never took risks, and now I want something different. This country is changing. Every day we read in the papers about new people coming here, about new ideas. My generation has seen the bad times—we grew up to a world war, struggled through a depression and then another war on top of that. It probably has defeated some people...but some like me have become tougher because of having to struggle. I want you and your children to have a better life, but nobody hands it to you on a plate—you have to work for it. And I think you are willing and able to do that and to succeed. That's why I'm prepared to give you the money, because I know you won't let me down."

At first Cliff refused to go along with Minnie's idea—but when he realised that she was determined to take the risk, he ran the suggestion past Harry, his future partner. Harry was totally against it at first. "I want to be an electrician, not a counter jumper," he said.

"You probably will have to be at first...at least part of the time, but once the contracting side of things takes off, we can find someone for the shop. Minnie is right, all these new people are going to want electrical appliances—we can make sure they know about the other side of the business and we will be the first they'll think of when they need an electrician. I don't know why we didn't think if ourselves—it just has to work," Cliff assured his friend.

Harry went home and discussed it with his parents, who, being business persons themselves, saw the logic in Minnie's suggestion. He returned, much reassured, and announced that his father had offered to loan him money to supplement his savings. They had more than enough funds to set up shop and buy the initial stock.

The next few months were a steady learning curve for the two young men. Each stayed on in their respective jobs but spent every spare moment in finding details of suppliers and checking out what was available, what was popular and selling well...and in searching for premises. Almost to order, the local shoe repairer decided to retire from business, and his shop in the local shopping centre was up for rent. It was a fairly narrow shop, but it had a good showcase window and its depth made up for the small frontage. Better still, there was a residence above the shop, which would be ideal for storage of stock and for the onsite repair business.

Realising that it would be best if he lived locally, Harry at first volunteered to camp in the upstairs rooms above the shop—but Minnie and Sandra would have nothing of that.

"There are two bedrooms not being used in our house—it will be years before I need them for the children," said Sandra.

"I agree, I wouldn't dream of letting you stay there all alone. You're almost part of the family already," Minnie said as she hugged the lad. "There's always room for one more in this household."

So, Harry became a permanent member of the family. To the girls, aged fourteen and twelve, this tall, fair-haired twenty-year-old in their midst added a note of excitement to their home. Angie developed a huge crush on Harry, who thought of her as just a child and was totally unaware of her feelings for him. Although many of her schoolmates were already well-developed young women, Angie, to her misery, still looked very much the child that she remained in Harry's eyes. To her chagrin, Shirley, two years younger, was already more physically developed than she, with a womanly shape and blossoming breasts. Angie's chest remained flat as a board and her hips stayed almost non-existent. She even went as far as to ask her mother to take her to a doctor. "There must be something wrong with me. I might as well be a boy—that's what I look like," she despaired.

Minnie avoided the temptation to smile at her daughter's distress, remembering how desperately aware she had been of her own shortcomings at Angie's age. "Some people develop more quickly than others—I was a bit like you when I was young—and then suddenly overnight I realised I had turned into a woman. You must be patient, there's no way of hurrying things up. It won't be too many years before you will be trying to look younger than you are. I'm not going to spend good money on having a doctor tell you that."

Angie was forced to reluctantly accept her mother's words and while silently pursuing her unrequited love, she secretly checked her body for signs of maturation every night before going to bed. All the adults—other than the object of her passion—were aware of Angie's crush, for her ability to materialise on the scene whenever Harry was around would have been obvious (as Cliff put it) "to blind Freddy." As he looked on Angie as a younger sister, Cliff resisted the urge either to kid her about it—or point it out to the oblivious Harry.

Thirteen

Jack

The man living in her back yard was from the start a puzzle to Minnie. Although always polite and friendly, initially Jack volunteered nothing of his past to her in their frequent conversations. He received no personal mail; his only friends were the few mates he had at the local pub and nobody seemed to know where he originally came from. He didn't seem particularly lonely, but only after some persuasion on Minnie's part did he reluctantly join in the family social occasions.

As he became more a part of the family group, Jack relaxed a lot in Minnie's company. Gradually, over afternoon cups of tea in his little domain, he felt more comfortable and related the story of his life.

He hadn't had a family...at least not since he was six years old. His father was only an unpleasant and vague memory...his mother not much more. The day she dressed him and his older brother in their school clothes and took them on the tram to the city was clear in his head, even though it was almost sixty years ago. He recalled being puzzled as to why she was crying and why she held both their hands so tightly. Questions went unanswered, as she led the boys from the tram stop to a large red brick building. His first impression as they entered the place was coldness, even though it was a warm sunny day outside. The two boys were left sitting side by side in the hallway, while their mother was led away by a woman in a nun's habit. Neither boy spoke, each overawed by the unfamiliar surroundings and the worry that something was about to happen, together with the feeling that the something was not going to be good.

Finally, his mother returned alone. She hugged both of her boys in turn, saying, "You will be staying here for a while until I can find us somewhere to live. You be good boys and remember I love you. I'll be back soon to visit you."

She led them down the corridor, knocked on a door at the end and opened it. Inside, they saw the same nun who had spoken previously to their mother. The Sister smiled at them, said "Come in boys," and gestured toward two chairs in the room. She nodded at their mother, who repeated the words, "I'll be back." She turned and left the room without looking back and Jack never saw his mother again.

He spent the next eight years of his life in the Holy Mercy Orphanage. Because of the difference in their ages, he and his brother lived separate lives, slept in different dormitories and rarely had a chance to speak to one another. Somewhere in the course of those years, his brother disappeared from the scene—whether he had run away, been claimed by their mother, or died, as many of the children did from the infectious diseases that often spread through the crowded rooms—Jack was never to know. Many years later he decided to try to find out about his brother, only to discover that the old records had been lost in a fire and that, although there were still some of the original staff, it was impossible for them to recall one boy out of the thousands who had passed through the doors.

Life in the orphanage was hard, but not as bad as some of the stories he heard in subsequent years from others who had been in similar situations. The boys were treated strictly but fairly well. They were reasonably well fed, clothed, educated and taught the scriptures by the nuns, but treats of any kind were rare, nor were there any personal kindnesses. He made no real friends among the other boys and longed for the day he could leave and find what the outside world held. When he was fourteen and attending the local high school, Jack one day packed his spare underwear and shirt in his school bag, left as if he were heading for school and walked around the city streets until he saw a sign in a shop window that read, "Boy wanted for odd jobs." He applied for the job, was hired and never returned to the orphanage. He slept in the doorways of buildings, scrounged in garbage bins for food and washed himself in public toilets until his first pay day. Once he had money in his pockets, he found a room in a boarding house, saved his money and started out on the life that was to be his more or less for the next four decades. He drifted from place to place, worked at various jobs, made few friends and, remembering a mother who had deserted him, was largely distrustful of women and found himself uncomfortable in their presence.

He was twenty-five years old in 1914 when the war started. Times were tough and, along with thousands of others, Jack joined up for the three meals a day and the chance of overseas adventure. The recruitment posters told of the glory of serving one's country; the recruitment sergeant told them nothing of the horrors that awaited them in the trenches—but in fact nobody had an inkling of what was to come. This would prove to be a war like no other that had preceded it, the first really mechanised warfare carried out on a large scale. The soldiers from the colonies were under the control of the generals in England, who utilised them as little more than cannon fodder in Gallipoli and in the trenches in France.

Jack survived the war virtually unscathed. He toyed with the idea of staying in the army, but decided he had had enough of institutionalised life and landed back in Sydney with his discharge money, no belongings—for he had had nowhere to leave his few possessions when he enlisted—and nowhere to live. Back to yet another cheap boarding house and, along with his fellow ex-servicemen, the discovery that jobs in Sydney were virtually nonexistent. After a month of fruitless searching with his money running out, he hopped a freight train in the hope that wherever it was heading would offer more work than there was to be had in the city. He ended up in Bourke and from there gravitated up to Queensland, working when he could, sleeping rough and seeing a lot of Australia in the process.

The Depression years that followed the Wall Street crash were even harder than those that came before. Jack was only one of thousands of men on the road "humping the bluey," travelling from place to place by whatever form of transport they could bum a lift or hide on, or slogging on tired feet along dusty roads, seeking work or a handout. The outbreak of the Second World War saw Jack too old to enlist, which he would not have willingly done, even if they would have taken him—he had seen enough of warfare to last a lifetime. It also saw him back in Sydney, fifty years old, savings virtually nil and with nowhere to live.

He was never quite sure what brought him to the northern beaches, but it must have been inspiration, for he ended up one October morning having a beer at The Royal Antler Hotel in Narrabeen. It was a quiet day; the barman was in a chatty mood and asked Jack where he came from and where he was staying. "Nowhere and nowhere" was the answer—and did the barman know of anyone who needed an odd jobs man, for Jack badly needed work.

"As a matter of fact I do," was the reply. "You come back here around four this afternoon when Jim Carmody comes in. Only the other day he was saying he needed someone to help out around the house. Him and his missus run a boarding house down on the lake. Jim's getting a bit long in the tooth and he's finding all the gardening and upkeep a bit much these days. You could be just the bloke he's looking for—you're no spring chicken yourself, but you look pretty fit to me. If you're interested, I could give you an intro to him."

Old Jim took one look at Jack's wiry frame, decided he liked the look of him and insisted on taking him home with him that evening. Mary, his wife, put on a few more potatoes and fed Jack the first home-cooked meal he'd had in many a year. They showed him the shed in the back yard—it really was a shed in those days, but was weatherproof and comfortable enough with the folding bed Jim took from under the house. That evening they made an arrangement that they would see how each liked the other and if it worked out, Jack had a job for as long as he wanted.

It worked like a charm for both parties. Jack and Jim became firm friends and the wanderer had a home of his own for the first time in his life. In his travels Jack had picked up many skills, not the least of which was carpentry. He gradually turned the basic wooden shed into a little self-contained home, furnished it with bits and pieces picked up here and there, and when it became obvious to all parties that he was there to stay, the Carmodys paid to have electricity connected and insisted on installing the small kitchen.

The crunch came when the Carmodys decided eight years later that they were finding the running of the guesthouse to be too much for them and they would have to sell up. "Don't worry about your job, Jack," Jim Carmody assured him. "I'm sure the new owners will let you stay on. This place would fall to pieces without you."

Jack was not as optimistic. His experiences of the outside world and those who lived there had not given him as much faith in his fellow men as had his good-hearted employers. His heart sank every time someone came to inspect the place, but by this time the war was over, there wasn't the money around for this sort of business and the place didn't sell. Then, Mary Carmody suffered a stroke and died two days later, and a devastated Jim was left to struggle on alone. His health failed quickly after this, and when it became obvious to him that he wouldn't last much longer, he called Jack in for a conference.

"Jack," he said, "I've been worrying about what will happen to you after I'm gone. I am leaving this place to my two boys, who I hardly ever see these days. I would like to think that they would give you a home for life, but much as I hate to admit it, I think they are more interested in money than in honouring their old man's wishes. So, I've decided to make it legal. I've had my solicitor draw up a document that gives you tenancy of your home for as long as you live, unless you decide to leave of your own free will. To make it legal, you will have to pay what they called a "peppercorn rent" of five bob a week—the lease is as tight as it's possible to make one, and as long as you pay your rent, nobody on this earth can make you move. When this place sells, you go with the property and you pay the rent to whoever buys it. As well as the lease I've had it all laid out in my will, along with a little sum of money in thanks for all you've done for Mary and me over the past years."

Jim died three months later and Jack was left there alone, wondering when the house would be sold, regularly paying his rent to the agents each week and worrying about who would be the next owners. He had been reassured by the solicitor that his home was safe when he was paid the hundred pounds that Jim had left him, but he knew that someone who didn't want him around could easily make life so miserable for him, that lease or not, he would have to move on.

He continued to look after the grounds and regularly checked the big house for any work that needed done and spent many a night lying awake wondering whether he would once again be homeless.

So, when Minnie and her family moved in, he quickly found that his worries were over. He had been on friendly terms with Jim and Mary Carmody, but they had kept their distance and he had kept his. Other than having the occasional beer with his landlord, Jack had been left to his books and his garden.

Right from the start, Minnie would have nothing of this—once she trusted Jack, which she did almost immediately, she wanted him to feel that he was a welcome part of the family. She made sure that everyone respected his privacy, but when it came to occasions like Christmas and birthday celebrations, Jack was always automatically included in the festivities. He found that he loved it, and although he had always thought of himself as a loner, he discovered the enjoyment that can be found in the company of people whom he liked and who liked him. The Carmodys had given him a home—Minnie Sherwood had given him a family.

Fourteen

Family business

The new shop was an immediate success, and the electrical contracting business, although slow for the first six months, was improving on almost a weekly basis. At Minnie's suggestion, Cliff had several hundred flyers printed advertising the new shop, as well as the repair and installation business. The girls and Jack took on the task of ensuring that every home in a wide radius received a copy and there was no doubt that it helped considerably in getting the new enterprise off the ground.

Harry was uncomfortable about dealing with customers in the shop, so Cliff tried as much as possible to allocate the repair and installation work to his partner, who being younger, was happy to leave managerial decisions to Cliff. Once the non-retail side increased, it quickly became apparent that they not only needed another van, but also a helper in the shop to free up Cliff for working outside on the road. Minnie helped out at first on her days off, but really preferred to be a silent partner in the enterprise—besides which she enjoyed her job at the haberdashery shop and felt that to give it up and work full time again was a retrograde step. She enjoyed her days at home with

Sandra and the children and liked the balance of work and home that her part-time job allowed. She left it to Cliff to interview applicants for the shop assistant's position, for she assured him that if he were going to be a businessman he had to learn how to select and deal with staff.

He settled on a middle-aged woman, Margaret Johnson, who was a recent arrival in the area, widowed and living with her semi-invalid mother. She had previous retail experience in Melbourne, good written references and seemed the ideal person for the job.

Margaret seemed at first to live up to Cliff's expectations, but as the months progressed she often arrived late for work, looking haggard, giving the excuse that she had been up all night with her mother. When Cliff complained about this, Minnie asked him to show some compassion. "Her life can't be easy," she said. "Half an hour here and there doesn't make much difference in the long run." Other than her lateness, Margaret was very good with customers and Cliff agreed to balance this against her unreliability.

Several months into her employment, on Margaret's rostered day off, Cliff came up against a worrying situation. A customer brought a faulty radio back for repair under warranty, which their records showed had never been sold. The customer had brought the original receipt with the radio; it was in Margaret's writing and on a hunch that he never could explain, Cliff rang Sandra asking her to look up the records for the day of sale. Sandra came back with some disquieting news. "That docket...in fact none in its number series was included in the daily records." It required very little imagination to realise that something was sadly amiss. Their employee was obviously selling stock and pocketing the proceeds. How many other appliances had she "sold" without declaring the money? The only way to determine this was to conduct a comprehensive stock take, which Cliff, Harry and Minnie did overnight. The outcome showed that there were around a dozen items for which they couldn't account. Making allowance for clerical errors, it became apparent that their trusted employee had been feathering her personal nest to the amount of several hundred pounds.

Next morning, Minnie joined Cliff in the shop awaiting Margaret's arrival at work. She was late as usual, and being confronted with the evidence, she at first denied all knowledge of it. Finally, as it became apparent that a dummy sales docket in her handwriting could not be explained away, the woman broke down in tears.

"I was desperate," she sobbed. "My mother's medical bills were growing and I just didn't have enough money to pay them. Please don't call the police. If I'm sent to jail, my mum will die—she has nobody else. I will work for you for nothing until I've paid back the money. Please give me this chance."

Minnie and Cliff looked at one another and shrugged in unison. What could they do? How could they prosecute this woman, who had only taken the money with her mother's wellbeing in mind? Minnie spoke for both of them.

"I can't really forgive you for what you have done. If you had come to us with your troubles, we would have found some way of helping you out, but I understand that sometimes people do things in desperation they would never think of doing otherwise. You obviously can't afford to work for nothing, so we will deduct a pound from your wages each week until the debt is paid." She walked to Margaret, who was sobbing uncontrollably and laid a hand on her shoulder. "Right now you are too upset to work, so I want you to go home and spend the day with your mother. I will work for you today and you'll be paid for the time. We employed you on trust and I want your word that we can trust you in the future. Is that clear?"

Margaret clung to Minnie and thanked her, saying that she would be forever grateful for what she was doing. "I will be the soul of honesty in future. I promise you that on my mother's life."

"Then home you go; we'll see you here tomorrow morning with no recriminations." Minnie gave the woman one last hug and saw her out the door. Cliff, who had remained silent throughout, ran his hand through his hair, saying doubtfully, "Gee, Mum, I really hope we've done the right thing."

"Only time will tell," said his mother-in-law. "We will just have to be more vigilant in future. We have been too trusting and it doesn't do to be that way in business."

"I'm not sure I can continue to work with Margaret, knowing what she did. Can we really trust her to be honest?"

"Only time will tell," repeated Minnie. "Right now, I have a shop to pay attention to and you have jobs out on the road. As far as Margaret is concerned, we will just have to wait and see."

The wait wasn't terribly long. Next morning, nine o'clock came with no sign of Margaret. Cliff waited until nine-thirty, then rang Minnie at home. "It looks as if Margaret isn't coming today. Now what do we do?"

"We'll have to visit her at home and find out what's going on," said Minnie in exasperation.

Fortunately, Harry was in the upstairs workshop, so he was recruited to mind the shop while Cliff and Minnie drove to where Margaret lived in a flat underneath a house close to the hotel. They arrived there to see no signs of life; the blinds were drawn and there was no answer to their knocking. Finally, a woman came from above, obviously the owner of the house.

"You can knock all you want," she said. "You won't find anyone home, now or in the future. I'm afraid the bird has flown. Did an overnighter, she did, owing me three weeks' rent. I only discovered it when I saw the milk still on her doorstep. Not only that, she took off with half the contents of the flat—that boyfriend of hers must have loaded it all into his truck. I heard a lot of banging last night, but paid no attention—I'm so used to all the noise and carry on that happened down there all the time."

"But where could she have taken her invalid mother? I thought she lived there with Margaret. What about her?" asked Minnie in distress.

"Mother? What do you mean? She didn't have any mother; she lived there alone—except when the boyfriend was there. In fact, I don't think she had a father either—if you get my meaning. She is a right trickster that one, so full of excuses, always finding some way of talking you round. I'd reached the point where I was about to throw her out, but she convinced me she was coming into some money soon and I trusted her. Now, see where trusting gets you—never again!"

Minnie and Cliff looked at one another and echoed her words in unison. "Never again." They commiserated with their fellow sufferer and made their way back to the shop in crestfallen silence, then filled Harry in on what had happened in the past half hour.

"Well, we're back to square one," said Minnie. "I suppose we'd best report it to the police, although something tells me our erstwhile employee will never be seen in this area again."

"How do we ever trust anyone again after that?" said Cliff.

"You just have to," Minnie replied. "I'm sure there are more honest people than dishonest. We were just unlucky and got one of the bad ones."

Cliff refused point blank to trust his judgement again. "I thought that Margaret was the ideal person for the job; her references were good and everything seemed fine. How about you have a go this time, Mum? I'd feel a lot better if you made the decisions; you've had more experience with people than I have—after all, I'm just an electrician." Feeling that maybe she had put too much on Cliff at this stage, Minnie agreed to do the interviewing.

Her final choice caused some discussion at home, for she settled on a young woman from a completely different background. Marta Jacovic was an immigrant from Yugoslavia and lived with her parents on a farm in the nearby Warriewood Valley. Her English was quite good—certainly enough to get by on—but the major factor in her favour in Minnie's mind, was that she was fluent in both her native tongue and Italian. So many of the recent immigrants had little or no English and the knowledge that Marta could converse with them in their own language was a huge plus. These foreign refugees, "reffos" or "new Australians" as many people called them, were treated with suspicion in some of the local communities. Many Australians, with their mainly English backgrounds, looked on these newcomers to their shores with some trepidation. They looked different, dressed differently, ate vastly different food—and many "old" Australians, blissfully ignoring the fact that they themselves had no language other than their own, looked with disdain on how the newcomers struggled with English.

Minnie had come across some of these women in the shop and sympathised with their problems with trying to make themselves understood in a language of which they had little more than a grasp of the basics. Whenever she heard anyone criticising the new arrivals in the area, Minnie jumped to their support. "How do you think you would manage if you were uprooted from your own country and dumped somewhere completely foreign? These people have been through hell; they've probably lost half their families, their homes are gone and they are brave enough to face life in a completely new country. We should be going out of our way to help them, instead of looking down on them."

Cliff admitted to being doubtful at first about the new employee, but in no time it was obvious that Marta was proving to be the perfect choice for the job. Because she had encountered so much difficulty in being accepted, she went out of her way to please. She was a fast learner and, within weeks, the boys felt so at home with her that any doubts about her reliability flew out the door. Her skill with languages proved as helpful as Minnie had hoped and they quickly found that, where in the past they had dealt with people with Anglo Saxon names, their customer list now included names such as the Italian Bombadier and Picellos, and Yugoslavs with long unpronounceable names that it was hard to get their tongues around. With Marta in charge of the shop, the boys could give more time to their repair and installation work, which continued to grow steadily, much of it being due to word of mouth recommendations.

As 1951 drew to a close, the business was bringing in enough money to convince the partners that the gamble had been worthwhile. The boys were happy, Sandra was content with her little family and, with Minnie's help, she coped well with the clerical side of the business. It had been a busy year, with a few glitches, but all agreed that compared to some, their lives were almost perfect.

~ * ~

It was the hot, sticky time between Christmas and New Year in Sydney and the old guesthouse was full to overflowing, with every bedroom occupied. Minnie's sister, Kath, and her two step children, home from boarding school, were visiting for a few weeks while Arthur, Kath's husband, was away at a conference. It had been a busy family Christmas and the two women were taking it easy, feet up on the comfortable cane lounges in the sunroom. All four of the older children, much of an age, had left early in the morning for the beach, Cliff and Harry were at work and Sandra had taken her two children to visit one of her friends who lived nearby. Minnie and Kath had the house to themselves and the only sound that broke the silence was the occasional screech of a seagull and the comforting whirr of the push mower as Jack cut the front lawn.

Minnie sniffed the air. "I love the smell of newly cut grass—but I wish Jack would leave it until it's a bit cooler, he's not a young man any more. There's no telling him, though; he does everything according to his own schedule and I've learned not to interfere. I really don't know what we'd do without him. Sometimes I feel like he's always been a part of our lives."

"You certainly landed on your feet here," said Kath, making a sweeping gesture with her arm to encompass the whole place. "Look at you—you're almost unrecognisable from the woman you were ten years ago, you've lost loads of weight and look younger now than you did then. What a change there's been in all our lives."

"Well, my life keeps me constantly on the hop and I wouldn't have it any other way. I still wish that Tom could have been here to share it all with us—but that wasn't to be; however I agree with you, our lives have really changed in such a short time. It seems like only yesterday that you were adamant you would never marry and I was a housewife in the western suburbs, contending with all of Gramma's nonsense." She paused and smiled. "If only I'd known then that I would have so much to thank the old girl for in the future. Without her, I would still be a simple housewife in Leichhardt, with never a thought of working, or being in business. Sometimes I can't believe it myself."

Kath grinned and reached down to stroke Frankie the cat, who was sharing the room with them. "I couldn't agree more, sister mine. If someone had told me I'd be living in Wahroonga in ease and comfort,

I'd have told them they were nuts. I'd still be stuck in that dinky little semi, with nothing to look forward to other than the pension when I was put out to pasture. We've both come a long way in a short time and, if we were praying people, we should be giving thanks to him up there for how much our lives have changed."

"You're right," smiled Minnie. "There are very few clouds on my horizon at present. And I'm not worrying too much about those anyway—if I've learned nothing else in this life it is that things have a way of sorting themselves out."

Fifteen

Angie

There was, in fact, a cloud on Minnie's horizon and once again it was to do with her daughter Angela. Whereas Shirley, her youngest, sailed through life happy to go along with almost everything that was asked of her, Angie had always, even as a very young child, been fiercely independent. Having completed her Intermediate Certificate in December, her junior high school days were over. She was due to start the two years leading up to the Leaving Certificate at a new school when the summer holidays ended in late January. It had always been thought that, later, Angie would go on to university, or at least that was the assumption of Minnie, whose plans for Johnny to get a degree had been dashed years ago. Now she pinned all her hopes on her second daughter. Angie, it seemed, had different thoughts on the subject.

Since she read her first Dickens novel at the age of ten, Angie had been obsessed with a desire to go to England. She read everything about that country she could lay her hands on—the most recent being Nancy Mitford's wonderful humorous novel, The Pursuit of Love. Angie felt an immediate affinity with Jassy, one of the daughters, whose whole life centred around the desire to save enough money to escape to the outside world. Angie's plans were much along those lines, so she had squirreled away every penny she could save from pocket money for her own "running away money." It soon became evident that it would take forever to save enough to fulfil her dreams as she had decided that until she saw and experienced England, and London in particular, she would not rest. The prospect of another five years of study didn't fit in with these plans. She needed money to accomplish her wish to travel—and the only way to get that was to work for it. A week before Christmas she announced to her mother that she wouldn't be returning to school in January, and that as soon as the holiday season was over, she intended to go out and get a job.

"Doing what?" a shocked and annoyed Minnie retorted. "The only place you would get work is in a factory or shop—you have absolutely no qualifications for anything else."

"Working in a shop is good enough for you. Why wouldn't it be for me?" argued Angie. "If I go to uni, probably the only job I would get is as a teacher—and I certainly don't want to do that." She grinned cheekily. "I could imagine nothing worse than having to teach kids like me!"

"You could have a point there. I've no doubt some of your teachers would agree with you, but Angie, there are lots of other things you could do...you could be a doctor, or a journalist, or anything you wanted to be."

"I certainly couldn't be a doctor. Not with my maths and science marks—and if I wanted to be a journalist, I could get a cadetship at one of the newspapers—that's what my friend Sophie has done. But I don't want to be a journalist; I just want to go to England. I'm sure that once I get there things will sort themselves out."

Exasperated, Minnie jumped up from her seat and grasped her infuriating daughter by the shoulders. "Things don't just sort themselves out. You're talking like the fifteen-year-old you are."

"Well, they did for you," said Angie, shrugging off her mother and looking fiercely around the room.

"Not without a lot of hard work and worry...and you seem to be going out of your way to give me more. Nothing we have has come easily," said Minnie, thinking to herself, Well, some of it has, but I'm not going to admit it to this selfish little monster.

"Oh Mumma, I realise that; you have always worked so hard! I didn't mean to be nasty about it, but I really don't want to stay on at school. It's all very well learning French and Latin, but they certainly don't give me any qualifications to get a job. In many ways, I wish I'd gone to a domestic science school like Shirley. At least there they learn shorthand and typing. My school has taught me nothing useful at all."

"What you've learned is useful to someone who is going on to university. That's what I've always thought you would do and that's what I thought you wanted, as well."

"The trouble is, nobody's ever asked me what I wanted to do. Everybody...you...the teachers...everyone took it for granted that because I get good marks, I wanted to go to uni. I don't know what I want to do—but I do know what I don't." In spite of her seriousness, she couldn't help smiling at the expression on her mother's face. "I know that sounds confusing and I suppose it is because I am confused. I'm sure it will all work out in the long run, but right now all I want to do is go out and get a job and start saving to go overseas—'cause I know I'll never be happy until I get it out of my system."

Realising that it was pointless to argue further at this juncture, Minnie asked Angie to think it over and they agreed to discuss it again in the New Year. Minnie's thoughts were that it was a passing fancy and given time, Angie would come around. So, she put it all out of her mind and concentrated on enjoying the holidays with her family.

True to her promise, Angie said no more on the subject and threw herself into enjoying the holidays and the company of her new step cousins. She and Shirley had been nervous about these strangers coming to visit, but they found them to be friendly and outgoing. Dan Forsyth was a month or so older than Angie and his sister Rhonda was the same age as Shirley. The four of them had a wonderful time at the beach, embarking on fishing trips in the rowboat, going together to the Saturday afternoon matinees at the local picture theatre, and generally spending every possible moment in one another's company.

They took off on expeditions to explore the bushland on the other side of the lake and came home with bunches of wildflowers to rival the roses that Jack so carefully nurtured in his garden. Dan and Rhonda loved the relaxed life in Narrabeen, which was so different from theirs, which had been spent largely in boarding schools since their mother's death. They were much more sophisticated in many ways than Angie and Shirley, for their father's money had allowed them to travel round the country and overseas, staying at much more glamorous places than Minnie's rambling old house, but they said again and again that this was the best holiday they had ever had. The girls felt much the same way and the four of them became close friends, swearing they would stay that way forever.

~ * ~

The Christmas and New Year holidays had passed, the decorations were down and slowly things were returning to normal. The family had enjoyed every moment of their break, taking full advantage of all the area had to offer. They had gone en masse to the New Year's Eve Surf Club concert, laughed themselves silly at the antics of the burly lifesavers who, dressed as women, sang the current popular songs in high pitched falsettos. It had been a wonderful time, and although Minnie had put Angie's plans out of her mind, her daughter certainly had not.

Angie waited until Kath and the children had gone home, and everyone was back at work; then, knowing that the time to return to school was getting perilously close, she cornered her mother in the kitchen, grabbed a tea towel and started wiping the dishes that Minnie was washing. Surprised to see her daughter helping out without actually being asked, Minnie remarked, "To what do I owe this honour? Usually you're nowhere to be seen when there's work to be done."

Angie grinned sheepishly, for the remark was all too true, and in spite of the fact that she knew it would change her mother's cheery attitude, she was determined to press her case. She waited until the last dishes were washed and dried, then before Minnie could escape elsewhere, she spoke up.

"Have you thought again about me leaving school? I haven't changed my mind. I know you had all sorts of plans for me and I am sorry to disappoint you—but truly, Mumma—I don't want to go back to school."

Minnie had hoped that the passage of the holiday period would have put all such thoughts from Angie's mind and she reacted angrily at the thought of once again having to deal with such a prospect.

"Angie, why in the name of heaven can't you be content to spend at least these next two years at school? You will be much older, more mature and better equipped to make decisions then. You are barely sixteen, much, much too young to think of travelling. You have your whole life ahead of you; why can't it wait until you have established yourself for the future? Besides which, you have to realise that you are a minor. You can't go anywhere without my permission...and I have absolutely no intention of giving it."

Angie pulled out a chair and sank into it, close to tears as she looked up at her mother and reached out to take hold of Minnie's hand.

"I know I'm too young to travel now, but I want to spend the next few years saving the money to do it. I really don't want to go back to school—they would be wasted years and I would hate every moment of it. Why can't you understand how I feel? Why do I have to do something for you, when it isn't what I want to do? This is my life—not yours. I might be young, but I'm old enough to know I don't want a whole lot of qualifications that would be useless to me."

She pushed back the chair and ran to her bedroom, closed the door behind her and fell on the bed, burying her head in the pillow to hide her sobs.

Back in the kitchen, Minnie collapsed onto the chair Angie had just vacated and tried to pull her thoughts together. Was she being unfair, she wondered? There was no doubt of the truth in some of the things Angie had said, for one of the reasons she had harboured such ambitions for her children was due to the fact that she had been forced to leave school at an even younger age than Angie was now. She, who had wanted so much to be a teacher, had been told there was no money for her to stay on at school and that she must go out into the workforce and earn money to help out the family. Her father was ill, her mother worked long hours to support them all, and there had been no alternative: she must leave the school she loved and take a job to bring in some badly needed money. Minnie had loved and respected her parents and had never resented the fact that circumstance had changed her own plans and yes, many of her plans for her children had been in a way a hope to relive her dreams through them. Until recently, she had assumed that Angie was as keen for higher education as she was for her daughter. It had never entered her head that the girl would feel otherwise.

It was obvious that if she forced Angie to stay at school, she would be confronted with two years of an unhappy, rebellious daughter, who she knew from past history was not one to hide her feelings. The prospect of her going out into the workforce without any qualifications whatsoever was unthinkable, for she knew that Angie had been correct when she'd said that nothing in her curriculum had qualified her for any job that would be available for someone her age. Was there some way to meet her daughter halfway?

She sat thinking for many minutes, then, having made a decision, she pushed back the chair and made her way to Angie's room. There were no sounds coming from behind the closed door, but deciding there was no point in delaying it any further, she turned the knob and entered the room. At first she thought that Angie was asleep, but when the girl raised a tearstained face to look at her, she sat down and took her daughter in her arms. Angie, who had stopped crying, began once again to sob and clung to her mother, saying, "Oh Mumma, I don't want to make you unhappy. But can't you please try to see it my way?"

Minnie pulled a hanky from her apron pocket and wiped the girl's face.

"I think I do," she said quietly. Then, before Angie could say anything, she held up a restraining hand. "I'm prepared to meet you halfway, for I realise that much of what you said to me was true."

She sat Angie up on the side of the bed, tossed some books from the bedroom chair and sat on it facing her daughter.

"I've decided to let you leave school, but I don't want you getting a job right away." When Angie opened her mouth to protest, she again held out a hand to stop her. "I can't let you go out into the world with no qualifications. It would not only restrict your opportunities here—but, if you are so dead keen to travel to England, you would have trouble getting a decent job there as well. And that's where I want us to meet halfway. You can leave school—I think I understand your reasons for wanting to—but I want you to go to secretarial college. I will pay for it, you can earn some money by helping out in the shop on Saturday mornings, and when you are qualified, you will have a good chance of getting a job that will pay much more than shop work. You can stay here in Sydney until you are eighteen and by then you should have saved enough to travel, and if you haven't changed your mind in the meantime, you at least have a good chance of finding a decent job in London. The Poms love Australian secretaries, so you would have no trouble getting work over there, and I will be able to sleep at night, not worrying about what is happening to my girl in a strange country. Think it over and let me know how you feel about all that."

Angie might have been young, but she was no fool and had worried a bit about her lack of experience and qualifications—although she would never have admitted this to her mother. What Minnie proposed was the perfect chance to get qualifications that would stand her in good stead almost anywhere in the world. Her face lit up and, misery forgotten, she hugged her mother. "Oh Mumma, that's the perfect solution. I don't mind spending time learning something useful—it was just the thought of two more years of trying to understand trigonometry and parsing Latin phrases that I hated. You are the best, most wonderful mother in the world—and I don't deserve you."

"Just so long as you realise that," laughed Minnie, as she returned her wayward daughter's hug. The two of them immediately set to looking in the phone book for local secretarial colleges. There appeared to be only one—and not being a person to waste time once her mind was made up, Minnie phoned them right away. Yes, there was a course starting in a few weeks' time and yes, they had a vacancy for another pupil. It wasn't exactly cheap, but Minnie worked out that as she would have had to fork out for a completely new school uniform and books for Angie at the new school, plus the extras that always seemed to crop up, she wouldn't be greatly out of pocket in the long run.

Angie, who realised the importance of the opportunity she had been given, threw herself wholeheartedly into learning what the college had to offer. As always, she learned quickly, for she had proven time and again in the past that she had the capacity to excel at subjects she liked. She even made a fairly good fist of the mathematics that were part of the syllabus, because she felt they served a purpose.

Six months later, the whole family turned out to her graduation ceremony, as she proudly accepted the prizes for best at shorthand and typing and for overall excellence. Minnie looked with pride on a daughter who had matured greatly in the past months, although she still looked a lot younger than her sixteen years.

Minnie and Sandra decided that they would have to do something to turn their pigtailed schoolgirl into a young woman who would be looking for work in the outside world. Angie was still slim as a boy, but she had beautiful dark hair and eyes and, although she didn't conform to the current popular image of the blonde and curvaceous woman, they decided to make the best of the girl's natural attributes. To the hairdressing salon she went, with orders to turn her unruly crop of long hair into something more adult. She came home with her pigtails gone, replaced by a gamin cut that, although not fashionable, highlighted her eyes and made her look a little older. The faithful sewing machine was again put to use, as Minnie ran up simple skirts and blouses that would be perfect for a young lady who worked in an office, and, complete with her new look and clothes, Angie was ready to tackle the world of business.

Minnie offered to accompany her on her quest for work, but independent as ever, Angie insisted on going alone. There was nothing available locally, but Angie was not interested in the local scene anyway. She reasoned that if she were eventually to work in a city environment in England, she needed to get a taste of what city work was like.

Because of her age, she found that she was only being considered for very junior positions, but her excellent results from the college stood her in good stead. She fairly quickly found what proved to be an interesting and rewarding job as assistant to the private secretary of a leading city lawyer. This rather intimidating lady was vastly overworked and Angie's job was to transcribe some of the notes her senior had taken and type them up, as well as take dictation herself for correspondence that was not considered of a private nature. The senior secretary had her own office, but Angie shared her workspace with other junior secretaries and clerks, so she had company around her own age. This meant there was always someone to join for lunch, either in the park or, on special occasions, at one of the many coffee lounges that had sprung up in the city in recent years.

The people she worked with were a fun crowd, who met frequently outside the office for trips to the movies, picnics and harbour cruises. She became good friends with Elsie Rogers, an English girl, two years older, who lived in Cronulla, as far south of the city centre as Angie's home was to the north. As a consequence, they usually met up in town, the halfway mark between their two homes, to share their mutual interest in football at weekends, or to visit Bondi Beach, which both of them thought of as the "rival" to the beachside suburbs where they each lived.

Knowing that Elsie came from London, Angie plagued her with questions about that city, telling her how much she was looking forward to visiting there when she had saved enough money.

"I don't understand why you should want to leave here for dreary old London," was Elsie's comment, when Angie told her of her ultimate dream. "It's cold, dirty, and there are no beaches. Wild horses couldn't drag me back there—you really are daft to want to leave Sydney for that."

"It has been my dream since I was small, ever since I first read about England. I know that Australia will always be my home, but something inside of me wants so much to go to England, that I know I'll never be happy until I do."

The two girls decided to agree to disagree on that point and settled into doing what young people have always done, enjoying life to the full. Australia, like the rest of the world, was at last recovering from the austerity of the war years and the shops were full of merchandise locally made and imported from overseas. Although she would have loved to throw caution to the wind and buy all the pretty clothes she saw in the department stores on her lunchtime forays, Angie held true to her main purpose and watched with satisfaction as her bank account grew and her dream of travel grew closer to becoming a reality.

It was a busy life and time passed quickly for busy people, even those as young as Angie, and before she knew it, her eighteenth birthday had come and gone and her savings had grown enough to pay her fare to England and allow her a reasonable time there before she found work. In the ensuing two years, her sister Shirley had also left school—for there had never even been a suggestion she stay on beyond official leaving age. She had never been more than an indifferent student, and when she asked her mother if she could leave school, Minnie had made no attempt to persuade her to stay. In a quick space of time, Shirley found a job working at the same department store in Manly where Minnie had worked in the past and had found herself a boyfriend, who worked in the shop's hardware department. Although she was too young, in Minnie's opinion, to have a steady boyfriend, Matthew seemed a sensible lad and in many ways it was better to see her youngest daughter confined to one partner. Shirley had grown up into every young man's dream of the perfect woman, blonde and curvy, and without even trying, she attracted the boys like flies. Angie, on the other hand, had never been on a real date, for most of the boys her age were put off by someone whose nose was forever buried in a book. Deep down inside she still harboured her crush on Harry, but by then she was old enough to realise he had no interest in her other than as a pseudo younger sister.

As Harry didn't feature in her current plans anyway, she put those thoughts behind her—other than dreaming of some future time, when he would realise his deep passion for her and sweep her off her feet. Her daytime thoughts were more practical, as she spent her lunch breaks booking her passage on a ship bound for Southampton and set about buying the few clothes she felt she would need overseas.

Elsie and her mother had proven to be valuable sources of information, wisely suggesting that she wait until she arrived in London to buy most of her warm clothes and her friend had presented her with a heavy overcoat, suitable to take on the English winters.

"I don't know why I brought it with me—it never gets anywhere near cold enough for me to need it here," Elsie said. "Believe me, you will need it over there, once the cold weather starts."

It was immensely heavy, made of flannel almost as thick as felt, with a padded tartan lining that could be removed if necessary, but because Elsie was taller and heavier, it somewhat swamped little Angie. Her friend assured her that the extra space wouldn't go astray, for in the coldest weather, even the coat would not be enough for someone used to Australia's weather. "You'll have plenty of room underneath for a couple of woollies if necessary," she remarked. When Elsie assured her that she would never want the coat returned, Angie asked her mother's help to shorten it a bit, which was possible, because the lining only came to just below the seat. There was no worry about her catching her heels in the hem, so the coat was given a good brushing and airing and folded away until the future when it was needed. For her birthday, the family had clubbed together and bought her a large solid suitcase and a smaller one to use for the internal travel she planned before she settled down in London. Her passage was booked for early March, which meant that she would have plenty of chances to be acclimatised before the winter months settled in.

"If you want to travel around, do it in the summer months. It's almost impossible in the winter and almost everything is closed anyway," advised Elsie. To Minnie's relief, Angie's ever helpful friend had written to her aunt who lived in Croydon and arranged a bed for Angie when she arrived—somewhere to stay until she found her own lodgings. Angie, too, was secretly relieved to hear this, for now that the time of departure was near; the enormity of what she was doing had at last sunk in. She had never spent more than a night or two away from her family, and the thought of being dumped alone in an unfamiliar city in a strange country was rather overwhelming. To have somewhere to stay, with people she could trust, meant she could take her mind off worries about arrival and leave it free to organise her departure.

<h1 style="text-align:center">*Sixteen*</h1>

To "the old country"

On Angie's departure day, the whole family, including Jack, piled into the two vans to see her off on her travels. Harry was the only one missing, as someone had to take charge of the shop—Marta was away on leave and Harry had, as he remarked to Angie when saying goodbye to her, "drawn the short straw." Disappointed that the object of her secret affections would not be there, Angie allowed herself the luxury of kissing him on the cheek, to which he responded with a huge bear hug—the type she sadly felt he would only give to a friend or little sister. Goodbye Harry, she thought to herself. Wait for me, I'll be back…but I've got a lot of growing up and things to do in the meantime.

Elsie and her mother came to see her off, with last minute instructions on what to do when she arrived in England, so it was quite a crowd of well-wishers that stood on the dockside waving to Angie as the ship pulled away.

SS Orcades sailed from Circular Quay, with the traditional trappings of paper streamers and a band playing the Maori's Farewell. Angie leant over the railing, holding onto the streamers connecting her with her family and friends, tears running down her face. Had it been possible at that moment, she would have run down and returned home with them. As the gangways had long since been removed, there was no option other than to wave goodbye and face up to the fact that she was on her way. When the streamers finally broke, she kept holding them for a while, then let go and watched them fall into the water below. Her last connection with the family had been severed and she was on her own, with almost a month ahead of her before she landed in Britain.

Sydney Harbour was very familiar to her from a lifetime of journeys on the Manly Ferry, but from the deck of an ocean liner everything seemed different. Looking at it with new eyes, Angie realised just how much she would miss it. As she frequently did, she thought of her father, of how much he had loved this beautiful harbour and this city she was leaving. She wondered how much time would pass before she returned. After the ship sailed out of the Heads, it was a very disconsolate Angie who returned to her cabin to sort out her belongings, only to find another girl her age—in much the same condition—sitting forlornly on a bunk and surveying what would be their home for the next few weeks.

Introductions proceeded, with each discovering it was the other's first trip away from home, and each of them already wondering if they had done the right thing. The cabin was tiny, with two bunks, one on top of the other, and a third situated on top of the small wardrobe area. Finally, having done what little unpacking was possible in the confined space, with no sign of any occupier of the third bunk in the cabin, they decided on "first come, first served," chose their own bunks and set out to fully explore their new home.

After the first few days of strangeness, of getting used to the movement of the ship and overcoming their initial seasickness, the girls settled into a routine, playing shuffleboard, watching films and spending very little time in their cabin, which was by far the least interesting and pleasant part of the ship. The third bunk remained empty for the whole journey, so Angie and Helen had the cabin to themselves, but there were much more appealing things to do elsewhere and they really only used the cabin for sleeping.

They parted at Southampton, where the ship docked early on a sunny Saturday morning, swearing eternal friendship and promising to keep in touch...but of course they never did. Helen was heading north to Scotland and, after waving her off, Angie searched for a public phone to call Elsie's Aunt Florence. Worried that something might go astray, she was cheered to hear the welcome in that lady's voice, as she gave Angie detailed instructions on how to get to Croydon. Fortunately, it was on the direct rail line from Southampton, so a relieved Angie gathered her belongings and set out on her way. Florence had looked up the train timetable and worked out when Angie would arrive, promising that someone would meet her at the station on arrival. That someone proved to be Florence's large and rather taciturn husband, who picked up Angie's big suitcase as if it weighed nothing, leaving Angie to carry the much smaller and lighter one. Feeling it obligatory to make conversation with this gentleman, Angie chattered away, her comments apparently falling on deaf ears—with even direct questions garnering nothing more than occasional grunts. Her heart sinking, Angie gave up and concentrated on keeping up with this giant of a man, who made little effort to slow his steps to her shorter legs.

"Oh dear, whatever have I let myself in for?" she wondered. After a five minute walk, they arrived at one of a row of two-storey, semi-detached cottages, not unlike those Angie had seen in Paddington in Sydney—but so very different from what she was used to at home.

Her fears were instantly dispelled when the front door opened to reveal a woman who was almost a carbon copy of Elsie's mother. Florence Paxton enveloped Angie in a huge embrace, instructed her uncommunicative husband in a loud voice, "Take those bags up to her room now, Frederick. Don't stand around like a dummy," and almost in the same breath said to Angie, "You must be exhausted after coming all that way. Come into the kitchen, love, and I'll make you a cuppa."

Angie was far from exhausted, her journey not having been really very long and her mind was buzzing from the sights of the English countryside she had seen on the way there. She decided that maybe Florence was referring to her trip from Australia, but regardless, she gladly agreed to the offer of the cup of tea. They passed down the hallway to the kitchen at the back of the house, which proved to be a large room with a scrubbed wooden table. It was obviously the hub of the house, making Angie feel instantly at home. So much of her own family's activities had centred around the kitchen table.

The table was already laid with china and a plate of scones, apparently all done in anticipation of her arrival. Touched at this kindness, Angie on impulse gave Florence a hug.

"Thank you so much for this—and thank you also for taking me in," she said.

"Why, it's nothing," dismissed Florence. "It will be lovely to have a young one around the house for a while. The place has been so empty since our Ronald left home. Please feel welcome to stay as long as you want."

She poured milk and tea into three cups, excused herself and walked back to the stairs leading upwards. "Tea's made, Frederick. Come and get yours while it's hot," she called out.

Her husband came lumbering downstairs, grunted once and, gathering up his cup of tea and a scone that his wife had buttered for him, left the two of them alone in the room and headed for parts elsewhere.

"Don't be put off by Frederick; he's a man of few words," explained Florence. "It's mainly because he's hard of hearing and so stubborn he won't do anything about it. I've asked him time and again to see the doctor about it—he could get a hearing aid on the National Health—but he refuses to accept there's anything wrong with him. He's really a very nice man, but people who don't know him get the wrong impression. He'd do anything for you, but don't expect any long conversations with him, my dear."

Relieved that Frederick's behaviour was not due to her presence in the house, Angie tucked into the delicious scones and happily chatted away to Florence, who plied her with numerous questions about the journey and the ship. Morning tea over, Angie offered to help wash the dishes, but Florence dumped them in the sink with the words, "They can wait for lunchtime, dear. Come on up and I'll show you your room."

As they mounted the stairs together, Florence explained that she had put Angie in the third bedroom, which was the smallest in the house.

"I'd have given you Ronald's room, but it's still so full of his things—mainly junk, but he won't throw any of it out. He's in the Navy, you know, and they have precious little space on board for much more than their everyday needs, so all his other stuff remains here and most likely will for some time to come. I thought you would feel more comfortable in a room which isn't full of posters and tennis racquets— you know what lads are like!"

Angie's memory of what "lads" were like was rather dim, it having been such a long time since her brother John had left home, but she thought that on the whole she preferred not to sleep in a room surrounded by someone else's belongings. The room allocated to her was indeed small—not much more than a box room, with little more space than for a single bed and a combination wardrobe and dressing table. The bed was very high, so she was relieved to see that there would be room beneath to store her suitcases—there certainly wasn't space elsewhere. Still, it was clean and airy and that was all she needed.

"It's lovely," she said, giving the woman another hug. She sat on the bed and shyly asked the question that had been in her head ever since she'd arrived.

"What do I call you? It seems so formal always calling you Mrs Paxton. Do you mind if I call you Auntie Flo like Elsie does? She spoke of you so often I feel as if I've known you forever."

"Why, that'd be lovely," said her landlady. "There's always room in my life for another niece. I certainly do miss the one who went so far away, and her mum, who I was so close to. It's sad when families break up."

"I know it is," said Angie, recalling how much her mother had missed Johnny when he went away. "I already feel a bit lost so far away from mine, so it is great to find another Auntie so far from home."

"Well, this is your home for as long as you need it. I know you intend to move into London eventually, but it's your room for the time being—and this house is somewhere you can always feel free to come back to whenever you want."

Angie heaved a deep sigh, looked around the room and suddenly realised that she did indeed feel quite tired. She had hardly slept the previous night, partly due to last-night partying and partly to excitement about what awaited her in London. All this, together with the nervous tension about her arrival, the trip on the unfamiliar train and the walk from the station was suddenly taking its toll. She looked at her watch—it was only 11 am, but all she wanted to do right then was lie on this comfortable bed and relax.

"Do you mind if I have a bit of a rest?" she asked. "This is all so new to me, I all at once feel really worn out. Silly, this early in the day—but do you mind?"

"You rest all you want, my pet. I'll leave you to have a bit of a nap. The bathroom's down the hall if you need it—and you come down whenever you feel like it."

Florence left the room, closing the door behind her, and Angie lay on the bed, not even removing her shoes, intending only to rest her eyes for a second. Within minutes, she sank into a deep sleep, later waking to hear a clock somewhere striking three—surprisingly, she had slept for nearly four hours.

Embarrassed, she hastily straightened her clothes, tidied her hair and crept downstairs to apologise for sleeping right through lunchtime. Halfway down, she was surprised to hear several people talking and the sounds of laughter. The sounds were coming from the sitting room, so she peered around the door, only to realise that what she had heard came from a box in the corner. The Paxtons had a television set. Angie had heard about TV, which had been talked about a lot in Australia, but was still several years from being an actuality there. It had been the subject of much discussion in her family, for they had acknowledged the fact that when TV arrived, there would be a huge demand for it, and Minnie and Cliff had often spoken about finding larger premises in anticipation of this increase in business. So, she thought, this tiny flickering screen was what all the fuss was about. Angie stood there open-mouthed, fascinated by the fact that what was obviously a comedy show could be watched right there in the living room.

Florence, who had been sitting on a settee watching the screen, turned around—sensing Angie's presence in the room.

"So, you're awake at last," she said. "I peeped in at you a couple of times and you were dead to the world. I hope the sounds of the telly didn't wake you up."

"No, not at all," replied Angie, and indicating the set, she remarked, "It's fascinating, isn't it? I've never seen television. We don't have it in Australia."

"I didn't know that," said Florence. "England's had it since before the war, although they stopped it over the war years. Fred and I only got our set last year, for the coronation—the Queen, you know," she added. "We thought it would be lovely to see it—we made a huge party of it, all the neighbours—those who didn't have their own sets— came in and we had champagne to drink to Her Majesty's health. She looked so lovely; we were so proud of her."

"I went to a newsreel theatre to see it, in colour," said Angie. "I ended up sitting through the whole thing twice; it was so lovely. Then, when the Queen and Prince Philip came to Australia just before I left, I saw them several times in Sydney. She really is beautiful, isn't she!"

"She's a lovely lady in every way and a real credit to her father and mother. We miss the old king—he was so strong and brave through the war years—but now we have this lovely young queen; it's almost a sign that things are getting better. Poor old Britain suffered a lot in those awful years."

Florence rose from her seat, walked over to the set and turned it off. "You must be starving, young lady, sleeping all that time. I've saved some lunch for you—and it's time for another cup of tea, so let's us both head for the kitchen."

Cups of tea, it proved, featured very strongly in the Paxton household—Florence loved her "cuppa," as Angie was to discover. She quickly felt at home in the house, as she was made so welcome that any sense of discomfort disappeared almost immediately. Nervous about Fred at first, she found that Florence had spoken the truth, and

Angie soon realised that part of his lack of communication was due to shyness. His deep blue eyes held a constant twinkle, which she hadn't noticed at first, and once she learned to speak up clearly, she found him responding with actual words. The initial steps of communication were laid when she automatically hugged Florence before going to bed that first night—and then thinking it rude not to—Angie hugged Fred, too. Surprised, he recoiled a little at first, then hugged her back and gave her a little wink. From then on, they felt comfortable with each other and although he remained a man of few words, Angie became as fond of him as she was of Florence.

After a day or so of settling in, Angie made her first train journey into London. First impressions were rather disappointing, for everything looked so dingy and dirty to eyes accustomed to the relative cleanliness of Sydney. Many buildings were still decked with the decorations from the coronation a year ago, but the thing that made the most impression on her was how much war damage still remained. With the war nine years in the past, she had more or less expected everything to have been set right by then. When she mentioned this to Florence, it was pointed out to her just how extensive the devastation had been.

"There just hasn't been the public money to fix everything," she was told. "The authorities made a big rush in the months coming up to the coronation. A lot of work was done, particularly in the city centre, but so much of the housing that was destroyed hasn't yet been replaced. They've built some new places, which are much better than people had before, but nowhere near as fast as is needed and many people aren't too happy about moving out of the areas they grew up in. Lots of these new places are in estates, specially created for this purpose and a long way from anywhere and anyone many of these people have known all their lives. They've also started building some extremely tall buildings that are all flats. I don't like the idea of this. Cramming hundreds of people together in one place is asking for trouble, in my opinion. It's no wonder people like my sister and Elsie, your friend, have packed up and decided to have a completely new start on the other side of the world."

Florence repeatedly stressed the point that there was no hurry for Angie to move on and she made the girl feel so at home there was a strong temptation to stay put. However, although this safe haven was very tempting, Angie really wanted to strike out on her own and decided that once she found a job, she would start looking for accommodation closer to the city. She had originally planned to travel throughout Britain before settling in London, but when she realised the size of the city, she decided that, for the time being, she would concentrate on getting to know it better, to hopefully discover what it was that made this the greatest city in the world.

Once she felt a bit less overwhelmed by the place and had put aside her preconceptions, Angie set off each day armed with her Authentic Map of London, with plans to visit all the main places of interest first; then, when she had reached the point where she had some vague idea of the general layout, to strike out further afield. Never having been one in the past to visit galleries or museums, she found a new world opening up to her as she roamed through the vast halls of the Museum of London and discovered the treasures in the various art galleries and churches. She discovered that, although she hadn't found the London she had always dreamed of, the reality was even more exciting. She wrote home to her mother several times a week, enthusing about the wonders she had seen, and any semblance of homesickness (which had been fairly strong at first) disappeared as she discovered this whole new world. Certainly the weather left a lot to be desired, for although it was summer, it seemed to rain almost all the time, but Angie didn't allow a bit of water to stop her in her tracks. She spent some of her limited money investing in a waterproof mackintosh and galoshes to cover her shoes, but resisted any urge to invest in any of the other beautiful clothes on sale in Selfridges and Harrods. This could wait until she had a job and, hopefully, the funds to splurge at last.

After several weeks of almost daily trips afield, Angie realised she must put an end to her adventures and look for work, or she would face the prospect of running out of money. Florence Paxton had at first refused to accept any payment, but her mother had stressed to her that she must always pay her way, so Angie insisted on giving that kind lady a couple of pounds a week to cover her meals. "My mum would kill me if I didn't," she said as she handed over the cash.

Angie had left Sydney armed with the addresses of several employment agencies that specialised in placing visitors from overseas, so she set about phoning them to make appointments for interviews. She was rather worried to find that jobs were not exactly coming out of the woodwork, particularly the temporary ones which she had hoped to find. After several forays that brought no results, she decided to take the search into her own hands. Every morning she bought the papers and scanned the Help Wanted columns for secretarial positions. Eventually, she reasoned that there really was no need to seek short-term work, for at present she had no plans to move on, so she started applying for all positions that sounded even vaguely likely. Immediately, it became apparent that her age was something of a drawback, so she decided to add a couple of years when ringing for interviews, in spite of the fact that she still didn't really look her eighteen years. One plus, in Angie's opinion, was that the English diet had added several pounds to her weight and, as a consequence, she had actually acquired a few curves.

More than a week passed with not a single interview and Angie was beginning to feel that she would soon have to wire home for some money, either to keep her going—or worst case scenario—pay for her passage home.

If need be, I'll scrub floors rather than have to do that, she thought to herself, as yet another phone call drew a blank. Then suddenly, as fate has a habit of doing, she was called in for two interviews in one day. Both positions were in the heart of London; one was for a small law firm, which Angie felt, with her two years of legal experience in Sydney, she could do with her hands tied behind her. The other was more of a challenge, working for Thomas Page, a man who described himself as an "entrepreneur." This was a term that Angie had never heard, but it seemed he was a person who dabbled in several fields, as an agent for various performers, and had interests in several businesses. It was in one of these, a placement agency for hotel staff, that secretarial help was needed. Charlie Henderson, the manager of the agency, was at the interview and Angie warmed to him immediately. There was something about him that reminded her of her father, although there was absolutely no physical resemblance between the two. In fact, he couldn't have been more different, standing not much taller than Angie's five feet and being rather rotund in build with a pronounced cockney accent. The resemblance was more in the eyes—he had the same brilliant blue eyes that she recalled from her dad.

I would like to work for him, she thought. If they offer me the job, I'll take it.

They, in fact, offered her the job on the spot, for Charlie told her later that he felt the same affinity with her. He had called his boss aside and told him, "She's the one," to which Thomas Page had replied, "Then let's hire her."

As easily as that, Angie's immediate future was secured. She never regretted her snap decision, for Charlie Henderson turned out to be a great person to work with. As she came to know him, she found that he had originally been one of Page's theatrical clients, an old time song and dance man, who found that in an increasingly sophisticated world, his type of performer was no longer needed. Everyone who met Charlie loved him, and when it became almost impossible to find work for his client, Page sat him down and told the man what he'd already known deep down inside.

"Charlie, you and I both know that the world has passed you by and this is how it stands—you are not getting any younger and it is only going to become harder for you as time goes by. You can keep on grabbing the occasional spot in god awful, out of town places, or you can take on what I'm about to offer you."

Page had gone on to explain that he wanted someone he trusted to run the agency. "I know you have no direct knowledge of the hotel business, but you haven't spent all those years staying in hotels of all shapes and sizes without gaining a fair idea of what goes on there and who does what. The pubs always tell you what they're looking for anyway, what I need is someone with an eye for people and one who won't cook the books and cheat me at every opportunity. The last manager grabbed everything he could lay his hands on and then flew the coop. I really need someone in a hurry and you would be helping me no end if you took it on."

Charlie had at first refused point blank. "I've never worked in an office in all my life. I wouldn't know where to start."

"You don't have to know. You'll have a secretary who knows the business back and forwards. She will show you the ropes and answer all the questions. She's an excellent woman and I'd give her the manager's job if she would take it, but she has an invalid husband, who is getting worse and it's only a matter of time before she has to give up work completely. She was the one who alerted me to what was going on in the office, unfortunately a bit too late for the man to be caught, which was partly due to her sense of loyalty. It was only when she realised how bad it all was that she came to me, but the culprit must have sensed there was something afoot and disappeared into the blue. Charlie, you need a job; I desperately need someone I can trust; it's logical you should give it a try. If after a month or so you decide it isn't for you, then we'll call it quits with no regrets on either side?"

With nothing to lose, Charlie had taken on the job and after an initial period of terror, found that he liked it. After forty years' insecurity of never knowing where the next penny would come from, having a steady income made his life much easier. He found that he had a natural affinity for dealing with people and, five years later, could not imagine doing anything else. Sadly, the secretary, who had been his lifeline in the early days, finally found she had to leave as her bedridden husband had nobody else to look after him.

Angie was a trifle worried about taking over from someone who had been in the position for so long, but Charlie went out of his way to make things easy for her. The old secretary had left voluminous notes, explaining every detail of the job, but Angie really didn't need them, as her boss was so undemanding and so easy to deal with that she almost immediately felt at home there. As it was just a two-person concern, she found that she was involved in almost every facet of the business. After a month or so, she felt comfortable enough that when Charlie asked her to take over interviewing some of the clients, she overcame her trepidation about dealing with people years older and found she quite enjoyed the experience.

The only drawback about her job was that it afforded Angie no opportunity to meet young people her own age. Her life seemed to be centred around the job, exploring London, and what she had come to think of as "home" with the Paxtons. The time had flown and Angie was comfortable living where she was, but as summer passed into winter, and spring was on the horizon, she decided it was time to get moving and look for accommodation in the city. She made a few attempts to look around and had answered several advertisements for sharers, but it was an eye opener to her to see what was on offer and the conditions in which many fellow visitors to London were content to live. Nothing she had seen so far had private bedrooms—they were all shares—and Angie, tidy by nature, knew she could not sleep comfortably surrounded by someone else's mess. Florence continually stressed that there was no need for her to hurry, so Angie had the luxury of being able to keep looking, hopefully to find somewhere she would feel more at home.

Thus it was one Saturday, that feeling somewhat depressed after looking at yet another dingy basement flat, Angie was surprised to hear a male voice calling out her name. She turned around to see a young man running towards her—an unfamiliar young man at first—but as he came closer, she realised to her surprise that it was Daniel Forsyth, her Auntie Kath's stepson. He picked Angie up in a bear hug and swung her off her feet, before planting her back on the ground.

"What in heaven's name are you doing here?" she cried. Excited, she stepped back and saw that the skinny youth she had spent holidays with nearly three years ago, had grown taller and filled out into an attractive young man. "My, you've changed!" she added.

"I could say the same thing about you." Dan grinned and looked her up and down. "Amazing—you've turned into a woman while I wasn't looking. I wasn't sure it was you at first and fully expected to get the brush off from some strange beauty who thought she was being accosted by a madman."

"Oh, it's me all right, still the same old Angie. But really, I can't believe it's you. Whatever are you doing in London? Nobody told me you were coming—I'd have laid out the red carpet for you or something. Are you staying long? Where are you living?"

"I'm here for eight months, give or take…and the answer to the other question is at a flat in Paddington that my dad owns." He smiled at Angie's look of amazement and added, "Sometimes it's handy to have a father who's dripping with money. He visits England often for conferences and stuff and snapped this place up cheaply way back during the Depression. Dad and Mum used to come and stay here a lot when Rhonda and I were little. Sometimes they'd bring us with them, sometimes farm us off on various relatives. Since Mum died, he hasn't used it much; Kath isn't interested in travel, so he has rented it out on and off. It just happened that it was vacant when I decided to come over, so he's given me the keys…it's mine for the duration."

Angie stood there open-mouthed at this story, then laughed and shook her head. "Oh Dan, I can't believe it—you are so lucky. If you could see the place I've just looked at and some of the others I've seen. Squalor would be a complimentary word about most of them. And there you are living for free in luxury in Paddington!"

"It's far from luxurious. It is quite old and a bit rundown and as for the free bit—my dad worked my fingers to the bone for the months before I left, both at home and in the office. He got plenty of free labour in exchange for the so-called 'free' accommodation."

He took Angie's arm and turned her around, saying, "There's a nice little teashop just around the corner. How about we continue this conversation over some tea and buns? Don't know about you, but I'm starving."

Angie grinned. "Always. Particularly since I came to England. I've eaten more in the past three months than I have in all the rest of my life. It must be the weather."

Settled at a corner table, refreshments on order, they continued the conversation. It appeared that Dan, having finished high school, was taking a year off before starting university. "I'll be doing medicine, probably be a GP at first; I'm not sure at this stage whether I want to specialise in anything. I'll wait until I'm through and then decide, for it all seems much too far in the future to make any plans. After all those years of study, with a lot more ahead, I decided it would be good to have a year off and London seemed a good place to spend some of it." He hung his head in mock embarrassment, then grinned cheekily. "I have to admit, it does help to have a Dad who's loaded. A couple of my mates are working at places like Woolworths to have enough cash to take the year off."

The grin faded from his face, replaced by a serious expression. "I really did do a lot of work for Dad before I left. You do believe me, don't you?"

Equally serious, hiding her amusement, Angie replied, "Of course I do." She glanced down at his hands, which showed no signs of ever doing anything approaching hard work. "Fingers to the bone, that's what you worked."

They spent the next hour filling one another in on what had been happening in their lives. Angie told him about her job, of where she was living and of her so far fruitless search for a flat in the city. When she finished, Dan grabbed her hands, saying, "I've got an idea. Why don't you move in with me? There's two bedrooms in the place and I'm rattling around like a single pea in a pod. I'd been planning to look for a flatmate, someone to have a laugh with, and that was part of the arrangement with Dad…to pay some rent, which would help with my living expenses. I'm not a total leech, you know; I won't be completely living on 'Daddy.'"

Angie couldn't restrain herself any longer; she burst out laughing. "Oh Dan, it isn't exactly hard labour, living on the rent that someone pays for your father's flat."

Then, turning serious, she shook her head. "What you are suggesting sounds wonderful. But I'm not completely sure it would be a good idea. I don't think my mum, or your dad for that matter, would like the idea of us living there together. I think my current landlady, who has become like family to me, would feel the same."

It was Dan's turn to laugh. "Hey there, girl…you talk as if this is the nineteenth century. This is 1955, not 1855. Lots of girls and men share flats these days—and it isn't as if I'm Jack the Ripper. I'm sure I can convince your landlady that I am not going to invade your bedroom and ravish you. I am, after all, a sort of cousin. I'll tell you what…how about you come with me right now and have a look at the flat? If you decide you don't want to move in, I will never mention it again. Were you heading anywhere when I met you? Do you have the time?"

"I was actually heading somewhere similar to where we are right this minute. I told you, I'm always hungry. After an afternoon of trudging the streets, looking at places that resembled the local tip, I really needed some sustenance."

"Feel better now?" said Dan, as he dumped another rock cake on Angie's plate, just in case she wanted it.

"Heaps better. And how can I resist—looking at the flat—not this," she said as she smiled and replaced the cake on its plate. She stood and picked up her handbag. "Come on, you sweet talking, non-Jack the Ripper, let me have a look at this place I've heard so much about."

Dan picked up the bill and stopped at the counter to pay for their teas, then opened the door to usher Angie out to the street. Familiar with the good manners of most Englishmen by then, Angie smiled at the thought that it was not something she had grown up expecting of fellow Australians. There's a lot to be said for what they teach in those fancy boarding schools, she thought, as Dan took her arm and guided her to the inside of the footpath.

Paddington was not far away from where they were in Lancaster Gate, but Dan, looking at Angie's high heels, said, "I think we'll get a taxi," and proceeded to hail one. On the short journey he remarked, as he had before, "I can't believe that in all the millions of people in London, I should run into you."

"My mum would say it was fate; she's a great believer in things like that. Personally, I prefer to think it was just a coincidence."

"That it certainly was. You probably won't believe this, but only yesterday I wrote to Kath, asking for your address. I'd heard you were over here and wanted to look you up. And here you are! And here we are," he said, as the taxi drew up outside a large Victorian building.

"This is all very grand," remarked Angie as they entered a marble floored vestibule.

"Decayed grandeur would be a better description really. It used to be a private residence but was converted to flats back in the thirties; that's when Dad bought it, when prices were low due to the Depression. I don't think anyone has done a lick of work on the building since." He led her up a flight of stairs and opened one of the four doors on the landing above.

"Da-dah! Welcome to home—and excuse the mess, I wasn't expecting any visitors today."

The door opened straight into a living room, which was indeed a bit messy, but nowhere near as bad as some Angie had seen in recent times. This room led to the kitchen, which was in the state to be expected of a nineteen-year-old male living alone. Unwashed dishes lay in the sink and the remains of breakfast still stood on the table, but under the mess it was obvious that the place was basically clean.

"There's a cleaning lady who comes in twice a week; she's due on Monday, so that's why everything is such a mess."

"Have you never heard of picking up after yourself? Or washing the dishes?" remarked Angie, with a smile in her voice.

"Heard of them, never tried them," was the reply.

"Well you would have to learn how in a hurry if I move in here. I'll have you know I run a tight ship, young man. There'd be no taking off and leaving things undone in my house."

"Then I'd best not show you my bedroom. Come on and I'll show you yours instead."

Down the hall they went, past the bathroom, which was similar to most English bathrooms, having a bath, but no shower. Angie had found that hard at first, but had eventually become quite fond of her daily soak in the tub. Like the rest of the flat, it was as Dan had warned her, very much of its era, but equipped with all the necessities. He led her to a closed door at the end of the passageway, which opened to reveal a large room, furnished in the Art Deco style, with a bay window opening to a tiny balcony.

"Oh my goodness! Now this really is grand; it's like stepping back into the past."

"All this can be yours, madam, at a very reasonable rental. And pray, I ask you, look out at the view from your window."

The view was indeed lovely, for the room overlooked a small, walled garden on the far side of the road. Lush green grass was surrounded by mature trees and bushes and on one side there stood a summer house in the style of a Chinese pagoda.

"Ours," said Dan, gesturing in its direction.

"What do you mean, ours...do you mean it's yours?" asked Angie in amazement. Dan nodded and led her back to the kitchen and to a bunch of keys hanging on a hook.

"Ours—yours. To use whenever you want. The garden belongs to this building and all the tenants have keys to it. You obviously like the garden. What do you think of the room?"

What could Angie say, other than it was perfect? Right in the heart of the city, close to the Tube, and where almost every other place she had looked had been dark and dingy—this flat was full of light.

"Oh Dan, I am so tempted! It really is lovely and it would be such fun sharing it with you—but what will everyone think?"

"Everyone doesn't have to think. This is between you and me. How about we tell any of the everyones who ask, that there's another girl sharing with us? Then they won't disapprove, and in the case of the people back in Australia, they aren't here to find out otherwise—and neither of us are going to spill the beans, are we?"

"I suppose it might work, but it would be awfully deceitful. I hate telling fibs, even if it is only to keep our parents from worrying. I'll have to think about it; on one hand I would love to live here, on the other I think I would feel forever guilty about lying to my family."

"Well, why don't you sleep on it?" He went to a table in the hall, tore off a piece of paper, checked the telephone and wrote the number down, then handed it to Angie. "Think about it and call me here tomorrow morning. I won't give you any longer; otherwise, you will think up more reasons to talk yourself out of it. You really have nothing to worry about...we will just be like brother and sister—we'll be fine."

Of course, they weren't. Of course, Angie overcame her doubts and moved in, and of course being two healthy young people, they didn't stay like brother and sister for long. At first, each went out of their way to keep their distance, until one warm summer evening when Angie brought home a bottle of wine she been given by one of the hotel owners. Common sense should have told her that to drink half a bottle of wine with a young man she found increasingly attractive was a sure step into his bed. A month after she moved in, her Art Deco bedroom was used only for clothes storage, and they both gave up any pretence of living apart and spent every night together in the master bedroom. Dan, her pseudo brother, became the centre of Angie's life, and although she kept up the pretence of having another flatmate with Florence Paxton and in her letters home, for the first time in her life, Angie was in love. Gone were her dreams of Harry. Those she thought of as her childhood fantasies. Dan was here and now and he seemed to love her every bit as much as she did him.

At the office, Charlie Henderson immediately noticed the change in Angie. How could he not, for the girl had changed almost overnight. He felt he should at least say something, for he had grown fond of his young assistant and was worried that what she was doing could end up with her being badly hurt. He had met Dan on several occasions and liked him. Charlie knew about the fictional other "flatmate" and finally decided it was time for someone to speak to Angie. He had daughters of his own and felt every bit as protective of Angie as he had been of them in the years before they married. Calling Angie into his office one afternoon, he pulled no punches.

"I hope you know what you're doing, living alone with young Dan. He's a good lad, but it just isn't right that you two should be shacked up the way you are. I'm as broadminded as the next man, but you are both so young and I'd hate for anything to happen to you," he said, feeling a bit too embarrassed to go into any details.

"If you're worried about me having a baby," Angie, who considered herself a "modern" woman, stated outright. "No need to worry about that; I've found out all about taking precautions. I know I'm much too young to be having babies—that's something I'll think about in the future."

"You're also too young to be living alone with a young man. I'll bet you haven't told your mother about what you two are up to."

"My mum's much too old fashioned to be told about it, so it's best she doesn't know. Now, Charlie, I know you have my best interests in mind, but we're just fine and you don't have to worry about me," she said politely, but in such a tone of dismissal that Charlie realised he could say no more.

For the time being everything was, as Angie had said, "just fine," but one thing to which she hadn't given much thought was the fact that Dan was only in London for a short visit. As the months flew by, the two of them had a wonderful time exploring London. In what seemed like no time, summer had come and gone. Aware that the good weather would not last much longer, Dan persuaded Angie to take a fortnight's vacation so that they could see something of Britain together, and for this purpose, they scraped together enough money to buy a battered old Ford coupe. Dan already had a driver's license and he persuaded Angie to obtain hers. Determined to see Britain from Land's End to John O'Groats, they made a fair attempt at seeing as much as the two weeks allowed them. They visited castles and cathedrals, climbed mountains and collapsed in laughter at the sight of the English beaches, which compared so poorly in their eyes with those they knew so well back home. Aside from that, they mutually agreed that, although everything was so different from what they had grown up with, nothing could compare with the beauty of the English countryside. Even the weather co-operated, with warm sunny days most of the time, and the few that were rainy gave them the opportunity to snuggle up in whichever small hotel they were currently staying and catch their travelling breath for the next adventure. Fully aware that they would be turned away from most country pubs and Bed and Breakfast places if they tried to book in as singles, they decided to pass themselves off as a married couple, so before they left London, Dan bought a plain wedding ring from a local pawn shop and put it on Angie's finger, saying, "I'll get you a real one, one of these days."

Maybe so, but when they returned to London and looked at the calendar, it suddenly became clear to them that the time was fast approaching for Dan to return home. Part of the tradeoff with his father was that he would be home before Christmas. The Indian summer, so unusual in late October, was coming to an end and so too was their relationship—at least for the time being. They had talked of marriage, but only in the future, for there was no doubt in either's mind that Dan must go back to Australia and complete his studies. Having grown up surrounded by the medical profession, Dan knew enough about the life and income of a new doctor to be well aware he would not be in a position to support a wife for many years to come. Although Angie's heart ached at the prospect of losing him, she knew that she had to face one of two alternatives. She could either return to Australia and spend the next five years as Dan's girlfriend, or stay on in Britain, at least for the time being.

"I'm not ready to go home yet. There's so much more I want to do and see before I settle down," she explained. "I know from seeing my mum and sister, that once I'm married and have children, my days of freedom will be over. If I could be with you all the time I would give up on that, but if we can't be married right away, I don't want to be over there waiting for you. I'd rather do it here."

There was no practical alternative that Dan could suggest, so he was forced to accept Angie's decision. He had pointed out to her unsuccessfully that there was no reason on this earth that she shouldn't come back with him as his girlfriend, but he hadn't bargained with the fact that he was dealing with a girl who had decided at fifteen that Britain was where she wanted to be. Britain was where she would remain and nothing, as always, would sway Angie when she had decided something in her life.

What remained in her mind was the problem of where she would live once Dan returned home. He had strict instructions to place the flat back in the hands of the estate agent and Angie knew that even if she could find someone to share with her, the rent Dr Forsyth was expecting was way beyond her means. Her halcyon days were coming to an end and she must face the prospect of looking once again for somewhere in London…with the knowledge that there was not even a slight possibility of finding something that compared with the Paddington flat. She could, of course, return to live with the Paxtons, but after more than six months of independent living, the prospect of the tiny room in suburban Croydon, even with Auntie Flo looking after her, was far from appealing. Besides, if one phase of her life was ending—albeit for the time being—Angie felt that she needed something new.

Even before Dan left London, Angie's life was turned upside down by an unforeseen event. At seven on the Wednesday morning before Dan was due to leave, the phone in the flat rang unexpectedly. Thinking at such an early hour it must be a call from Australia, almost certainly for Dan, Angie left it for him to answer.

"It's for you," he called out to Angie, who was in the kitchen and had just taken a mouthful of buttered toast. "Someone called Thomas Page."

Surprised, for she had only met the "big boss" a couple of times since her initial job interview, Angie quickly wiped her hands on a tea towel and ran to pick up the phone. What on earth would make Mr Page call her at home, she wondered?

"Hello?' she hesitantly said, absentmindedly wiping her mouth with the towel she still held in her other hand.

"Angie, forgive me for calling you this way, but I'm afraid I have some bad news to give you. It's Charlie. I'm sorry to tell you he died last night. I thought it best to let you know right away. I didn't want you going into the office and finding out when you got there, for I've had to post a notice on the door that it is closed for the time being and the reason why."

He went on to tell her that Charlie had suffered a fatal heart attack on the way home. It was too early to know any funeral arrangements, but it would most likely be the coming Friday.

"The office is closed, so there's no point in your going there. I will keep you posted about when the funeral is to be. Your salary will continue on as if you are at work, and as this has happened so suddenly, I'm not quite sure what is going to happen in the coming weeks."

Angie stood in the hallway thunderstruck, the tea towel slipping from her grasp as she assimilated the information she had just received. Impossible as it was to believe, Charlie, who had been so full of life the previous evening, was dead. She thought of what it would mean to her job and to her life and wondered how she could face the office when the place would remind her so much of Charlie's exuberance and kindness. He had been like a second father to her and she felt this loss almost as much as the younger Angie had done for her real father. Numbly, she thanked Thomas Page and stood in the hallway, the phone still in her hand even after Page had hung up, tears streaming down her cheeks. Dan, who had headed down the hall when she took up the phone, returned to find her still standing there several minutes later.

When she saw him, Angie threw herself into his arms sobbing uncontrollably. It took some minutes before she calmed down enough to explain what had happened. What really upset her most was the fact that, within days, she was losing the two men who meant everything in life to her, along with the fact that what had become her home for the past many months would also be taken from her. When she woke that morning she had known that although she was losing Dan, the job that she loved would remain constant. Without the support of her friend and mentor, Charlie, how would she cope?

Dan took the phone from her hand and replaced it on its hook. He led Angie to the kitchen, sat her down and, after turning off the stove that she had left burning, felt the teapot and found it was still hot. He poured her a cup of tea, added milk and two spoons of sugar, recalling from his school First Aid lessons that this was good for someone in shock, for that most certainly was Angie's condition at the moment.

"What am I to do?" Angie cried. "Even if I still have a job, I don't want to work with anyone else—some stranger. I know I would hate it."

"Charlie was a stranger to you when you first worked for him," reasoned Dan, holding her hand with one of his as he fed her the tea as if she were a baby. "Honey, you've had a tremendous shock and I know you were very fond of Charlie, but everything will be fine. I'm sure of that."

"You're going away and leaving me, too; it's all very well you saying things will be fine. You won't be here to find out one way or another."

"Then come home with me—that's what I've wanted you to do all along. Back home, you have your family and I'll be there whenever I can be. It's not too late to change your mind." He led Angie to the bedroom and sat with her on the bed, holding her in his arms until she stopped crying. When her weeping subsided to the occasional sob, he tilted her face up to his. "You okay now?" he asked, handing her a handkerchief.

Angie nodded numbly and blew her nose, but continued to lean on Dan, too wrung out to speak yet. When she regained her composure, they sat together talking over the whole situation. In spite of everything, Angie said she still did not want to return to Australia.

"I'll wait and see what Mr Page has to say. Funnily enough, Charlie only said to me the other day that he had a feeling there was something afoot as far as the company was concerned. He didn't know what, but now, seeing that Charlie's dead, I wonder if this will bring it all on sooner. Whatever happens, I'm sure I'll get another job and I can always move back to Auntie Flo's. I don't want to go home—not yet."

Dan knew that it was pointless to argue with her, and sensing that Angie needed to get her mind off the future, he suggested they head out to see the Changing of the Guard, a ceremony they both really loved.

"I know Charlie wouldn't have minded," he said when Angie wondered if it was the right thing to do. "The last thing he would have wanted was for you to sit around moping." Realising the truth of this, Angie agreed and changed from her work clothes into pants and a shirt. Together, they went hand-in-hand towards the Tube station, joining the throngs of workers city bound, of which Angie had expected to be a part only a few hours ago. When they reached Victoria Station, they left the workers behind and made their way in the direction of Buckingham Palace. With plenty of time on their hands and with no knowledge of when Charlie's funeral would be, they treated this day as their last one together. After the changing ceremony, they headed for Horseguards, then on to Trafalgar Square to feed the pigeons with some of the bread they had saved for this purpose.

Angie tried hard to keep a cheerful face for Dan's benefit, although her thoughts were full of worries about what the future held. Finally, they topped the day off by changing into their best clothes and having a slap-up meal at a restaurant that normally would have been beyond their means, both thinking that they needed something special to remember in the time until they would be re-united.

Next day they stayed in the flat, hoping to hear some news from Thomas Page. As the afternoon passed with no call, Angie decided to try to contact Page herself and was lucky enough to find him available when she phoned his office.

"Oh Angie, there has been so much going on, I completely forgot about you. The funeral is at eleven am tomorrow. I don't have the full details with me, so I will put you back to my secretary. I want to see you here in the office, so ask her to arrange an appointment for you on Monday. Are you okay? I know that you and Charlie became very close and it's been a hard time for everyone. He was a great little guy and we will miss him a lot."

The appointment made, Why does he want to see me? Angie wondered. Well, she would have to wait until Monday to find out, so there was no point in fretting over it.

Now that they knew the funeral was the next day, she and Dan decided to spend what would be their second-last night together at home with some fish and chips. Tomorrow would be an early night, for Dan was due to fly out early on Saturday, first to New York and then home to Sydney. He had told the estate agent that the flat would be vacant in a fortnight's time, so Angie had two weeks to sort her life out, either by finding another flat or moving back to Croydon.

It poured rain at the funeral and, in spite of umbrellas, the strong wind determined that everyone was thoroughly soaked. Charlie's brother had arranged a wake, which the young couple attended briefly, but after paying their respects to the widow and her daughters, Angie and Dan decided not to stay. This was their last day together and it was too wet, cold and miserable to do anything outside, so they made their way back to the flat, lit the fire and snuggled up in their dressing gowns, both trying to put the approaching separation out of their minds.

Dan was flying first to New York, where he would stay a couple of days with relatives before taking another flight across the continent and on to Sydney. Angie was keen to accompany him to the airport, but Dan asked her not to come. "I would rather remember you here than leave you at the airport to come back alone. Anyway, airports are such dreadful places at the best of times."

Angie, who had never flown in her life, or even been to an airport, was unable to comment on this. At first, she was adamant that she preferred to stay with Dan right up to flight time; however, when he explained to her that they would be separated soon after he checked in, Angie finally agreed to say her goodbyes at the flat. The New York flight was an early one, which meant that Dan must catch the airport bus at 4 am. They waited in the dark and cold, thankful that yesterday's rain had at least disappeared, but by the time the bus rounded the corner, Angie was shivering inside her layers of clothing and Elsie's old coat, which she had brought from Sydney in what seemed like another lifetime ago.

They had only time for a quick goodbye kiss before Dan loaded his bags on the bus and leapt aboard, standing on the back platform to wave until the bus turned another corner and disappeared from view. Angie stood for a few minutes looking towards where it had disappeared, then heaved a sigh and made her way back home. Alone.

Once inside she shed the heavy coat and boiled the kettle for a warming cup of tea. Two goodbyes, she thought, one yesterday, another today. I wonder, will the day after tomorrow bring another one? She spent that day and all of the next trying to relax and catch up on her reading, but constantly found herself gazing into space, the book on her lap, forgotten. It was proving very hard to put thoughts of the future out of her mind.

Whether precognition, or just plain fate, Angie's thoughts about another goodbye proved to be true. Monday morning, she arrived at Thomas Page's office at 9 am, dressed for work, as she hoped that his news would be that he was reopening her office that day. Any such hopes were dashed almost immediately, for after thanking her for coming and briefly remarking on the funeral, he got straight down to business.

"I'm not reopening the agency; there doesn't seem much point in doing so, for even before Charlie died I had other plans. I had long since decided that it really had little to do with any of my other interests, so I'd put out a few feelers in the hotel industry and had in fact found a buyer who is due to take over in a month's time. Any enquiries in the meantime will be handled here in my office, which means, Angie, unfortunately there is no longer a job for you. In appreciation of the great job you've been doing for the past year, I will pay you a month's salary in advance, plus the Christmas bonus you would have received if the agency were still operating." He opened a drawer in his desk and removed a large envelope.

"In here is a cheque for any salary outstanding, plus the payments I just mentioned. There's also a reference, describing your contribution to the business and inviting interested persons to phone or write me for a personal recommendation. I would gladly offer you a position in any of my companies if such vacancies were available, but unfortunately there are none. I am sure you will have no trouble finding another position, for the market is crying out for good employees such as you."

Angie had said hardly a word during the whole meeting, and when Page rose and held out his hand to shake hers, she could do nothing more than transfer the envelope to her left hand and shake the proffered hand. She murmured a few words of thanks, which seemed appropriate in the circumstances and was shown to the door, where Thomas Page again shook her hand and wished her well. The whole meeting had taken only ten minutes.

Back in the street, Angie headed for a tearoom, sat down and ordered morning tea, opened the envelope and checked out its contents. The payment was a very generous amount, much more than she might have expected, and the reference was all she could have hoped for. None of that could alter the fact that she was unemployed, with Christmas only weeks away and chances of finding anything at that time of the year almost nil. The generous payment would have to be spent wisely, for with little savings—having only recently spent so much on her holiday with Dan—it seemed apparent that unless a miracle happened and she found work fairly quickly, a move back to Croydon would be almost imperative.

Everything had happened so suddenly, it was only after finishing her first cup of tea that she started to think about what Page had said. Remembering how Charlie had remarked a week ago that something was afoot, she realised he must have heard something on the grapevine about the business being up for sale. This knowledge gave her further thoughts about Charlie's death. He had returned that last afternoon from a meeting with Thomas Page...had he perhaps been given the news that his job was no longer there? She knew that Charlie was constantly in debt, and not being blessed with either youth or much in the way of qualifications, could his subsequent heart attack been brought on by worry? She wracked her brain to try to recall how Charlie had acted that afternoon...but couldn't recall him being any different than usual. But then, being Charlie, he wouldn't have shown it anyway. Forever the clown, he would have masked his feelings, knowing all too well that she would soon be out of work as well. Angie stuffed the papers back in the envelope and poured herself a cup of tea. It was pointless thinking any of that, for only Thomas Page would know the answer and she was fully aware there was no point in going down that road.

The day had barely begun and, since she could think of nothing she wanted to do, Angie returned to the flat. With Dan gone it seemed empty and uninviting; even lighting a fire made no difference to that feeling, and finally, unable to contain herself any longer, she sat on the floor in front of the flames and sobbed her heart out.

Seventeen

A new twist in the road

Angie spent the next few days in much the same mood, only making trips out for food and fresh air, and her depression was heightened when the regular weekly letter came from her mother. The big news was that her sister Shirley was engaged and the wedding was set for the coming April. I know that they are both very young, her mother had written, but they are perfect for each other and Shirley has never had any ambitions, other than to be married and have children, so I've given them my blessing. The other news was that Harry had a girlfriend, which the previous year would have devastated her, but Angie, whose thoughts were totally taken up with Dan Forsyth, smiled and reflected on how childish she had been only a short while ago. Whatever could she have been thinking to imagine that Harry was the man for her? However, the fact that her sister, almost two years younger, was to be married, with any hopes of marriage for Angie years in the future, made her even more miserable, although she knew that her current situation was largely of her own doing. Now, feeling so alone, without a job and with the prospect of having to move, for the first time she began to wonder if she should have returned to Australia with Dan. The good weather had disappeared; it was cold and bleak and the letter from home spelled out to her the difference between there and London. Mid November, it could already be beach weather at home in Narrabeen, where there were blue skies and sparkling water, unlike the dark, cold, littered streets of London. For the first real time since her early days in England, Angie was overcome with a huge dose of homesickness.

Deciding eventually that moping was really getting her nowhere, Angie picked up the phone and rang Thomas Page's office. With all that had happened in the past week, she had overlooked the fact that she had left some of her belongings at the office on that last day. She still had a key to the office but felt that she should ask permission before letting herself in; after all, she no longer worked there.

"Of course, you can," was Page's reply when she asked. "But I will have to meet you there, because I've put a padlock on the door for security reasons and I'll have to open it for you. Besides that, I want to talk to you; I was, in fact, just about to ring and see if you were home. I've heard about a position that might interest you, something very different from what you've been doing, but it could well be a very interesting job. Shall we meet there at three pm?"

Burning with curiosity, Angie agreed and hurried to change from casual to more formal clothing. There was something about her former employer that made her feel he would disapprove of her turning up dressed in jeans and a Sloppy Joe.

She arrived at the office to find no sign of Thomas Page, so she scribbled a note on a page torn from her diary, telling him that she was in the adjoining office. She tucked it under the padlock and headed for the next door office, as she wanted to take this opportunity to say hello and goodbye to Rosa, the lady who worked there. They had shared many a chat over washing up in the tearoom and walking together to the Tube at knock off time.

Rosa was pleased to see her and they sat together discussing recent developments and pondering over Angie's hopes for the future, until Thomas Page put his head around the door.

"Sorry I'm late," he said as Angie rose, kissed Rosa on the cheek and followed him towards her old office. As he undid the padlock, they shared views on the vagaries of London traffic and transport. Page opened the final lock and ushered Angie into the room. After only a week of disuse, the place looked and smelled deserted and Angie hastened to open the windows—even London's polluted air was preferable to that in this sad, unloved place.

Angie went straight to her old desk and removed the photos of her family and several other personal belongings on the desk and in the drawers. These she put into a carrier bag she had brought with her, then turned to Thomas Page, who had spent the past few minutes in the office, riffling through some papers on Charlie's desk and then seated himself in the swivel chair behind the desk.

"You said there was a job that you wanted to tell me about. Has something come up within your organisation?"

Page shook his head and gestured towards a chair on the other side of the desk. "No, still nothing on that front. I think I mentioned that this is something very different, and indeed it is. You may not be interested in trying for it, because of its out of the way location, but I heard about it last night, immediately thought of you, and decided you should at least be told about it."

He leaned the chair back, stretched his arms behind his head, and continued, "I am a member of Trafalgar Country Club, a very exclusive retreat and golf course situated out in the countryside. You've probably never heard of it; few people have. It was formed back in the twenties by several very rich and important people and has a restricted membership—mainly to the aristocracy and giants of industry."

He smiled. "You may wonder how I came to be a member of this club, as although I'm a fairly successful man, I could never be described as an industry giant—and as you may well be aware, I'm not a member of our esteemed aristocracy. However, my father-in-law is. My wife, before she married me, was the Honourable Catherine Dupledge. Her father was one of the founding members of the club and, when we married, he pulled the necessary strings to gain me membership. It is a fascinating place; many of the members have never played a round of golf in their lives...they belong to the club for the prestige and its exclusivity. It has residential facilities, an excellent kitchen and is somewhere they know they can relax without any pressures, hidden away from the ever increasing eyes of the public press. If anyone of any note visits the country, they can bring them there for a meal, or even a short stay, knowing that there is no fear of interruption by outsiders.

"Trafalgar has a full-time manager, who is not a member as such, but serves on the board in his capacity of Company Secretary. Because the place is so remote, his is a live-in position, as it is for the accountant and the manager's secretary. We tried a couple of times to fill this latter position from the nearby village, but none of the applicants lived up to expectations, mainly because they tended to gossip among their friends and families of what went on at the club. None of this was anything of a salacious nature, but it did make its way into the press, causing great dissatisfaction among the members. Since then, we have only employed outsiders and found it has worked much better in the long run. It's this position that I thought you might like to apply for, as it is about to fall vacant."

Stunned, for it was indeed a very different job from anything she had imagined or contemplated, Angie sat there speechless, unsure what to say in response. When she made no immediate comment, Page continued.

"At first I thought you are much too young for such a responsible and remote position. But then I thought of how you have conducted yourself over the past months. Charlie kept me well informed of all you have been doing and I know that much of it exceeds the position we gave you originally. Charlie particularly remarked on how well you related to the clients in a one on one situation. Personal contact with the members is a very large part of the requirements of the job at Trafalgar; indeed, it is the most important. The actual secretarial work is minimal and the scope of other work involved depends very much on what is needed at the time. As an instance, weekends—which would be required as part of your working week—are when the club is busiest. Sundays, in particular, are when there traditionally is a large buffet luncheon and members drive down from the city just for this occasion. Some of them combine it with a round of golf; others, as I mentioned previously, just relax and take in the country air. On these occasions, you would be expected to greet them and their visitors, seat them in the dining room and generally make them feel at home. So, it's tasks like this that made me say how different this job is. More public relations than secretarial, but we need someone who is qualified to carry out those duties as well."

He leaned back in his chair and looked directly at Angie, who so far hadn't uttered a word.

"What do you think?"

Angie shook her head.

"I don't quite know what to think. It is so different from anything I've done before and would be such a change of lifestyle; I must admit I'm a bit overcome by the thought."

"I didn't expect you to say yes immediately and, anyway, the decision is not mine. Think it over and if you're interested, you would have to go to Trafalgar for an interview with the manager and secretary and board. One of those board members is my father-in-law and it was from him I heard about the vacancy. I told him about you then and there and he seemed quite interested, but the decision is not up to him alone."

"How soon would I have to decide?" asked Angie, continuing before he could reply. "In many ways it would solve my current problem. In just over a week, I will have to move from my flat. I won't actually be homeless, I suppose, for I could move in with friends—but something such as this, coming up when it has, makes me wonder if it isn't meant to be."

"The position is more or less vacant immediately. The present incumbent is leaving before Christmas, which doesn't leave a great deal of time for breaking in her replacement. The manager is thinking of conducting interviews starting next Monday and I have to say, without making any promises, the fact that you come highly recommended, plus your immediate availability, would count very much in your favour. Let's see, it is Thursday now, what say you think about it overnight and call me in the morning? If you're interested in applying, I might even be able to arrange an interview for you sooner, over the weekend to be exact. I was planning on going there Sunday; you could come along as guest of my wife and me and I'm sure we could somehow fit in an interview while we are there. Think about it, call me early tomorrow, and if you're interested I will phone around and drum up a couple of board members to sit in on the interview. How does that sound?"

Feeling somewhat overwhelmed by the suddenness of it all, Angie could do little other than agree to think it over, but she was already tempted to go on Sunday, for she realised she had nothing to lose. She thought it amazing that such a simple procedure as employing what sounded like an office dogsbody should entail an interview complete with board members, but at the least she would be assured of a trip out into the countryside, a free meal and a glance at how the other half lives. She gathered together her belongings and shook hands with Page, who rose from his seat and walked her to the door.

"Until tomorrow," he said, at which she nodded, took one last look at the place where she had spent so many happy hours, and left the building, her head spinning with all she'd been given to think of in the last half hour.

Back at the flat, Angie realised she was ravenous. She had missed lunch while getting ready to meet Thomas Page, so she decided to have an early dinner. The task of preparing the meal gave her the chance to put off thinking of the proposition she must consider before tomorrow morning; then, having eaten, she took her cup of tea into the living room and turned on the television to watch Hancock's Half Hour, a show that usually left her in stitches. Not so today; she had too much on her mind to enjoy the antics of Tony and Sid, so she turned it off and sat gazing into space. What to do? There was really nobody she could ask for advice. She thought fleetingly of calling her mother in Australia and to hang with the cost, but a look at the clock told her it would be 4 am in Sydney, which was hardly a suitable time to be ringing for motherly advice. She knew that Florence Paxton also would happily listen to her, but lovely lady though she may be, Angie doubted she would be a great deal of help in these circumstances.

"Well, I've made my own decisions so far and most of them seem to have worked out reasonably okay. Obviously, I have to do so again," she said out loud, gathered up her cup and saucer and taking them back to the kitchen. Piling all the dishes into the sink—they could wait until morning—Angie turned out the kitchen light and went to bed. That seemed as good a place as any to lie and contemplate her future.

After mulling over the whole situation, she finally decided she would call Thomas Page and say she wanted to attend the interview on Sunday, if he were able to organise it at such short notice. As he was offering her the opportunity to visit the country club, it would, if nothing else, be an interesting experience and a day away from the flat. Angie had never been to anywhere remotely like that and doubted such a chance would ever come again. She would have a good look around, go through the interview and then make her decision. It, after all, was hers as well as theirs. She could always tell them if she wasn't interested. Satisfied at this, she turned out the light and slept better than she had in days.

~ * ~

"Good," said Thomas Page, when she rang him Friday morning. He arranged to pick her up from the flat at ten thirty on Sunday. "It's at least an hour's drive out to Trafalgar, so if we make good time, we may be there in time to arrange the interview before luncheon. Otherwise, something tells me you won't have much appetite if it lies ahead of you," he said jokingly.

Angie's immediate worry was what to wear. She had added to her wardrobe over the past year, but mainly with work clothes and casuals. She had a feeling that none of those would be very suitable to dine with the rich and famous. She didn't want to turn up looking like a poor relation of the Pages', so she decided to spend some of her bonus money on a new outfit. If nothing else, it would keep her occupied and take her mind off what lay ahead.

Knowing that her budget would not stretch to shopping at Harrods or Harvey Nichols, Angie headed for Kensington High Street, where many small, boutique style shops had sprung up over the past few years. She settled on a sage green suit of light wool, suitable for the current weather, which, after the few wet and windy days, had reverted to reasonably warm weather, so unseasonable for this time of year. She then splurged on matching shoes and handbag—and having a trial run in front of the mirror back at the flat, she thought she looked well enough turned out to confront the upper classes on their home ground. The green of the suit highlighted her eyes and her hair, which she now tinted a deep auburn.

"You don't look too bad at all for an interloper from the Colonies," she said to her mirror image in her very best posh voice.

Angie's only worry was the possibility that the weather could change again, but by Sunday it held out beautifully and she breathed a sigh of relief. After a quick breakfast, she dressed herself in her new finery and waited on the footpath for Thomas Page's car. She had failed to ask what make of car to look out for and peered anxiously at every car that passed her by, invoking many a strange glance and several complimentary whistles from the occupants of passing vehicles.

She had expected something good, but was not prepared for the chauffeur driven Daimler that pulled into the kerb. Thomas Page, who was travelling in the front seat next to the driver, leapt out and opened the back door for Angie, ushering her into the luxurious interior, where his wife Margery was sitting, along with a distinguished-looking gentleman, who was introduced to her as Lord Montgomery Dupledge, Margery's father.

"Don't be misled by all this finery," stated Page. "This car and all its trappings belong to His Lordship; I drive a much less imposing Morris Oxford. As Lord Monty was coming to Trafalgar this weekend anyway, we decided to do it in style. If nothing else, it will give you something to write home about to the family in Australia."

Page excused himself and returned to the front seat, while Angie, trying to be as unobtrusive as possible, checked out her companions and surroundings. Margery Page, who she had met briefly at the funeral, was a tall, pale English beauty, slightly past her prime. His Lordship was a large man of the type one could imagine having played rugger in his youth. He was ruddy faced, heavy without being corpulent, and sporting exactly the type of curling white moustache that Angie had always imagined a lord would have. After grunting an amiable greeting, he settled back in his seat and said barely another word for the progression of the journey. His daughter, on the other hand, hardly stopped talking. She questioned Angie on her family in Australia… which, like the young Queen, she referred to as "Orstralia" much to Angie's secret amusement, and generally kept up an endless stream of chatter about everything and nothing, ranging from the unpredictable weather to the difficulty in buying so many things "all these years after the war." To her relief, Angie was not expected to add much to this one-sided conversation, so she spent most of the time nodding and making agreeable noises, while wondering how a seemingly sensible man like Thomas Page managed to put up with such an onslaught of words. No wonder he chose to ride in the front, where she could see through the glass partition that other than exchanging the occasional word with the driver, he sat back and relaxed in his seat.

One thing that Margery Page's chatter achieved was to drive any thoughts of nervousness from Angie's mind. She was too busy keeping up with the "conversation" and concentrating on giving the correct facial expressions to allow her thoughts to dwell on what lay ahead. This didn't stop her from watching the scenery, which, once they left the city behind, was lush and gleaming from the recent rain.

Forty minutes into the journey, they entered a fairly dense forest. "Oh good," said Margery Page, "he's taking you along the scenic route."

It wasn't very scenic at first, unless one considered endless trees scenery, Angie thought. Then, after a few minutes, the trees started to thin out and they emerged once again into the sunlight. They stopped at the top of a small hill and the countryside that lay below them was indeed scenic, with a small village in the foreground. A mile or so beyond this lay what Angie realised must be their destination. A stand of poplars served as a windbreak to the rolling greens of the golf course and in the background stood what could only be described as a fairytale castle.

The chauffeur had stopped the car on the rise and Thomas Page climbed out of his seat and beckoned to Angie, who joined him on the roadside.

"Our destination," he said, with a sweep of his arm. "What do you think of it?"

"Oh, it's beautiful," said an excited Angie. "What an amazing building; I've never seen anything quite like it."

"And you certainly won't again. Although it looks very old from this distance, it is actually only a century old. It was built in the 1850s by an eccentric American, who made his money in the California Gold Rush. He'd always dreamed of being English landed gentry, came here and bought up all the land around, demolished the perfectly good country house that stood there and built his version of what he thought a country squire should own. He only lived there for thirty years or so; then lost everything in the US stock market crash of 1893. The bank resumed Trafalgar to cover some of his debts and other than having a couple of tenants over the years, the building was allowed to deteriorate until the founders of the country club were looking for suitable premises in the late 1920s. One of the board members was chairman of the bank that held the mortgage on Trafalgar. He suggested it as a possibility and assured his friends that they would be able to acquire it at a good price, because it was considered something of a white elephant. There was some resistance from the more conservative members, as they hadn't envisaged something as "fancy" as that, but when nobody came up with anything more suitable, they backed down...and now those who are still around pat themselves on the back at what a bargain they found, and talk of its uniqueness, forgetting completely how much they objected to it in the first place."

"Well, it certainly looks unique from here; I can hardly wait to see it up close," Angie remarked as they climbed back into the car.

When the car started up again, Thomas Page swivelled around in his seat and opened the sliding glass door that separated the driver's section from the passengers in the back.

"As my wife has probably told you, there is a more direct way of getting to our destination, but I deliberately asked Charlton to come this way, so that your first view of Trafalgar would be from up above."

Angie thanked him for his kindness and thought to herself how she had always considered him to be a fairly remote person. Obviously, Thomas Page at home was very different from the rather blunt man she had encountered in the business environment.

They made their way down from the hillside and took a road that skirted around the village and approached the clubhouse from the side. They drove through imposing wrought iron gates, along a driveway on the edge of the golf course and pulled into the parking area, where several cars, some as imposing as theirs, others rather more ordinary, were already parked.

"It tends to be something of a hodgepodge of architecture," remarked Page, as Angie looked up at the building they were approaching. "Some of the more outrageous features were demolished when the club undertook the necessary renovations. However, it was decided not to take too much away, as it would spoil the appearance of the whole place and most people are quite happy with how it turned out."

He looked at his watch and said, "You ladies might like to freshen up a bit while Lord Dupledge and I try to see if we can rustle up another board member." To his wife he added, "We will meet you in the bar in a few minutes, darling, so give Angie a quick look around and we will see you then."

Massive bronze doors stood open wide, ushering them into a spacious hallway, resplendent with large vases of flowers on either side of the entrance. To the left were three rooms with closed doors, to their right was another doorway which opened onto a lounge area, where several people were sitting at tables or on settees. This room had large windows that looked directly out on the wide expanse of the golf course.

Before the party separated, a young man in a dark suit came forward and shook hands, first with Lord Dupledge and then with

Thomas Page. He took Margery's hand and kissed her lightly on the cheek. "I see you made good time in getting here," he said.

Page took his arm and directed him towards Angie, leading both of them away from the others. "Angie, I would like you to meet Leslie Moulton, the manager and Company Secretary of Trafalgar Club. Leslie, this is Angela Sherwood, the young lady I told you about."

The usual pleasantries were exchanged and after saying he would see them later, Moulton excused himself and left.

"Leslie will be sitting in on the interview process, so it was good that you were able to meet him beforehand," said Page as he led Angie back to his wife. "We will see you again soon," he remarked before he and Lord Dupledge headed off in the same direction Leslie Moulton had taken.

Margery Page guided Angie towards a staircase at the rear of the hallway, saying, "Let's powder our noses. There's a loo downstairs, but I thought you might like a peep at the upstairs rooms, where the house guests stay, so we'll use the upstairs one and then have a quick look around before we join the menfolk."

"I'm surprised he is so young—Mr Moulton, I mean," Angie remarked, "I imagined someone many years older, to be in a position such as his."

"Oh, he's in his mid-thirties I think, but very good at his job. We ladies in particular really love him and he is, in fact, something of a lady's man." Margery gave a little gasp and covered her mouth with her gloved hand. "Thomas would really be cranky with me if he knew I'd said that. Please don't misunderstand me. Leslie is always extremely circumspect with the staff and anything else he gets up to outside, he is smart enough to ensure it gets no further." She gave a little giggle and blushed slightly. "My husband always says my mouth will get me into trouble one of these days. Please, I beg of you, don't tell him I said any of this."

Angie laughed and assured her she would never breathe a word. As if she would. Did the silly woman think that Thomas Page took her into his confidence, or she him, for that matter?

They tidied up and did a quick sprint around the unoccupied bedrooms, which lay open. The rooms were comfortably, but not particularly richly, furnished. Most had the same outlook as the lounge downstairs and Angie thought to herself how lovely it would be to wake in the mornings to look out on such a view.

The two women came downstairs to find the men already waiting. They rose as the women approached and Angie smiled to herself—she loved the way English men did this. There was an addition to the party…an extremely old gentleman, dressed in tweeds. He was introduced as General Attard, the club's President, and Angie realised it was his portrait—that of a much younger man, clad in army uniform—hanging over the large fireplace.

"The general has agreed to make up the interview panel," said Thomas Page. "Leslie Moulton is waiting in the boardroom, so shall we make our way there? Margery, this should not take very long, so if you will excuse us, we will rejoin you as soon as possible."

The boardroom, which smelled of beeswax polish and cigars, was furnished with a bookcase that took up one wall, a sideboard and a long table, with six chairs on either side. Thomas Page seated Angie in one of the chairs, before moving to the other side to join Lord Dupledge, the general and Leslie Moulton, all seated facing her. The interview was conducted by the latter, with none of the others taking any part in proceedings. It was like no interview Angie had ever had, for other than a quick perusal of Angie's reference from Page, which was handed on to each of the others in turn, it mainly consisted of what Thomas Page had already told her about the position. When he finished speaking, Moulton asked two questions of Angie: "Do you realise that you would be expected to work on weekends, when most others are at leisure?" To which Angie answered "Yes," feeling no need to enlarge further. The second, after a whispered exchange with General Attard, was, "You are very young. We wonder if you would miss your friends and lifestyle living in such an out-of-the-way place?"

"I really haven't made any friends my own age since I've been in England," was the reply. "I have a fiancé, but he has returned to Australia and we won't be thinking of marriage for at least five years."

Moulton, looking puzzled, asked a further question. "If your fiancé is in Australia, why have you stayed in London?"

"Because while he is studying, we can't be married. Besides, I like England," said Angie, smiling.

"Well, we're glad to hear that!"

That, it appeared, was the end of the interview, as the three men rose, thanked her and gestured to Angie to follow them. Page took Angie's arm and led her back to his waiting wife.

"I think you can safely assume that the job's yours—if you want it," he said as he pulled out a chair for Angie. "I think the old boy quite liked the look of you." He gestured towards the general, who was standing in the doorway, deep in conversation with Leslie Moulton.

Moulton left the general, who had spied some friends and wandered off in their direction. He walked over to them and pulled up a chair next to Angie's.

"How soon can you start?"

Decision time. Angie had not expected to be hired immediately and had anticipated a wait of a couple of days, which would give her time to decide whether she wanted this unusual job or not. Deciding it was best to be completely honest, she replied, "I'm not one hundred percent sure I actually want the job. This has all happened so suddenly—can I please have some time to think it over?"

"I quite understand. This is a position that means a complete change of lifestyle and we wouldn't want you to take it on if you have any doubts. We would, however, like a decision within the next couple of days, to enable us to interview others if you decide against it. Can I ask that you let me know one way or another by Tuesday afternoon?

Angie agreed and there was no further discussion on the subject for the rest of the afternoon. Business completed, they headed into the dining room, where a sumptuous buffet, both hot and cold, was waiting. Starving by then, Angie made good use of all it offered, thinking that this was how she would live if she came to work at Trafalgar. Moulton had mentioned to her that her meals would be taken in the main dining room, instead of with the other staff members, who had their own facility. When she considered the offer of free accommodation, and excellent meals into the bargain, it was a very tempting proposition.

When the chauffeur dropped her back at the flat, Angie climbed the stairs, her head buzzing with all she had seen that day. She looked around the place she had come to think of as home and thought, If I can't stay on here, I might as well give Trafalgar a try. Decision made, she spent the rest of the evening writing home to tell them of this next move in her life.

First thing the following morning, she called Leslie Moulton, told him that she wanted the job and asked when they wanted her to start.

"You can move here whenever you want. The room that would be yours is still needed by Frances, the lady you are replacing, but there are other rooms we could give you for the time being."

He explained that they were coming into the quiet period, as the members mostly stayed away in the winter months.

"We are busy coming up to Christmas, have a big New Year's celebration and then there's precious little going on until late February. We have the occasional in-house guest, but those who come here for the golf find other diversions in the winter months. Your greatest problem could well be boredom, but you are welcome to make use of the library, which is quite extensive."

Great food and paid to read! That was Angie's idea of heaven on earth.

"If it is okay with you, I would like to come on the first of December, for that is when I have to vacate this flat."

"Splendid, that fits in with our plans perfectly. You can spend a couple of weeks with Frances learning the ropes and, by the time the busy festive period arrives, you will know enough about your job to take over from her with no problems at all. Now, how do we get you here? What I suggest is that you take the train to Pontonville, which is the closest village, and I will arrange for the club's bus to collect you at the station."

"I won't need that," Angie responded. "I have a car and I can drive there if I am allowed to keep it on the premises." Dan and Angie had discussed whether to sell their car, but thinking it might come in handy, Dan had signed it over to Angie before he left the country. The Ford was still parked on the street where they had left it after their last trip and Angie felt pleased that she still had the use of it, for it would allow her the freedom to travel around on her days off. She wouldn't feel so remote with the knowledge that her car was there whenever she needed to escape, without being dependent on others for transportation.

Surprised, for not too many young women owned cars or even drove them, Leslie Moulton said it would be the perfect solution and, yes, there would certainly be no problem with her keeping the car at the club, as there was a staff parking space at the rear of the building.

"We will see you on the first then. If you have any problems, feel free to phone me at any time."

Angie spent the next few days packing her belongings and cleaning the flat, after which she made a trip out to visit Flo and Frederick Paxton to tell them about the unexpected change in lifestyle that awaited her. She decided to drive out to Croydon, rather than taking public transport, just to make sure that everything was working properly in the car. The faithful old Ford started almost immediately, which was surprising after being stationary for so long, particularly in the weather, which had turned decidedly colder.

Flo welcomed her with a big hug, was a bit doubtful when she heard about Angie's new job, and assured her that if it didn't work out there was always a room waiting for her with them. Angie ended up staying the night and drove back to Paddington the next day full of excitement about what lay ahead.

December first dawned cold and crisp. Angie was up at first light, gathered her bags together, gave the already cleaned kitchen and bathroom a final wipe over and took the linen to the local laundry as the agent had instructed. She brought the car around to the front of the building and packed her belongings in the back, returned and made a final check of the rooms, locked the flat and left the keys in the mailbox as the agent had requested. Then, with a deep sigh, she consulted the road map to make sure she knew where to go, started the car and headed off into what she mentally acknowledged was the unknown.

The route Angie took to Trafalgar was not as picturesque as on her previous trip, for she took the "short" way, which passed through the village of Pontonville. She stopped off briefly in the village, walked around the streets and checked out the local facilities. These were the closest shops to where she would be living and she was curious about what the place had to offer. Not a great deal—it was a typical English village, not much more than a hamlet really, but the necessities such as a village store and post office were there and Angie didn't anticipate needing much more than those two had to offer. For anything further afield she had the car. She called into the local pub and had a ploughman's lunch, as she thought it would be a bit much to turn up at the club and expect to be fed immediately. After a further look around the shops, she returned to the car and continued the rest of her journey.

Eighteen

Narrabeen

Back in Australia, there had been many changes in the two years Angie had been away. One that shook the whole household was the sudden death of Jack, who had passed away quietly without any fuss in much the same way he had carried out his life. Minnie had noticed him one morning sitting on the water's edge, leaning against a post, with his fishing line in the water. It was only when she saw him still there hours later that something in his posture made her suspicious and she went down the garden to check on him. Bob, who was lying by his side, jumped up when she arrived, whimpering as if he sensed something wrong. One look at the old man told Minnie that he was gone and that there was nothing anyone could do for him. She called out to Cliff and Harry, who were home, it being a Sunday, and the two men carried Jack into his cabin and laid him gently on the bed.

Knowing that Jack had no relatives, Minnie happily paid for his funeral, feeling it was the least she could do in thanks for his years of service. There was a surprisingly large turn up at the funeral, for the old man was well liked in the area, and at the small wake afterwards there was many a tale told of services and good turns he had carried out in his years in Narrabeen. To Minnie came the task of sorting out his few belongings and notifying the authorities of his passing. Jack would be missed, but she felt happy that her family had managed to bring some sense of belonging into his lonely life.

She toyed with the idea of renting out the little cottage but dismissed it with the thought that she didn't want strangers traipsing through her yard. Six months later, when Shirley and Matthew announced their engagement, Minnie offered them the cabin rent free, to give them the chance to save for their own home eventually. She made a few additions to the little cabin, notably a shower room, for Jack, used to roughing it all his life, had happily showered in the laundry under the big house. Minnie felt that the newlyweds would much prefer having their own bathing facilities on site, so Cliff installed a hot water service, which would also give them hot water on tap for washing up and cooking.

The businesses were doing really well. The electrical contracting concern had become so popular that the boys had employed two apprentices and they were so busy that it increasingly became impossible for them to give any time to the retail store. Reluctantly, Minnie gave up her job at the haberdashery shop and spent more time involved in the two businesses. Sandra, with two active children to look after, was finding little time for the book work and needed help with that, so Minnie divided her time between helping her daughter and spending time in the shop.

Another big change was underway, for the long-awaited inception of television was about to arrive. The small premises where they had started had long since outgrown its present use, and with no adequate showroom facilities, the rush was on to move to larger premises before the September launch of Sydney's first television station. Public interest in television was huge; for months before the opening, people were enquiring about the price and availability of sets and the partners agreed that a move to somewhere more suited to their proper display was imperative.

Fortunately, there was a new development underway only a few doors from where the shop was located. Minnie approached the developers and was able to persuade them to change their plans around slightly, incorporating two planned shops into one on the promise of signing a three-year lease in advance. Everything happened in a rush. With Shirley's wedding in July and the new building completed three weeks later, it was a very busy few months for all involved.

Minnie had offered to make a dress for Shirley, but her youngest daughter, having inherited some of her mother's practicality, opted to wear Sandra's dress, which fitted her perfectly. It was a trifle too long, but she compensated for this by wearing higher heels. Cliff was to give Shirley away; Andrew was to be a pageboy and Amy a flower girl, so all the local family were involved in one way or the other. Minnie's son John, Annie his wife, and their three-year-old daughter came from Melbourne for the event, so the only missing family member was Angela far away in England.

Nineteen

Trafalgar

Angie's first few months in the new job flew by like the wind. As Thomas Page had predicted, it proved to be unlike any other job she knew of or even imagined. There were many people to get to know, dos and don'ts to learn and a whole new way of life to which she had to adapt. The closest comparison she could make to it would be life on an ocean liner, for Trafalgar was an encapsulated world of its own. One was aware of the world outside and even ventured out into it on occasions, but mainly life was completely absorbed in the place and what went on inside.

She found that there were two distinct strata of staff: the upper (of which it seemed she was one) and the lower, mainly comprised of the kitchen employees and barmen. The former ate in the main dining room and were waited on by the latter, who seemed not to resent this fact, accepting it as "how things should be." Coming from Australia, where to her knowledge no such social barriers existed, Angie found the division a bit hard to understand.

When she felt more comfortable about discussing this with

Leslie Moulton, her boss admitted that at first he, too, had found it strange.

"I've come from a working-class background. If I had continued on doing what my parents did, I would be one of the servers—not the served," he remarked with a smile. "I've the war to thank for my rise in stature. I was fortunate enough to be involved in administration during those years, to rise through the ranks and to meet the right persons in the process. One of those happened to be Colonel Roger Attard, the son of our esteemed President. He took an interest in me and encouraged me to take on further studies when the war ended. We kept in touch and when this position became vacant, he persuaded me to apply for it. To my amazement, I was hired and here I've been for the past six years."

He raised his hands in the air in completion. "So that's how I made the transition from server to servee. A very enjoyable one, I must admit."

Angie found her new boss very easy to work with. He was a pleasant, easygoing man, with a sense of humour and wide-ranging interests. As she had been told at the initial interview, Angie's secretarial duties were few. Her duties were varied and she found that Moulton gave her the latitude to take on anything that she perceived needed doing.

When large functions were held at the Club, and on Sundays when the main activity was the elaborate luncheon she had enjoyed on the day of her interview, Angie was expected to greet the members, preferably by name—and fortunately, her good memory allowed her to quickly learn those of the frequent visitors. Something as demeaning as money changing hands was frowned on by the board, so a system of chits was in force and another duty, which terrified her at first, was for Angie to approach each party once they were seated at table, work out who was the host, enquire how many members (one price) and how many guests (slightly more) and have the host sign the chit she had prepared. It was here that she discovered a marked difference between the attitude of what she could only think of as the "Landed Gentry" and those members who were mainly leading businessmen.

The former were almost without exception pleasant and gracious to her, the latter often less so, sometimes to the extent of rudeness.

When she remarked on this fact, Leslie Moulton smiled wryly. "There you have another example of the class system. All the 'Landed Gentry,' as you call them, have been used since childhood to dealing with staff. They have been taught to treat their 'lessers' with politeness and respect; the others are those who have only been allowed membership since the war, when economics forced the older members to allow them entry. They are mostly nouveau riche and money is their only god; they look with contempt on those aforesaid lessers and treat them accordingly. There are, of course, exceptions to this rule—your friend Thomas Page being one of them—but remember he has upper-class connections too, which does make a difference."

Angie smiled to herself at the description of Thomas Page as her friend. Hardly, she thought, but understood the analogy and developed a personal game of picking out the wheat from the chaff among the members, based on Moulton's description. Only rarely was her guess incorrect.

Gradually, she came to know everyone on the staff, liking most of them, with two main exceptions. One was Tom, the head barman, who was obsequious to the members and unpleasant, verging on rudeness to Angie for reasons she found hard to fathom. Did he resent having to wait on her at table, she wondered? Surely he must understand that it was not of her choosing. The other, who had more direct impact upon her, was the lady who kept the accounts. Emily Warburton was a widow, fiftyish, a woman of set habits and exaggerated bigotry. She looked down on people of colour, the "wrong" religions (i.e. anyone other than C of E) and colonials—which naturally included Angie—and did everything in her power to make the girl feel inferior. Through some sort of synthesis, Mrs Warburton was great friends with Tom the barman, fluttering her eyelashes girlishly at him when he came to the table, and he in turn, treating her with the same, in Angie's opinion, false obsequiousness he lavished on the members. Angie could avoid Tom most of the time; Emily Warburton unfortunately resided in the office next door to hers, so she was a more constant thorn in Angie's side. As Mrs Warburton only worked three days a week, living in for those and going home to London on the other four, mealtimes and evenings on her absent days were a lot more relaxed and friendly than when Angie's nemesis was present.

Her special friend proved to be the person she initially dreaded working with, for Francis Chalmers was a tall, stooped, elderly gentleman and hardly at first sight the ideal working companion for a young woman. Chalmers dressed impeccably in dark suits and appeared to have no particular duties. He had been with the club since its inception and the members referred to him as Head Steward, but he carried out no waiting duties, spending his time in greeting them all by name, taking coats from the ladies and running any little messages for those who were in residence. He also spent time in the office with Angie, assisting her in the sorting of the chits that had been signed by the members, for he recognised every signature and was an invaluable help when Angie found it impossible to recognise the name from a scrawled signature. Chalmers ("call me Frank") was a gentle, good natured, amusing man, a mine of information about all the members, and a source of many funny anecdotes about them. Angie found him a joy to work with and a buffer against the occasional nastiness that emanated from the room next door.

"Don't pay any attention to her; she doesn't deserve your tears," he whispered to Angie on an occasion when she was visibly upset by something Mrs Warburton had said. On a quiet day, when there was nobody there but the two of them, he filled Angie in on Emily Warburton's background. She had no children, had lost her husband in the war and spent her time away from the club looking after her deaf, bedridden mother. Not, Angie thought, a happy life and maybe the woman had reason for bitterness, but surely there was no reason to take this bitterness out on her, or the waiting staff, who also were frequently the recipients of her sharp tongue.

Angie's relations with the other staff were good. She often had need to visit the kitchen and took the time to get to know the people who worked there. The two chefs, who alternated shifts, were as dissimilar as chalk and cheese. Bill, the head chef, was a thin wiry man with a pronounced cockney accent, while the second chef, Con, whose real name was Cornellus, was a tall, slightly overweight Dutchman, his rosy cheeks and roly-poly body making him look much more the quintessential chef than his skinny superior. Angie was really interested in what went on in the kitchen, often asking the chefs questions about what was being prepared and, sensing her genuine interest, the men were usually happy to explain and demonstrate their techniques.

The kitchen and house staff, like the barmen, were all residents of the local village. They were collected from their homes in the mornings and returned home after their shift in the small bus that the club kept for this purpose, as well as for picking up supplies. As Angie gradually got to know each of them and heard stories of their lives, she came to feel as if she were a part of one big family. There was always something going on at the club, so she never had the time to be lonely, or to be homesick.

Part of the fun of the job was that she never knew who would turn up on the doorstep. Although to her knowledge there were no celebrities among the membership, Trafalgar was a place where visiting performers and dignitaries were brought by the members to relax in peace and quiet away from the eye of the public and increasingly inquisitive news media. In one week alone, Angie met the glamour couple Vivien Leigh and Laurence Olivier and the visiting American actress Bette Davis. To see these movie idols of hers in the flesh was something she would never have expected in her wildest dreams.

Most of all, she enjoyed meeting and watching the visiting aristocracy. Here, at last, was the England she had read and dreamed about. She loved the way they spoke and looked and actually one day met the woman who had first inspired her wish to visit England. It had been the novels of Nancy Mitford, the oldest of the fabled Mitford sisters, who had years earlier captured her fancy. When she heard that the author, on one of her infrequent visits from her home in Paris, was to visit the club, Angie was beside herself with excitement. She was not disappointed, for that lady, who had epitomised and dictated everything the upper-class English could aspire to in the years between the wars, was still beautiful and elegant in her fifties. She graciously agreed to sign Angie's well-read copies of her books. What more, Angie wrote home to her mother in Australia, could I ever hope to have in this life or the next?

At first she missed Dan terribly, but very quickly, as she became involved in the day to day business of the club, she found it hard at times even to recall what he looked like. Initially she wrote to him twice weekly; he on the other hand, was a sporadic correspondent and, after a couple of months, Angie found herself only writing to Dan after she received a letter from him. Finally, after more than a month of silence, she received one saying that he thought they should put their relationship "on hold" for the time being, that he had started dating one of his fellow students, as it was too lonely waiting for her to decide when to come home.

As this apparently meant an end to their somewhat indefinite engagement, Angie at first felt rather slighted, then on reflection realised that she was nowhere near as devastated as she would have been six months earlier. Her feelings for Dan, as previously those for Harry, seemed to her those of another, younger person. Her life was different and she felt years older than the girl who had come to Trafalgar just six months ago. And she was developing other interests.

Part of the reason Angie was so happy in the job had to do with an increasing attraction to her boss, Leslie Moulton. Spending so much time in close proximity to an attractive man can either spell disenchantment or passion, and it was the latter that started to overtake Angie's life. He showed no sign that the feeling was mutual, but she felt a glimmer of hope because he chose to ignore the difference of more than a decade in their ages, treating her as the adult she felt she was, spending many hours with her in the evening discussing books and the world in general, so that Angie felt he at least found her company enjoyable.

She had plenty of opportunities to witness his behaviour towards the wives of the club members and, recalling Margery Page's description of him as a lady's man, she kept an eye out for any signs of friendships other than those his job required. Most of what she saw seemed to be innocuous flirting, but one possible exception was a woman who spent a lot of time in the club, often without her husband, their closest neighbour Lord Hungerford, who had a large home on the far side of Pontonville village, which had in times past been part of his Estate. Hungerford was away most of the week, attending to his interests in the city, so his wife Cynthia was very much a free agent. She spent a lot of time at the club, lunching there and expecting Leslie Moulton to join her and spend time in her company. Angie doubted there was any romantic interest—the woman was in her late forties at least (which seemed very old to a twenty-year-old) for she had a daughter a few years older than Angie.

Cynthia Hungerford was indeed a handsome woman and had obviously been a great beauty in her younger days; however Rebecca, the daughter, was a carbon copy of her father, with large teeth and that horsey look many of the English aristocracy seemed to have. The resemblance to a horse was enhanced by a loud, whinnying laugh and as she treated Angie with condescension, obviously thinking of her as an inferior, she was not a young woman that Angie felt she could warm to under any circumstances. Lady Cynthia, on the other hand, was pleasant enough, if rather vague, a trait that seemed fairly common among the ladies of Angie's Landed Gentry.

As these two were the most frequent female visitors to the club, Angie felt she had little competition there. Not that her boss showed any signs whatsoever of being interested in her beyond the confines of work and a pleasant friendly attitude in their leisure hours. Very much like her past unrequited love for Harry, Angie came to accept that her feelings were not returned and did her best to disguise the fact that she felt a strong attraction to the man.

The possibility that he may feel some attraction in return first became evident one day when the two of them collided accidentally, rounding a corner from opposite directions in a corridor. Was it her imagination, or did he keep hold of her rather longer than the circumstances necessitated? He bent his head down towards her and then shook his head, stepping back and apologised, before asking had he hurt her. Flustered, Angie could do little more than shake her head.

They each continued on their way, with Angie wondering to herself, Did I just imagine it—or did he seem to like holding me? There seemed no answer to that question and when next they met, each acted as if the episode (if there had been one) had never happened.

One summer night, when Angie had been at the club for eight months, the whole thing came to a head. There was a laundry room on the premises, run by Mrs Toddy, a formidable lady, who worked there two days a week. A large function was planned in the dining room the next day; Mrs Toddy was home confined to bed with the flu, and one of the maids discovered rather late in the day that they were short of clean tablecloths for tomorrow's luncheon. Rather than keep one of the girls back to launder and iron them, Leslie Moulton said he would wash them himself and asked Angie if she would mind giving him a hand with the job once they had eaten their supper. Angie readily agreed and together they piled the cloths into the large washer/dryer. Leslie was familiar with the operation of the machine, as it had been installed at his suggestion, a cheaper alternative in the long run to sending the linen out to the only laundry in the district, many miles away.

It was hot in the room; there was no seating and, having spent most of the day on the run, Angie mentioned that her feet were sore. "Take off your shoes," Leslie said. He pulled down some clean towels from the shelf, and strewed them across the floor. "The machine will take a while yet. Make yourself comfortable and rest while you're waiting; I only need your help with the ironing." He set up the rotary ironer, which would be the next step in the process once the cloths were nearly dry, and wiped his brow saying, "Whew—it's hot in here. I could do with a cool drink. I'll get one for both of us." This said as he left the room. He returned a few minutes later with a large bottle of lemonade and two glasses, set them on a little stool, then looking down at Angie, said, "You look so comfy there. Mind if I join you?"

He poured the lemonade, saying, "Hardly champagne, but more suitable in the circumstances, don't you think?"

Angie agreed, took a grateful sip from the glass he handed her, smiled and reached out her glass to touch his in salute. Her heart was pounding, for this was the closest she had ever been to him, and instinctively she knew for certain that he felt the same way towards her. He smiled, set his glass back on the stool and took Angie's glass from her hand, setting it next to his. He reached across, cupped her face in his hands and ever so gently kissed her. "I've wanted to do that for ages," he said, releasing her face and moving his hands down to her shoulders.

"I've wanted you to do it—for ages," Angie smiled and said.

He pulled her close so that they were lying body to body and kissed her again. This time Angie was left in no doubt that he was as attracted to her as she was to him. Then, both realising that they could be interrupted at any moment, they pulled apart, straightened their clothes and turned their attention to the job at hand.

The tablecloths were soon dry enough to iron, so they removed them from the machine, then gathered up the towels from the floor and put them in the machine to wash.

As they went about the job of feeding the tablecloths into the rotary ironer, neither made any mention of what had happened earlier. It was only when the job was complete, the towels were washed, dried and folded away that Leslie took her in his arms again.

"Come to my room later," he said. "I've had a taste of you; I really want some more. That's if you do—I hope you want me as much as I want you?"

Angie reached up and ran her fingers through his hair, thinking to herself that it was almost like living in a fantasy, for this was what she had dreamed about for many months.

"I'll come. I want more of you as well."

Together they went down to the TV room, where Chalmers had fallen asleep in front of the set. Leslie turned off the set, roused the old man and gently told him it was time he went to bed. When they were alone again, Leslie said to Angie, "Give him half an hour to get settled, then come to my room; the door will be unlocked and you needn't knock. I'll be waiting for you. It wouldn't really matter much if Frank knew about us; he would never breathe a word to a soul, but just the same, it's best we keep it to ourselves."

When all was quiet in the building, Angie made her way from her room in the old servants' quarters to Leslie's, which was situated adjacent to the visitor's bedrooms. She turned the handle on the door and entered the room to see Leslie wearing a dressing gown standing at the window, looking out on the grounds, which were illuminated with light by the full moon. He turned to her and held out his arms and his kiss this time was even more insistent than the previous one, as he lifted her as if she weighed nothing and laid her on the bed. Hardly able to believe what was happening, Angie gave herself up to the embraces of this man, so much more skilled in the ways of love than Dan had been. She stayed with him until dawn was starting to break, then hastily made her way back to her room, climbed into her narrow bed and lay there thinking of all that had happened that amazing night. Her whole world had changed with the knowledge that Leslie felt the same as she did. She would have wished to shout it to the rooftops, but he had explained to her that it must remain their secret for the time being.

This night set the scene for what was to follow for many months to come. Leslie explained to her that any suggestion of their relationship would mean the end of both their jobs; therefore, they had to practise extreme caution so that nobody suspected a thing. They kept their night-time meetings to occasions when, as on the first evening, there was nobody else in residence other than Frank, who, even if he suspected anything, would never give their secret away.

Over the months, as she lay in Leslie's arms, Angie found out more about this man whom she loved so deeply. His ambition was eventually to have his own country hotel. "I am in a position to save almost every penny I make while I'm in this job. Another year or so, and I will have enough put away to leave and do it." They talked at length about a life away from the club, where they would no longer have to keep their love a secret. No more sneaking around when nobody could see; they would be husband and wife, answerable to nobody—and it was the promise of this that kept Angie going, when sometimes she wished she need not be forever on guard, that she could accidentally give away to the world how she felt about this man.

It was doubly hard to suppress her jealousy when she witnessed Leslie flirting with the various ladies of the club. Although he assured her they meant nothing to him, she found it increasingly hurtful when he was asked to their homes for dinner parties and occasionally was called upon to squire one or another to social events.

Cynthia Hungerford, because she lived so close, was the most frequent of these ladies, but Leslie assured Angie that the woman was a frightful bore. "She talks of nothing other than clothes and the people she's meeting—or worse still, I have to listen to the goings-on of that awful daughter of hers. It's hard to tell the difference between Rebecca and the horses she's forever riding. Trust me, neither of those ladies spell any threat to our relationship. I only pander to them because they and the old Lord can be so helpful with contacts for our future."

On the lonely nights when he was off on these social occasions, often staying away overnight, Angie shed many a quiet tear over her situation. She was not happy about being a guilty secret, for that was what she felt she was. More and more she wondered why their relationship could not be brought out in the open. Surely they could still do their respective jobs as husband and wife—but every time she suggested this to Leslie he vetoed it. "I'm sure the board would not agree," he said in a tone of finality.

In spite of all this, she still enjoyed the job and loved the countryside. Since childhood she had always been an early riser, so before breakfast she would often don her walking shoes and explore the course and its surrounds. The stands of forest on the perimeter were so very different from the land where she had grown up, so much greener, with a stillness she had never encountered in the Australian bush. To come upon a fresh clump of mushrooms (or were they toadstools, Angie was never sure), lightly coated with the morning dew, was like something out of a storybook.

From home came news of Shirley's wedding and the huge boom in business, now that television was up and running in Australia. Harry had moved out into a flat of his own and he and his girlfriend had announced their engagement. Sandra's son Andrew was in his last year of junior school—when to Angie he had seemed not much more than a baby when she left home. It was amazing, the changes that nearly four years had brought about. She still wrote regularly to her mother, telling of the activities in the club, but never breathing a word about her relationship with Leslie Moulton. For some reason she could not define, she felt that Minnie would not approve of her clandestine activities. She tried to justify it all to herself, for after all they were both free agents, but by instinct she knew that her mother would be less than happy to hear about how she was behaving.

She and Leslie did manage to steal a couple of days together away from the club. Angie was ostensibly going on two week's holiday to France, but in reality only stayed away for one. They worked out an arrangement whereby she would call the club, pretending to be a relative of Leslie's, with the news that there had been a family emergency. When she called, the phone was answered by Frank Chalmers; her heart pounding, Angie lowered her voice an octave and put on her best BBC voice. If Frank suspected anything he gave no indication, and soon she heard Leslie's voice at the end of the phone. He made the correct replies, in case anyone was listening, and said that he would leave as soon as possible.

Their pre-arranged meeting was at a railway station sufficiently far from the club that there was no possibility of being seen by anyone they knew. Angie left her car there and they continued in his to a small hotel where she and Dan had stayed on their trip across England. Miles away from anywhere, they felt sufficiently safe to walk the streets of the nearby village and go for long treks over the moors. Angie had felt a bit worried that the people in the hotel would remember her, but she had changed quite a lot, her hair was longer and back to its natural colour—and she was with a different "husband," so the chance of being recognised was almost zero. For this stay, she brought out the ring that Dan had given her, wondering what his reaction would be if he knew.

After their two blissful days of freedom, Leslie drove Angie back to pick up her car; he returned to the club and she drove on into London to spend the rest of her holiday visiting Flo and Fredrick.

Having heard nothing from him in more than a year, Angie was surprised to receive a letter from Dan Forsyth. He wrote as if nothing had happened, and with no explanation of why he had broken the silence but did mention that his relationship with a fellow student was over. When was she returning to Australia? he asked. Angie smiled to herself, thinking that surely he didn't expect to take up where they'd left off, when he had all but dumped her. Dan and all the people in Australia seemed like another world to Angie, who felt convinced that nothing on this earth would make her want to return for anything other than a holiday visit. Her life was in England now, her future with Leslie. She still missed much about the lifestyle back home, but her plans were for a completely different life from that she had left behind.

For another year, Angie's life went on in much the same way. She felt reasonably sure that nobody on the staff suspected her relationship with Leslie was on more than a friendly employer/employee basis, for each had gone out of their way in public to avoid any show of affection. The possible exception was her friend Frank Chalmers—who had asked her on several occasions if everything was all right—making her think he probably was aware of the relationship. Hiding her feelings and constantly watching what she said and did was becoming more and more of a strain, and Angie wondered just how much longer things could go on the way they were. When the change came, it was at a time and in a way she least expected.

When she answered a knock on her bedroom door one morning quite early, Angie expected it to be one of the housemaids wanting to ask her a question, as they often did. To her surprise, she found Frank Chalmers standing in the doorway and one look at his face told her that this visit was not a frivolous one.

"Frank, whatever is wrong?" She took his arm and ushered him into her room, swept some papers from a chair and sat him down, for the old gentleman's face was ashen pale. Wordlessly, he handed her the local newspaper. "Read this," he eventually said.

Angie took the proffered sheet and sank on the bed, expecting to read some dreadful report of an accident. To her surprise, it was opened at the social pages, and at first she shot him a puzzled look, then gasped in shock, as she read the headlines.

Engagement announced of local club manager to daughter of Lord Hungerford.

At a private function last evening, it was announced that the Hon Rebecca Hungerford is to wed Mr Leslie Moulton, the Secretary/Manager of the Trafalgar Club. The Hon Rebecca is well known in equestrian circles, while her fiancé engaged in an army career before joining the exclusive club some years ago. The young couple will reside at Hungerford Hall and in London, where Mr Moulton will be pursuing business interests, etc. etc.

Frank rose from his seat and headed for the door. "I'm so sorry," he said, "I thought you needed to read it and have some time before you came downstairs."

At the door he paused. "You don't deserve this, you really don't," he said, his eyes glistening with tears. He left and gently closed the door behind him.

Angie sat frozen for several moments, the paper held limply in her hand. At first, she thought that maybe it was some awful hoax. She checked the date; it wasn't April first and deep inside the realisation came that it was all too true, along with what this meant to her and her dreams. She went to the window and looked out, expecting everything to look different, but nothing had changed. The rolling greens were still there, a squirrel was hunting for nuts around the big pine tree and the sun was coming up over the hill, exactly the same as it had yesterday. For the world, nothing had altered, for her it had come to a sudden end.

Finally the numbness turned to anger; she flung the newspaper across the room, hastily donned some clothes and set off down the hallway, first retrieving the offending paper from the floor. With it in hand, she headed for Leslie's room in the other wing of the house among the guestrooms. It occurred to her as she approached the door that she had never been there in daylight; all her visits had been clandestine, hidden away at night, as had her relationship with the man who she now realised had been playing her for a fool.

She opened his door without knocking, surprising him standing half-dressed in the middle of the room. "What in heaven's name…" he started to say, then, seeing the paper in Angie's hand, mumbled, "Oh… you know."

Angie threw the newspaper at him. "Yes, I know, don't I? What a lovely, cowardly way it was for me to find out. You didn't even have the guts to tell me what you were up to, did you?"

"I didn't want to hurt you," he said, making Angie take a deep breath at the stupidity of this remark. He tried to take her by the shoulders, but she shrugged him away. "Angie, this is an opportunity in a million. Lord Hungerford is giving me directorship of one of his companies, something I have always wanted. How could I refuse an offer like that?"

"So, he's buying you as husband for his horse-faced daughter. I suspected there was something going on behind the scenes there, but all along I thought it could be Lady Cynthia—I never for one moment thought you would sell yourself for someone you've always professed to dislike. And all the time you were making love to me, you were…"

"I've never touched her—what do you think I am?"

"You've never touched her! Spell it out—don't you mean never fucked her—you certainly are going to have to in the future. I'm sure they expect you to be more than a puppet husband. You're going to have to fuck her again and again, or I'm sure she'll complain to Daddy if you don't." Even as she spoke, Angie was surprised at the words coming out of her mouth, words she would never have used in a million years, but right then they seemed the fitting ones, as she poured out her anger and disillusionment at the man who stood before her, a look of bemusement on his face.

"So what happened to our fantastic future together? What about our wonderful country pub? When did you suddenly decide to be a King of Industry?"

He shrugged. "When they made me the offer, I suppose. All the other was a pipe dream; this is reality. By marrying Rebecca I instantly acquire prestige and riches I would never have made in a pub in a million years."

He took her by the shoulders and this time she made no move to shake him off, just stood there listening numbly to the words coming out of his mouth. He reached down and tilted her head up to his, then uttered the words that hit her like a slap in the face.

"Angie, this needn't be the end for us. You can move back to London and find a flat. I'll be in the city most of the time; Rebecca will stay here with her horses during the week. You and I can go on the way we always have."

Angie flung away from him so violently that he was nearly thrown off balance. She went to slap his face, then pulled her hand back and said slowly, her fury evident in each word, "So, on top of betraying me in every possible way—you now want me to be your whore. Or is that what I've been all along? Your little bit on the side, the dumb little love-struck idiot, who you sweet talked into keeping our little secret. I've half a mind to go straight to Lady Cynthia—or your beloved fiancée—and tell them what you've been up to the past few years."

To her surprise, he smiled at this remark; then she realised why.

"Cynthia knows, doesn't she?" He nodded. "What about Rebecca?" He shook his head.

She sank down on his bed and put her head in her hands, then looked up at him, hating him with a strength she didn't know she possessed. "That poor girl... I wonder does she have an inkling of what she's getting into? I've half a mind to tell her what you just offered me, but I haven't the heart. I don't much like her, but she's never done anything to me. I think I'll just have to let her find out for herself just what sort of a bastard you are."

She stood and looked him up and down. "Oh boy, I certainly hope you get what you deserve—everything! Goodbye Leslie, I can't say it has been nice knowing you."

Calmer than she could have imagined possible, she walked back to her room and unaccountably stripped the unmade bed, throwing the sheets and blankets in a heap on the floor. She then opened the door and made her way to Frank's room, where she felt almost certain she would find him. She was correct, for he opened the door the moment she knocked; he had been waiting for her. She walked over to the old man and hugged him. "Thank you for being so kind. Thank you for everything."

"Are you all right?" he asked.

Angie grinned hopelessly, her eyes full of tears. "I suppose I am...now. I really have no alternative." She took his hands in hers. "Frank, I need some help. I'm leaving, as soon as I can get my things together. Will you give me half an hour and then come to my room? I'll need some help carrying everything down to the car. And I don't want anyone else to know I'm going. I'm sure he will make up some sort of story about my sudden departure—and to be honest, I don't much care what he says. My car is parked near the cellar entrance; I'll leave that way. Will you help me please?"

He hugged her and gently kissed the top of her head. "Of course. Anything I can do to help. That mongrel! If I were a younger man I'd..." She cut him off. "He isn't worth it, Frank. I realise that now. I've been a silly little fool and you are a wonderful friend. Now, I must get going." She looked at her watch. "Half an hour, knock on my door and I'll be ready to go."

She went to the box room and found her suitcases, took them to her room and threw her clothes into them, making little effort to fold anything. All she wanted was to be far away from the place as quickly as possible. She picked up the bedclothes from the floor, took the sheets down to the laundry and folded the blankets neatly at the foot of the bed. When she was sure that no trace of her remained, she sat on the bed and waited for Frank.

Together they carried the bags down the back stairs, to Angie's relief meeting nobody on the way. She didn't feel strong enough to have to make explanations. When everything was stowed away in the back seat, she shut the door, turned and hugged her friend and helper.

"Thank you again, Frank, for everything. You are the only thing I will miss about this place. I now realise that everything else has been a childish fantasy. I suppose it was high time I grew up—but I certainly didn't expect it to be this way."

He opened the driver's side door for her and closed it gently when she was seated. "Will you write to me and tell me how you are?" he asked.

"Forever. Will you write back?"

"Forever." He bent down and kissed her on the cheek. "Take care, little one, and try to remember that all men are not the same."

So choked up with tears that she couldn't speak, Angie squeezed his hand, attempted a smile and turned on the engine. As she pulled away, she waved to her friend, then drove nonstop until she was outside the gates of Trafalgar. There she stopped momentarily and looked back at the place that had been her home for two years. Thinking she never would have dreamed that she would leave this way, she shrugged, turned her eyes away and drove blindly towards the village.

Twenty

Aftermath

London seemed the obvious place to go, so Angie headed the car in that direction. Unfortunately, the road led past the grounds of Hungerford Hall, a further reminder of her humiliation. How she would have loved to drive up to the door and speak her mind to Lady Cynthia, but Angie knew it would be a waste of words and had no doubts about who would come off worse in any confrontation. In the distance she could see a figure on horseback. I wonder if it's the bride-to-be, she thought.

"Poor bloody girl," she muttered aloud and drove on.

As she drew closer to the city, Angie had to make a decision about where to stay. She knew she would only have to make a phone call to the Paxtons to be made welcome there, but she felt too shattered to make explanations, or even to talk to anyone, no matter how understanding and kind they may be. She stopped off around eleven at a country pub and ordered some food, for as ever, her appetite was unaffected by her state of mind. As she ate, Angie tried to consider where she could stay at least for that night, then remembered a guesthouse near Victoria Station—one of the clients she had dealt with in her previous job.

Having never actually met the proprietor in person, she felt it would be a place she could stay, more or less anonymously, with no need to have to make any explanations. All she wanted was to be undisturbed, in a room where she could think over what to do with the rest of her life, or to be more precise, her immediate future, for right then she had absolutely no idea of what to do next.

She headed for the nearest post office and asked to see a London directory, wrote down the phone number and, armed with lots of pennies, entered the red telephone booth outside the shop. Yes, the Victoria Guesthouse had a single room available and the cheery woman at the other end of the line said she would look forward to seeing Miss Sherwood early that afternoon. With food in her stomach and somewhere definite to go, Angie felt a lot better, as she climbed back into the Ford and continued her journey towards the city.

Her room in the guesthouse was very sparse, reasonably clean and no more or less than Angie had expected it to be. Her room at Trafalgar had been not much different from this, situated as it had been in the old servants' quarters. This room would serve her purpose for as long as she needed it. All she wanted was a quiet bolt hole to recover from her shock and to reflect on what might lie ahead. Feeling suddenly tired, although it was still early afternoon, she stripped off her outer clothes, climbed under the coverlet and dozed for an hour or two. It was still light when she woke, groggy and initially wondering where she was—then the day's happenings came back in a rush. Immediately wide awake, Angie for the first time gave way to tears. She had been too angry to cry when confronting Leslie, too busy and preoccupied when packing or driving to London, but now, alone in a strange room, she sobbed her heart out as she thought of how all her dreams and plans had been so cruelly shattered. For the first time in her life, she realised how much things can change in the course of less than twenty-four hours. Yesterday she had a job, a lover and a future. Now the first two were gone and the third was very much up in the air.

For a while she thought of various means of recrimination against the man who had played her for a fool, then gradually realised that any move on her part would only make the situation worse for her. Without a doubt, Leslie would deny any accusations, saying she was just a silly, love-struck young girl. She knew that Frank could not be expected to uphold her claims—he had no home or job other than at Trafalgar and was an old man. She, at least, had youth on her side and felt that even without references she could talk herself into some sort of work fairly quickly. Even if she could make a claim, or take revenge by contacting Rebecca Hungerford and telling her what sort of louse she was about to marry, it meant reinforcing the feeling of worthlessness the morning's events had given her. With the newfound strength that had enabled her to act so far, she knew that the only way to go was forward. What had happened had happened and she had a life to live.

Her first move must be to let her family know she had left Trafalgar, plus write a short note to Frank at the club, as fortunately it was he who opened all the mail and would be able to forward any that came for her in the meantime. She dug a writing pad and pen out of her bag and dashed off a quick note to both of them, promising to write at greater length later when she had a definite address, but asking each to address mail to Flo's house for the time being. She dressed and went downstairs to beg some stamps from the landlady, then made a quick trip out to post the letters before nightfall.

For two days Angie stayed at the guesthouse, then as the shock gradually wore off and she was able to think more clearly, she started to crave human company. She called Flo Paxton from the phone box at the corner. "Can I come and stay for a while?" Flo asked no questions, just said, "Of course," so Angie repacked her bag, paid her bill and headed towards Croydon. Back in her old familiar room, unchanged since she had first slept there nearly four years ago, Angie found it hard even to think of all that had happened in the meantime. To Flo, she simply said that she had left Trafalgar because of personal problems and that lady wisely pressed no further for details. Angie had a roof over her head, but of what to do next she had absolutely no idea.

Realising that now she was back in London, the car was a luxury she no longer need keep, Angie drove it to the car yard where she and Dan had bought it in what seemed like another life. Pocketing the few pounds the dealer was prepared to pay, she caught the train back to Croydon. Her financial situation was far from bad; expenses had been negligible whilst she was at Trafalgar and almost every penny she earned for the past year or so had been banked towards her future with Leslie. Angie had enough funds to live without working for many months, so money was not really a problem. Her problem was just what those months ahead would bring.

Having walked out on her last job, she had little hope of finding another secretarial post, for her only English reference was from Thomas Page and lord only knew what story he had been fed. It looked increasingly as if she would have to take on waitressing or something similar, where a lack of experience could be easily overcome. Every few days she went into the city but found that the magic it had held for her when she first came to Britain was somehow missing. All she could see were crowded, dirty streets, and people clad in dark colours, which increasingly made her think of home. Home, where bright colours were everywhere, where the sun shone and even the rain seemed welcome, unlike the constant drizzle that seemed to envelop everything in London. Australia—Sydney—Narrabeen. Her family. Should she go there, where she could put the past years and her eventual humiliation behind her?

Was it admitting defeat, or was it the obvious next move to make? Angie wasn't sure, but one day when she woke to yet another grey morning, she made up her mind. She had seen all she wanted of England for now. Maybe someday in the future when the memories didn't hurt so much, she would return and possibly the magic would be there for her again. Right now, all she wanted was to get away and to see her mother and all the family. She decided the time had come to ring home.

It being summer, with Double Daylight Saving time in force, Angie knew that the time difference between London and Sydney was only eight hours, so if she phoned around 10 am, she could feel reasonably sure that her mother would be home, even if she had been working that day. She grabbed her dressing gown from the hook on the back of the door and went downstairs to find Flo in the kitchen, cooking Frederick's breakfast.

"Do you mind if I make a long-distance call to Australia?" she asked. "I'll ring afterwards and find out the cost. It's so much easier doing it from here than from the post office."

"Of course, darling," said Flo. "Hope you know how to do it; I've never made a long-distance call to anywhere."

Having handled overseas calls on several occasions at Trafalgar, Angie was familiar with the procedure. She knew it was necessary to book the call in advance, so, thanking Flo, she rang the exchange and booked her call for ten o'clock. The next two hours dragged past, as Angie deliberated whether she was doing the right thing. She had almost talked herself out of it when the phone rang and she picked up the receiver to hear the tinny voice of the operator. "You have a person-to-person call to Mrs Minnie Sherwood in Sydney, Australia. Mrs Sherwood is on the line, please go ahead."

No going back now...Angie could hear her mother's voice on the line, saying, "Hello, hello. Is that you Angie—is everything all right?"

The connection was dreadful; it sounded as if her mother's voice came from a tunnel, but it was still unmistakeably Minnie on the other end of the line. Fighting back tears, Angie choked out, "Yes, Mumma, it's me. Everything is okay; I'm fine. I'm calling to say I've decided to come home. That's if you want me?"

"Oh darling...as if you had to ask! Of course, we want you. You don't sound all right, are you sure? You're not sick or anything, are you?"

Angie laughed. "No...I'm not sick...or anything. A bit down at the moment, but nothing that seeing all of you won't fix."

"So, when are you coming? Have you booked yet?"

"No idea; I only decided this morning. I'll write or send you a cable as soon as I know for certain the dates. It's so good to hear your voice. How is everyone at home?"

"We're all great. The shop is doing booming business. We're selling TVs as fast as we can get them through the door. Everyone's well and Johnny and Annie are bringing the kids up to stay for a week—we're so excited about that. Andy is doing really well at school; Shirley and Matthew are doing really well in Jack's old place. Bob is missing his old mate and will be pleased to see you. Oh—and by the way, Harry…" The operator cut in at this stage. "Your three minutes are nearly up, do you wish to extend?"

Minnie quickly spoke up, "No darling, don't extend—this must be costing you a fortune. Write soon, we love you!"

"I love you too, Mumma," Angie said, as the line went dead and tears streamed down her cheeks. She replaced the phone on its cradle, thinking, Well I've done it now. She hoped it was the right thing, for there was no going back on the decision, or Minnie would think the worst. Angie was all too aware of what "or anything" meant and if she didn't turn up in Australia, obviously not pregnant, her mother would probably go into panic mode. Little did she know that the mother she had always thought of as old fashioned was well able to cope with daughters, pregnant or otherwise. It would be many years before Angie appreciated just how capable her mother was and how much she had accomplished over the years since she was a simple housewife in Leichhardt.

She waited half an hour, then rang the exchange for the cost of the call, winced at how much—it really did cost a fortune to ring overseas. Next move must be a trip to the bank for the money to give Auntie Flo, who she knew would try to refuse it. Knowing the Paxtons' financial situation, Angie had no intention of leaving without paying for the call and would leave the money behind when she left, if Flo refused to take it.

Now that she had made her decision, Angie felt a lot more settled and was able to look back on what had happened without her anger towards Leslie clouding the situation. She regretted the fact that she had not said her goodbyes to the people in the kitchen. They had always been friendly and pleasant towards her and she would have liked to have had the opportunity to wish them all well for the future. She knew, however, that there was no possible way she could have stayed at Trafalgar for another minute. To have to spend any time in the company of the man who had treated her so badly would have been more than she could bear. The way she had left was the only possible one.

She did, however, feel rather bad about Thomas Page, the man who had been responsible for her working at Trafalgar in the first place. He had always treated her fairly and she felt that she had let him down in a way. Finally, she decided to write to him and, after several discarded attempts, sent off a letter:

Dear Mr Page,

I imagine that by now you have heard of my sudden departure from Trafalgar. I left for personal reasons, which I am not prepared to disclose, but feel that I should write to you and thank you for your help in the past and to apologise for any trouble my sudden departure may have caused.

It is not in my nature to walk out on a job in this way, but I assure you that I was put in a position where I had no other alternative. I have decided to return to Australia, but I leave with fond memories of my time working at the agency with Charlie. Of my years at Trafalgar I have mixed emotions—but once again, I am not prepared to go into any details of my reason for departure.

To you and your wife I wish all the very best and hope that you will accept my explanation that I had no choice other than the one I took.

Yours faithfully,
Angela Sherwood

He could make of it whatever he wished, but Angie had an inkling he may well easily read between the lines, in view of the comments his wife had made to her on her first visit to Trafalgar. She felt a lot better once she had sent the letter off, and also wrote one to Frank Chalmers, telling him that she was coping well and of her decision to return to Australia. She asked him to pass her regards on to all the staff (he would know which ones she meant) and gave him her address in Australia, asking him to write to her there, telling her of what had happened at Trafalgar after her departure.

Even though it had only been a few days since she'd left there, Trafalgar seemed like something experienced in a dream, which in a way it actually had been. She knew it would be a long time, if ever, before she could think of Leslie without an overpowering sense of betrayal. She would never understand how the man could have played fast and loose with her and dump her in such a cold-hearted way.

Although at first she had wanted to go straight to Australia as soon as possible, once she felt a bit less stressed, Angie decided to go home via America. She'd always wanted to see New York and, although it was on the other side of that continent, she decided also to visit Disneyland, the theme park that had opened a year earlier to huge publicity worldwide. Her mind was made up, when on a visit to a travel agency looking for ideas, she noticed a poster on the wall from Greyhound buses offering "A dollar a day in the USA." She quickly converted that sum to pounds and realised how cheap it was. The thought of travelling across America on the famous Greyhound appealed to Angie's imagination. She asked for brochures, bought a map of the United States and sat down to plan her journey.

She would cross the Atlantic by ship, spend a couple of days in New York and then two weeks travelling from New York to California and (hang the cost!) fly home to Australia from there.

The agency was really helpful, making suggestions on where to stay and in making bookings for all her accommodation in advance. It proved to be an expensive undertaking, using up about half of Angie's savings, but she had a now or never feeling about the whole exercise and, knowing how isolated Australia was from the rest of the world, felt sure it would be many years before she left its shores again.

Finally, a month after she returned to London, Angie said her goodbyes to Flo and Frederick and boarded the boat train for Southampton on the first leg of her "journey of a lifetime."

Twenty-one

Homeward bound

Angie had three days in New York and used them well, walking from one end of the island to the other. She went to the top of the Empire State Building, caught the ferry to Staten Island, gazed in awe at the United Nations building and Rockefeller Center, looked longingly at the wonderful shops, but bought nothing, for she knew that she must conserve funds, with no clear future in mind. Everything in that great city lived up to her expectations—even the rudeness of many of the natives and cab drivers was what she had expected. Determined, if possible, to see at least one Broadway show, she asked the receptionist at her hotel what was the best one running at the moment.

"West Side Story. It's a wonderful show. It's been running for over a year. Go to the theatre; they often have cancellations. You won't be sorry you saw it."

On that recommendation, Angie headed downtown and was lucky enough to get a ticket at an exorbitant price. After becoming immersed in the story of Tony and Maria and thrilling to the great music and dancing, she left the theatre feeling it had been money well spent.

She was somewhat put off when she eventually arrived at the Greyhound bus depot. It was rather grubby looking and some of the people waiting with her were a bit scary. Angie was determined to make the best of it and, once the bus was underway, found the person in the next seat was just an ordinary woman, much the same as she could have encountered on a bus in Sydney or back in London. That lady was amazed to hear that Angie came from Australia, showing a decided lack of knowledge regarding Angie's home country—something she was to become used to in the next week or so. Countless times she had to assure people that, "No, we don't keep kangaroos in our back yards, nor do we have those cute little koala bears as pets." Angie, who had never seen either species other than in the zoo, was amazed to find how little people in the US knew of Australia. Many actually confused it with Austria and asked her if she lived in the Alps.

Her bus ticket allowed her thirty days' travel anywhere on the Greyhound network, but Angie had no intentions of travelling for that length of time. She had relied on the advice of the travel agents back in London, who had suggested that she spend at least some of her journey in overnight travel—to save accommodation costs—and found that by freshening up at the depots in some of the less scenic parts of the journey, it had been good advice. One thing she had not realised was the vastness of the country she was travelling across and, although she saw some beautiful scenery, there were long stretches of emptiness. Angie also found that even the cities where she stayed overnight had a certain sameness to them. By the time she finally arrived in Los Angeles, nearly a fortnight after she left New York, it had all melded into one long, endless vista and she was left with the feeling that this was definitely not the way to see the US. She had a conviction that so many places of interest had been missed due to her lack of knowledge of the country. Her conversations with fellow passengers always seemed to be peppered with "Did you get to see so and so?" and more often than not, her answer was "No." When she settled into her Los Angeles hotel, she happily put her Greyhound ticket aside for the time being and told herself that the next visit to the States would be much better researched and her mode of travel would most definitely not be by bus. It had, however, been a fascinating experience; she had met some interesting people and seen (maybe too much of) some great scenery.

She was booked into the hotel for a week, a fact she was heartily glad of, for some time was needed to wash off the grime of travel and just relax, after so many days of being constantly on the move. She had bought her tickets to Disneyland from the agency in London. The agent, who had been to the theme park, assured her that she would need two full days to enjoy everything it had to offer. Although it was not high season, she was pleased to have had that advice, for so much time was taken up in the long queues to all the attractions. If the journey across country had been something of a letdown, Disneyland lived up to and exceeded all her expectations. The fun, glitz and excitement were exactly what Angie needed to take her mind off herself and she enjoyed every moment of it. Even the queues were enjoyable, for people spoke to one another and (as usual) were amazed to hear that Angie was Australian. She heard stories of menfolk who had spent time in Australia during the war and of distant relatives who had headed for its shores, never to be heard from again. If her sea trip, the days in New York, and the cross country journey had not erased most of her bad memories, the two days in Disneyland—taking her into a fantasy world—left her feeling more like her old self, the Angie who enjoyed life and was excited about what lay around the next corner.

She spent the rest of her week in Los Angeles on the tourist roundabout, taking the bus tour of stars' homes, examining the stars on the sidewalk outside Grauman's Chinese Theatre and going to Malibu Beach, which she thought much better than those she had seen in England, but not a patch on those at home. All too soon, it was time to head for the Greyhound depot for the last leg of her journey up to San Francisco, where she would catch the Qantas flight home.

The trip up the coastline to San Francisco was probably the most interesting part of her journey within America. Angie was swept away by the magnificent scenery and thrilled at the place names, so familiar to her from reading Steinbeck. Big Sur, Monterey, she almost felt she knew them intimately. San Francisco was equally beautiful, and she felt happy to have spent the extra money for a couple of nights there. This was a place she definitely wanted to return to, a magical city by the bay, unlike but somehow reminding her of Sydney.

An even bigger thrill was boarding the giant Qantas Super Constellation, made so much better by hearing the Australian accents of the crew, so refreshing after weeks of strident American voices. They were heading for the first stop, Hawaii, where she had splurged once again on two nights' accommodation. She spent the entire time either lying on the golden sand or luxuriating in the water, which was more like a tepid bath than the ocean she was used to. As she felt the last of her tension drain away, Angie started for the first time to feel as if she were really on the way home. The next stop was Fiji, where she had taken an overnight stay, and after a brief stroll away from the hotel, was pleased not to be staying any longer. The scenery was indeed beautiful, but the poverty everywhere, particularly in the Indian quarter, took away any enjoyment she might otherwise have felt in the place.

Back on the plane—next stop Sydney—home!

To Angie's delight, the plane circled over the city of Sydney before making its landing approach, giving the passengers a bird's eye view of the site of the old Bennelong Tram Shed site, where the Sydney Opera House was to be built. Although it was only a hole in the ground now, the thought that Sydney was to have a building unique in the world was something that filled Angie with excitement. A Manly Ferry was docked at Circular Quay wharf and she wondered if it could be the one her father had worked on all those years ago. That sight, more than anything else, gave her the feeling that she was at last back home.

Before she left San Francisco, Angie had sent a cable to her mother, telling her of the flight arrival time and had received one in return, assuring her that she would be met at the airport. She skimmed through customs in no time at all and emerged into the terminal, looking anxiously for familiar faces. No sign of anyone—maybe they were running late. Then she heard a man's voice calling her name and looked around to see a tall blond man coming towards her. Harry— but not really the Harry she remembered. How he had changed in four years! He had not been much more than a youth when she left and now very little of that youth remained. He had filled out and seemed taller and looked (she admitted to herself) rather gorgeous. He enfolded her in a huge bear hug, then stepped back to examine her head to toe.

"My, how you've changed," he said with a smile.

"For the better I hope—and so have you."

"I suppose we've both had time to do a lot of growing up in four years." Harry took the luggage trolley from her hands and, with his arm around her shoulders, led her towards the entrance doors.

"Where's everyone else?" Angie asked. "Is it just you to meet me?"

"Just me. I missed out on saying goodbye to you four years ago, so I volunteered to be your reception committee. Hope you aren't too disappointed."

Angie shook her head with a smile. "No Harry, not at all. I think it's great of you to come all this way to pick me up."

"To the ends of the earth. And why shouldn't I, when I'm meeting the best-looking babe in the whole place?"

"Aw Harry, you really have changed—you'd never have come out with something like that four years ago."

Laughing together, they made their way across the parking lot to the familiar Holden FJ Panel Van. It had been nearly new when she left and was bearing the signs of its years on the road but was unmistakably the same one that had transported her to the city four eventful years ago.

Harry deposited her bags in the back, unlocked the door and climbed into the driver's seat, then leaned across to undo the lock on the passenger seat. I'm really back in Australia, Angie thought. No more opening doors for the ladies here, but I really don't mind. I'm home and that's all that matters."

She climbed into the van and wound down the window to breathe in the October air, tinged though it may be with fumes of aircraft fuel. It was spring in Sydney and she intended to enjoy every moment of it. Very quickly she realised the fumes far outbalanced the fresh air and she wound it back up again.

The journey through heavy traffic was uninspiring and it was only when they pulled up to the tollgates on the Harbour Bridge that Angie had a real feeling about being homeward bound. As they crossed the bridge, she craned her neck to look at the harbour stretching out on either side. Nothing she had seen anywhere overseas could compete with this, she thought. Everything along the route was familiar and yet strange to her, but as they drove down the hill to the Spit Bridge, she gasped at the incomparable vista of sparkling blue water, dotted with the craft of weekend sailors.

"Oh, I'd forgotten how beautiful it all is!" she exclaimed.

"It is pretty special," agreed Harry, as they turned left into the winding road that led up the hill to the peninsula that contains the northern beaches of Sydney.

"Do you want to head straight home, or shall we take the scenic route?" he asked.

"The scenic route; home can wait a bit longer. I'd like to go down to Manly and look at the ocean."

"As madame wishes," he said as he turned the vehicle onto Sydney Road. Manly Beach was only minutes away. On arrival, he stopped the car halfway along the beachfront, bonnet pointed seawards, so they could see the whole panorama of sand and surf, stretching from Manly to Queenscliff, unequalled, many would say, in the world—and certainly so in Angie's mind.

Angie let loose a long sigh. "This is what I needed." She wound the window down again, this time to breathe in the fresh air, with its unforgettable flavour of the ocean. They sat there in silence for a few minutes, which Angie broke with a question. "I hope your fiancée didn't mind too much that you were picking me up?"

"Didn't anyone tell you? No fiancée anymore, not since about a month ago. She up and dumped me for someone who could 'offer her a better life,' whatever that means."

Angie reached across the seat and squeezed his hand. "Oh Harry, I'm sorry. No. I wasn't told—I wouldn't have asked otherwise."

He squeezed her hand in thanks. "Look, it's ancient history now. I was pretty broken up for a while, but I'm recovering. The thing that hurt the most was the way she did it."

"Oh boy, I certainly can relate to that!" exclaimed Angie, so vehemently that Harry shot her a questioning look." To her relief, he asked no questions and they lapsed again into silence, each lost in their thoughts.

Before them stretched the beach, almost deserted, for although it was a beautiful day it was still not warm enough for the weekend crowds to descend en masse. Some hardy surfers sat on their boards out beyond the break, hoping for a decent wave, and down on the waterline a small boy dug feverishly in the sand.

"Through to China." Angie broke the silence.

"Pardon?"

She laughed. "My dad always said that when we were digging holes, we were going through to China. That little boy just reminded me of it."

"Funny, my dad always said the same."

"Maybe it's a dad thing. Probably dads all over the world say something similar. I wonder if Chinese dads tell their children they are digging through to Australia?"

He grinned and shrugged. "Who knows!" Silence and their thoughts returned. Her hand was lying beside her on the bench seat and Harry softly put his hand on hers. At first she thought to remove it, then thinking that it felt rather nice, she left hers there.

Well, here I am back where it all started, Angie thought. I've spent four years chasing a childhood dream and it all turned into a nightmare. Now, it's a fresh start, I suppose, but I'm young and anything could happen. She looked over at the man next to her and thought, Maybe Harry was the one for me all along, or there's always Dan—he seems keen enough to resume our relationship. Or maybe it will be someone else entirely.

Enough of all this; people were waiting for her. She gently removed her hand from under his and smiled at him.

"Thank you for bringing me here Harry; this place means a lot to me. Now, let's go home."

Meet Ruth Reynolds

Born in Australia and living on Sydney's Northern Beaches, Ruth spent her working life in accounting, only fulfilling a lifelong ambition of writing after retirement. Her first novel One Step at a Time was published by Wings ePress in 2015, which, similar to Transitions, drew largely on her experiences and observations of those around her.

For more about Ruth, please visit her website at: ruthreynoldsau.wordpress.com

Works From The Pen Of Ruth Reynolds

One Step at a Time
Emma leaves London in 1920 looking for a new life in Australia and, through adversity, finds a future and a love vastly different from what she expected.

Transitions
Minnie Sherwood wants the best for all her children and is forced through circumstance to find inner strengths she didn't know she had.

Angie, her second daughter, leaves Sydney in 1954 for a London that exists only in her mind. When reality strikes, she too must cope and adjust to what life has to offer.

Letter to Our Readers

Enjoy this book?

You can make a difference

As an independent publisher, Wings ePress, Inc. does not have the financial clout of the large New York Publishers. We can't afford large magazine spreads or subway posters to tell people about our quality books.

But, we do have something much more effective and powerful than ads. We have a large base of loyal readers.

Honest Reviews help bring the attention of new readers to our books.

If you enjoyed this book, we would appreciate it if you would spend a few minutes posting a review on the book's ***Amazon page*** or on its Wings ePress, Inc. webpage ***at www.wingsepress.com***

Thank You very much.